PRAISE FOR THE
STEEL BROTHERS SAGA

"Hold onto the reins:
this red-hot Steel story is one wild ride."
~ A Love So True

"A spellbinding read from a
New York Times *bestselling author!"*
~ BookBub

"I'm in complete awe of this author. She has gone and
delivered an epic, all-consuming, addicting, insanely
intense story that's had me holding my breath, my
heart pounding and my mind reeling."
~ The Sassy Nerd

"Absolutely UNPUTDOWNABLE!"
~ Bookalicious Babes

INSATIABLE

INSATIABLE

STEEL BROTHERS SAGA
BOOK TWELVE
HELEN HARDT

WATERHOUSE PRESS

ISBN: 978-1-64263-138-8

For all the readers who've made it through twelve Steel Brothers books.

Thank you so much!

This wouldn't be possible without you.

PROLOGUE

Now I have what I need.

The wait is over, and I'm ready.

Ready to seek revenge.

Yet a duel rages inside me, tormenting me.

How could everyone have forgotten me? Left me to rot in hell? How? How? How?

No.

Won't go there.

Must be strong.

If only I could split off the weak part of me, leave it to putrefy in a swamp somewhere.

I must fight.

I must fight, and I must win.

CHAPTER ONE

Bryce

Silence on the other end of the line.

"Did you hear us?" I asked. "About the cufflink?"

Nothing. Maybe her battery had gone dead. If it had ... Was someone listening in? Had someone ...?

My heart hammered into itself, my chest heaving. "Marjorie? Sweetheart?"

"Sis," Joe said, his tone panicked. "What's going on?"

"Marj! Marj!" Franticness strangled me like a noose of fire.

Something was wrong. Very wrong.

"Did she say where she was?" Joe asked.

"No. I just assumed she was home. But now I'm not sure."

"Fuck," Joe said, pulling out his phone. "Keep that line open. I'm calling the cops."

"Marj!" I shouted again into the phone. "Marjorie! Talk to me! Damn it!"

"The cops are on the way," Joe said. "Keep that line open, whatever you do."

He didn't have to make the demand. No way was I severing my only line to the woman I loved.

No fucking way.

"We're coming, baby," I said into the phone, hoping

she could still hear me. "We're coming for you. I love you, Marjorie. Be strong. I love you."

"Fuck," Joe said. "Holy fuck."

I didn't reply. Worry for Marj consumed my whole body. I literally shook from head to toe. I'd never been so frightened in my life.

"We'll find her," Joe said. "We have to. We found Ruby, remember?"

Yes, the Steels had found Ruby. They'd pull out every source and more to find their little sister.

But...

What if it wasn't enough?

Vivid scenes exploded through my mind.

Marjorie falling, lying on the sidewalk hurt.

Marjorie being hit from behind and then dragged off somewhere.

Marjorie being drugged with chloroform, like Ruby had been...

My muscles tensed, and I rubbed at my forehead.

"Easy," Joe said.

"I love her. She's everything to me."

"I know. If I had any doubts before, which I didn't, they'd be gone now. Calm down, man. You're quivering."

I nodded, drawing in a deep breath.

Not a good time to lose it, not when the woman I loved needed me more than ever.

I silently thanked God that my mother and Henry were safe and out of the way in Florida. Then I turned to Joe.

"She was with Colin in the park. Do you think he had anything to do with this?"

Joe shook his head. "Colin wouldn't hurt Marj. His father,

on the other hand . . ."

Joe didn't finish his sentence. He didn't have to. If Colin was right, and his father had sold him to my father as a plaything to rape and torture . . . Well, then, he was capable of just about anything.

In his own way, he was as bad as my father had been.

I looked around. This was Steel country, the beautiful western slopes of Colorado. Snow Creek was a friendly small town. Psychotic creeps didn't exist in friendly small towns.

Except that they did.

My father and Larry Wade had proven that a hundred times over.

Granted, Ted Morse was from Denver. How he'd even gotten wind of my father was still a mystery to all of us, as was how he'd found out about Justin Valente, the poor kid Joe and I had invited along to one of our weekend campouts with my father.

Justin had never returned from that trip.

Joe was talking on his phone again. I lifted my eyebrows when he ended the call.

"No sign of her in the park. I say you and I get over there pronto and check things out ourselves. I texted Ryan and Ruby. I'd like her to join us if she can. In the meantime, we're going."

I nodded.

We couldn't get there fast enough.

★ ★ ★

I'd gotten control over my shivers, but the inside of my body still felt like a cold cavern with pointed icicles prickling me all over.

Marjorie.

We'd just found each other, decided to be together despite all the other crap surrounding us.

I couldn't lose her now. I just couldn't.

"Do you have Colin Morse's number?" I asked Joe. "He might know something. He was the last person to see her."

"I don't. Jade probably has it."

"Shit." I raked my fingers through my hair. "Someone has to tell Jade."

"That needs to come from Tal," Joe said. "With her pregnancy and all . . . Fuck!"

Two blues hovered around the park.

"Maybe the cops can get it," I said.

"Probably." Joe approached them.

I stayed at the bench where Marjorie and Colin had presumably been talking.

Nothing.

Fucking nothing.

Not even a dark-brown hair to indicate she'd been there.

"Damn it!" I said out loud.

"Hey."

I turned. Ryan Steel and his wife stood next to me. Ryan's eyes were heavy-lidded and troubled, and Ruby's blue eyes held sadness as well, but she was a pro. She got straight to work, her hands gloved.

"You sure this was the bench where she met Colin?"

"I have no idea, but it's the one closest to town, and I assumed she was in town when she called me. Reception is never great in this park."

"I don't think she was in town," Ruby said. "If she were, someone would have seen something. This park is usually dead weekdays during working hours. I'm betting she was still here."

Of course. That made sense. Why hadn't Joe and I thought of it?

I exhaled.

Because we were fucked up in the head with worry and fear.

Ruby eyed everything, leaving nothing to chance. She got down on her hands and knees and regarded the grass under the bench, threaded her hands through the thin carpeting of blades. I watched every move she made, my insides knotted, hoping she'd come up with something.

She didn't.

"Odd." She shook her head. "Or not so odd. If we're dealing with seasoned pros, they'd know not to leave clues. Or they'd leave blatant plants like they did outside the playground where Dale saw the stranger twice now."

"Damn," I said again. "Now what?"

"Now we look around. We ask questions. The cops are already downtown checking to see if anyone saw Marjorie. Do you have any idea where she might have gone in town?"

"She's got a new trainer at the gym," I said. "And she likes the smoothie place."

"I'm going to go ask some questions in town, then," Ruby said. "You two can come along if you want."

"I'll go with you." Ryan took her hand.

I felt like I was being tugged in two different directions. "I'll stay with Joe," I finally said. After all, Ryan loved Marj as much as Joe did, and he and Ruby didn't need me breathing down their necks.

Joe finished talking to the cops and returned to me.

"Anything?"

"Ruby didn't see any clues. She and Ryan headed into town to see if anyone saw Marj or Colin there. Did you uncover Colin's number?"

"Yeah. I got it, but he's not answering."

"Of course he isn't," I said. "Either he has Marj—"

"I honestly don't think so," Joe interjected.

"I don't either. Which makes me think whoever has Marj also has Colin." I shook my head. "This has my father's stench all over it."

"Your father is dead, Bryce. I saw it with my own eyes."

"I know. But he's haunting us. In the form of Ted Morse."

CHAPTER TWO

Marjorie

Darkness all around me.

Movement too. Jiggling movement.

And nausea.

Overwhelming nausea.

Then . . . the fear set in.

A scream rose in my throat, tearing through my vocal cords, and then . . .

Nothing. Nothing but suppressed gagging.

I was gagged. My mouth had been taped shut.

The nausea again, bile creeping up my throat like clawing acid.

I attempted a swallow.

I couldn't puke. If I puked, I'd suffocate.

Though I had no frame of reference, I sensed I wasn't alone. Someone else was with me. The presence of another body.

Fear. Dark fear. Panic.

God, the panic!

Marjorie, calm down. If you panic and throw up, you'll die.

No, I would not die. Not when I had so much to live for now. My family, including my new niece or nephew growing in my best friend.

Dale and Donny.

My brothers and sisters-in-law.

Henry and Evelyn.

And Bryce.

My wonderful Bryce.

A low groan vibrated next to me. I felt it more than heard it. It could have come from an animal, but if an animal were trapped with me, it would be moving in chaos. Maybe it was drugged.

No, not an animal. I felt sure of it. A person. A person was here with me.

I moved against whatever bound me. Though I couldn't see, I felt my wrists tied together in front of me. Also my ankles.

I breathed in deeply through my nose.

Air! Need air!

Calm down. Calm down. Don't panic, or you'll fucking die!

I was enclosed, so I needed to conserve air. If I panicked, I'd use more.

I wasn't claustrophobic.

But I also didn't know where the hell I was.

Once, in college, Jade and I had gone to a sensory-deprivation tank before finals. The advertisement had said that forty-five minutes in the tank was equal to five hours of sleep.

We were closed in, couldn't move.

And I'd never been more relaxed.

I closed my eyes against the darkness, trying to force my mind to go back to that place, that feeling of peace I'd had while being closed in, suspended in salty water.

But I wasn't suspended. I wasn't buoyant.

I was trapped, tied up, gagged, and in some type of moving vehicle.

God, the darkness!

A trunk. Was I in the trunk of a car? With no ventilation? The exhaust fumes would kill me. But I had to breathe. Had to fucking breathe.

Go back, Marj. Go back. How did this happen?

Bryce. I'd been talking on my phone to Bryce and Joe. I'd just seen Colin in the park, and he'd told me ... God, he'd told me ...

His father had sold him to Tom Simpson. Or so he thought. He was going to get me the documentation. He left. I called Bryce, and then—

Nothing.

Not until now.

Not until this hell.

Another scream lodged in my throat, unable to penetrate the gag in my mouth. I coughed, gasping.

Get hold of yourself! You need to stay calm!

How? How was I supposed to do that?

Think of happiness. Think of something that brings you joy. Anything. Anything.

Bryce.

Bryce loved me. I loved him.

He'd been on the other end of the phone when whatever happened had happened. He'd know something wasn't right. He'd come for me. He and my brothers would have a posse looking for me in no time.

In no time ...

No time ...

Don't go there. I have all the time in the world.

All the time in the world.

All the time in the world ...

★ ★ ★

I jolted against something hard. Whatever it was let out an *oof*.

Yes, another person was here with me. At least I knew it wasn't Bryce or Joe. They'd been at the ranch when this had happened. Still, knowing another person was here gave me some comfort and helped stave off the panic.

But who was it?

Colin? He'd just left the park when this occurred.

He was the most likely, but things never turned out to be the most likely.

Orange warmth punched my eyes.

Sunlight. I was blindfolded. How hadn't I realized it? Easy. I was in the dark, and I didn't stop to think about my eyes adjusting.

Again, I tried screaming, only to choke against the dirty gag in my mouth. Again, the nausea, the clawing acid.

And again, I had to stop it.

Movement. But *I* didn't move. The balance of the trunk shifted. Someone had removed the other person.

I stayed still. Easy enough since I was bound, but I was determined not to make this any easier on my captor, whoever he was.

Dead weight.

I'd be dead weight.

Within seconds, I was lifted from the confined space. I groaned as I was thrown against a hard body. My head bounced against a bony shoulder as we moved along.

A scream tried to force its way out of my throat once more, leading to more choking and gasping.

Air! I was outside now. I could tell because of the light streaming through my blindfold. Plenty of air around, I knew, but still I gasped.

Breathe in. Breathe out.

Calm down.

Calm down.

How was I supposed to calm down when I'd been kidnapped? Taken? Abducted?

Was this the norm for my family now?

I needed something to focus on.

Thump. Thump. Thump.

The rhythmic movement of the person carrying me.

Focus. Focus.

Then the orange warmth disappeared, and I was again left in darkness.

Gently—gently?—whoever carried me set me down on something soft.

"I'm so sorry about this," said a voice—a familiar voice, though I couldn't place it.

First the tape was removed from my mouth and I spit out the gag. All those screams that had been suppressed came out with a vengeance.

"Get away from me! Help me! Help me!"

"I'm not your enemy, Marjorie."

He removed the blindfold.

A blurry image slowly began to clarify. My mind was fuzzy, but I knew this person. This man.

"Dominic?"

"Yeah. It's me. I'm not here to hurt you. I'm here to help you."

"Are you responsible for taking my mother? Where the

hell *is* she, Dominic? You've taken a mentally ill woman against her will. You've taken me against my will!"

"Marjorie—"

"You transported me in the trunk of a car. I could have suffocated. Been killed by carbon monoxide!"

"You were in the back of a van, not a trunk. You were never in any dang—"

"The hell I wasn't! You did something to me. Knocked me over the head with something. What gives you the right—"

"I took you to save you, damn it." He stood and looked over his shoulder.

Another person entered the room, this one female.

"How is he?" Dominic asked.

"He's all right. Dazed and confused."

"So is she," Dominic replied.

Was he talking about me? "I'm far from dazed and confused. You'd better tell me what the fuck is going on right now, damn it! Who's that bitch? And who else is here with us?"

"Excuse me?" the woman said.

"Easy," Dominic said. "She's rightly upset."

"No one calls me a bitch and gets away—"

"Easy," he said again.

She quieted down, but she didn't look happy.

"Marjorie," he said. "This is my sister, Alessandra. My twin. She goes by Alex."

"Do you think I care what she goes by? Now untie my hands and feet so I can get the hell out of here. If my brothers find out what you've done, they'll fucking kill you."

"Alex and I aren't your enemies," he said quietly. "But we know who is."

CHAPTER THREE

B r y c e

Joe and I headed over to the gym. Marj's new trainer, Dominic, was the only other person who might have seen her this morning.

"We need to talk to one of your trainers," Joe said to the receptionist on duty, a new guy I didn't recognize.

"Of course. Are you interested in booking a session?"

Joe lifted one eyebrow. "Do either of us look like we need training?"

The guy's face turned pale. "Uh . . ."

Joe was going red. Usually I was the one to calm him down, but I was pretty nearly red myself. I wasn't going to tame Joe's hotheadedness today. No way.

"Dominic James," I said through clenched teeth. "We need to talk to Dominic James."

The receptionist eyed his computer screen. "We don't keep a schedule of the trainers down here. I don't even know if he's working today."

"Get us that information," Joe said. "Now."

"I don't have—"

I walked past him. "Come on, Joe. I know where the trainers' office is."

"Wait. You can't—"

"Watch us." I headed past the reception and up the stairs to the main floor where the weights and machines were.

Joe followed me briskly until we reached the small office. It was empty.

"Fuck."

"This is where you lost that card with the Spider's info on it?" Joe said.

"Don't remind me. I couldn't find it when I came in the next day. It probably ended up in the trash."

Before Joe could scold me further, a woman with short hair and buff as all get-out walked in. "Can I help you guys?"

"We're looking for Dominic," I said.

"He was in earlier, but he's gone for the day, I think." She eyed the computer screen. "Yeah. In fact, he'll be gone the next couple days. He's taking a few days off."

"Great," I said. "Who did he see this morning? Did he have a training session?"

"He did, but I can't give out that information. Gym policy. Sorry." She closed the scheduling window.

"We need his cell phone number," Joe said. "It's urgent."

"I can't—"

"Yeah. Gym policy," I said. "We get it. But my girlfriend is a client of his, and now she's missing. We think Dominic might have been the last person to see her."

The woman sat down at the desk and regarded the computer once more, pulling up files. "Looks like I can help after all. His two clients early this morning were both men, so your sister wasn't here."

"I still want his information," Joe said.

"I do too," I agreed.

"I'm sorry. My hands are tied." She clicked out of the screen once more.

Joe curled his hands into fists.

"Let's go," I said. "We've done all we can here."

"Why is he taking a few days off?" Joe asked.

"I have no idea."

"Who's his supervisor here?" I asked.

"Actually, that's me."

"You just let people take time off whenever?"

She rolled her eyes. "I know who you are. You're Jonah Steel, one of the Steel brothers. And you're Bryce Simpson. We all know who you both are. We know about both your fathers."

Joe's face morphed into a scowl. I expected him to growl at any moment.

"I don't owe you any explanation. Not after your father—"

This time *I* made two fists. "I am *not* my father."

"Look," she said. "I'm not trying to hit a nerve. But don't come charging in here making demands just because of who you are."

"We're not," Joe said through clenched teeth. "My sister is missing. We need to talk to Dominic."

"Dominic is an independent contractor. He eats what he kills here."

I cocked my head. "He eats what he kills? That's an interesting way to put it."

"For God's sake. If he doesn't work, he doesn't get paid. That's all I meant. I didn't ask why he needed the days off. It's not my place. He's not an employee."

Joe finally seemed to calm down. "I understand your position, but please. We need to get in touch with him. We won't say it came from you, okay?"

"I already told you he didn't see a female client this morning."

"Please," Joe said again. "What would you do if *your* sister were missing?"

She sighed. "All right. But if I get in trouble for this—"

"If you get in trouble for this, you'll be compensated," Joe said.

She scribbled on the back of a business card and handed it to Joe. "This better not come back to haunt me."

Neither of us responded.

We knew better than anyone that things you thought were dead and buried could always come back to haunt you.

★ ★ ★

"No answer," Joe said. "And it says the voicemail account hasn't been set up yet."

I grabbed the card out of Joe's hand. I had no reason to disbelieve him, but I had to hear it for myself. This was Marjorie. I had to be totally sure.

Sure enough. No voicemail account had been set up.

"What the fuck, Bryce?" Joe said.

"Just had to be sure."

"And you thought I was lying?"

"No. Of course not. I just . . . Fuck. I don't know."

"I get it, man. I do. But we have to work together. We have to trust each other. The minute you and I begin to doubt each other, we'll no longer be able to help Marj. Or my mom. Or Colin."

I nodded. He was right, of course.

I thought about Henry, about my mom. I'd been texting her hourly to check in. No doubt she thought I'd gone crazy, but I had to make sure they were okay. I couldn't worry about them on top of everything else.

Marjorie never left my mind. She consumed me, and a green sickness gnawed at me, forcing me to shut out the shivers that constantly threatened to erupt in me.

God, I loved her.

She saw past my emptiness, saw something in me that she could love.

I'd allowed myself to actually envision a future with her. The perfect mother for Henry and for the children she and I would have together.

Yes, I'd actually imagined more children, despite my horrific DNA.

Henry would love to have a brother or a sister, and Marjorie would be devoted to all her children, even the one she hadn't borne herself.

I had to find her. I just had to.

I could *not* lose Marjorie Steel.

"Now what?" Joe said, pulling me out of my head.

"Wish I knew. Did you try Colin again?"

"Yeah. Still not answering."

"Shit. And still no news from the Spider?"

"No. I called my friend from the club, the guy who set me up with the Spider. He hasn't heard from him either."

"Are they . . . friends?"

"I don't know, honestly," Joe said. "The whole thing is shady, to say the least. I mean, here's a hacker who won't deal directly with anyone, who doesn't want anyone to see his face."

"You said you trusted this guy."

"I do."

"Then let's talk to him," I said. "Maybe he can shed some light on what's going on."

"He won't know who took my mother or Marjorie."

"How do you know that? We need to check out all the possibilities."

"He won't see us," Joe said.

"Why the hell not?"

"Because . . . he can't risk being outed as a member of the BDSM club."

I looked Joe straight in his eyes. "Just who *is* this guy, Joe?"

He looked away. "I can't tell you that."

Chills hit the back of my neck. Whoever this guy was, he was somebody important. Someone who might be able to help us.

"Then tell me this. How does he know a high-priced secret hacker?"

"Because," Joe said, "he used to work for the FBI."

CHAPTER FOUR

Marjorie

"Who? Where's my mother? And why haven't you untied me? This is illegal, you know. Kidnapping. Assault. Battery. False imprisonment. My brothers will see you both behind bars."

Alex scoffed.

"Yeah, you, you dumb bitch."

"Dom, if she calls me that one more time—"

"You'll what?" I said. "Tie me up? Abduct me? Uh... I think you already did that."

"I'll crush your damned skull," she said.

Alex looked like she meant business. She was olive-skinned and dark-haired like her brother. She was also just as muscular.

"Easy, Alex," Dominic said.

"I don't have to take shit from this spoiled rich girl, Dom. That wasn't part of this deal."

"What do you expect when you take someone? She's pissed."

"This is for her own good," Alex spat back.

"Hello?" I said. "Still tied up here. I'd love to see how you'd act if someone kidnapped you and tied *you* up. I don't remember anything until I woke up in the trunk of the car."

"I told you. You were in the back of a van."

"Am I supposed to thank you for that? It sucked. What did you do? Drug me? And who was in there with me?"

"I'll untie you," Dominic said, "if you'll hear us out."

"I'm not sure you're the one who should be making deals," I said.

"Oh?" Alex said. "Seems like you're tied up and we aren't. Of course we're the ones who should be making deals."

"My brothers—"

"Aren't here," she said.

"They will be."

"They will be," Dominic said. "We're counting on it. And when they get here, I think they'll agree that this is the safest place for you."

"Was this all part of your plan?" I asked. "Train me for my company at lunch? Huh?"

"Marjorie, if I were interested in holding you captive, why would I train you? Make you stronger?"

Okay. A decent point. But I still wasn't buying.

"So you fake credentials to be a trainer, and—"

"Okay, I didn't go to UCLA. I don't have any college degrees, but I *am* a good trainer, and I do coach baseball, though not right now. Those two things just aren't my primary income source."

"No, I'm sure you'll make a lot more when you demand ransom from my brothers."

"Oh my God," Alex said. "Is this worth it? To put up with her shit? Let's dump her back where we found her. Give her a little roofie to forget she ever saw us. Anything is better than this."

"Alex, I'll ask you again to put yourself in her shoes. We

just took her against her will. She's pissed, and she has every right to be."

"Uh... still tied up here," I said. "You two can bicker on your own time."

"This *is* our time," Dominic said, "and we're being very well compensated for it."

"By whom? Not my brothers. No way."

"No, not by your brothers, but by someone who cares for you very much."

The only person other than my brothers who cared for me very much was Bryce, but he didn't have the money for this. Plus, he'd never order my abduction.

My mother? As far as she knew, I was a perpetual baby named Angela, and Talon and Joe were still little boys away at camp.

Colin? No. He cared for Jade and, by extension, me, but he didn't have the kind of money to pull this off.

"Who? Who, other than my brothers, can afford you?"

"I'm not at liberty to say yet," Dominic said.

"For God's sake. Untie me!"

"I will. If you promise to hear us out."

Before he could respond, another man entered the room.

"How's he doing?" Alex asked.

"He's scared, of course. Who wouldn't be after what he's been through? How's she doing?"

"She's not scared enough," Alex said. "In fact, she's a pain in the ass."

"*She* is right here," I said. "You can address me as a human being, despite the fact that I'm trussed up like a pig."

Alex ignored my remark. "Maybe give him something to help him calm down. It might be a while before we get—"

"Drug him? Whoever *he* is?" I yelled. "Are you nuts?"

"Marjorie," Dominic said, "we're trying to help him. And you."

"Who is he?" I asked, but I knew the answer before Dominic replied.

"Colin Morse," he and I said in unison.

"I want to see him," I said. "He'll listen to me."

"You're not listening to *us*," Dominic said.

"Actually," the other guy interjected, "she may have a good point. If he sees a familiar face, he might calm down."

"Finally, someone who is talking sense," I said. "Now if you'll untie me, I'll be happy to talk to Colin."

"You'll make a run for it," Alex said.

Damned right. She was no dummy. Not that it took the brightest bulb to figure out what I had in mind. But I was also concerned about Colin. Having been through captivity and torture at Tom Simpson's hands, he was most likely frightened beyond belief right now.

I was frightened myself, but though I didn't trust Dominic—and I especially didn't trust Alex—I no longer felt I was in any immediate danger. If they wanted to kill me, I'd be dead by now.

"I'll untie your ankles," Dominic said, "and we'll take you to see him."

I opened my mouth to complain but then shut it. I'd take what I could get. I could still run with my hands tied. Plus, I had to see Colin. Let him know I was here for him.

Dominic quickly unbound my ankles and pulled me into a stand. "Go with Dave." He pointed to the other guy.

Dave was tall and thin and clearly not related to Dominic and Alex. He was fair and blond where they were tan and dark-haired.

"We're not here to hurt you." Dave guided me out of the room, touching my elbow.

I whipped my arm away. "Don't you lay a hand on me."

He nodded, and I followed him into another room. The lights had been dimmed.

"The brightness seemed to bother him," Dave said.

Colin was lying on a couch in a fetal position, his legs and wrists bound as mine had been. Why would the brightness bother him? Then it struck me. He was reliving his captivity with Tom Simpson. He'd been kept in the dark, most likely bound as he was now. Tom probably turned on the lights when he . . . I didn't want to think about what he'd done.

I approached him tentatively. "Colin."

He whimpered. "No more. Please."

"Colin, it's me. Marj."

"Please," he said again. "Just let me go. My father will give you whatever you want."

Yeah, he really *was* reliving his former captivity. Today's Colin wouldn't expect any help from Ted Morse.

"You're not there anymore. You're okay. No one is going to hurt you."

In fact, Dave seemed to be concerned about Colin's well-being.

"Please. I want my clothes back."

"You're dressed, Colin. No one took your clothes."

"Why are you doing this?" he asked. "Why? Why me?"

I touched his face, but he jerked away.

"It's me. Marj. Marjorie Steel."

"Leave me alone! Please!"

"Look at me," I said. "Just look at me."

He opened his eyes wider, his pupils dilated from the darkness.

"Turn on the light," I said to Dave.

"He won't like it."

"Just do it. He needs to see my face."

Dave flipped the overhead light on, and I squinted against the invasion to my vision. I touched Colin's cheek once more. This time he didn't flinch.

"Look at me. It's me. Marj."

His eyes widened farther. "Thank God! Get me out of here."

"You're not in that basement, Colin. My brother Joe rescued you. Remember?"

He tried to sit up, tugging against his bindings. "Then where am I? Why are *you* here?"

"I don't know yet, but these people say they don't want to hurt us."

"I'm tied up." He looked me over. "And so are you."

"True. I don't know exactly what's going on yet." I turned to Dave. "Now would be a great time to explain it."

He nodded. "I'll get Dom and Alex."

CHAPTER FIVE

B r y c e

"So what?"

"We've been through this, Bryce," Joe said. "I can't tell you."

"Do you think I give a damn if our governor or anyone else is into bondage? Not to mention some former G-man. I care only about Marjorie, and so should you."

"You're right," he said. "Which is why I'm getting in touch with him. If he can help, I'll keep his cover. If not, all bets are off."

"And you still won't tell me who it is?" I paced around. "I can't believe you, Joe. Where's your famous hot head? What if Melanie were missing?"

Yeah, I'd gone a step too far. Joe grabbed my collar. "You think I'm any less worried about my sister and my mother—"

I broke his hold easily. "Save the tough guy act. I call bullshit. There's something else going on here. Who is this guy? Who is he? If he's no longer with the government, his career isn't in danger, right?"

"You think government officials are the only people whose careers are in danger if the public finds out they're part of the leather community?"

"I don't fucking know, Joe. I'm *not* a part of that community!"

"He's a lawyer in Grand Junction. In fact . . ." Joe stopped. "Oh, shit."

"What now?"

"He helped me find the facility in the city for my mother. After we brought her home from the place in California where my father had put her. Oh, shit."

"You think he has something to do with your mom's disappearance?"

"No." Joe was adamant. "This guy's legit, but there's a paper trail with his office. Those records are confidential. They're medical records."

"It was probably pretty easy for someone to figure out where your mother was," I said. "You, Talon, and Marj all went to visit her regularly."

"Yeah. But something still smells rotten."

Almost instinctively, I sniffed. Yeah, something did smell rotten, metaphorically speaking.

"If you can't tell me who this dude is, that's one thing. But you should be having a conversation with him right now."

He nodded. "That's why I've contacted him."

"The Joe I know would be hightailing it to his office right about now. And when you do, I'm coming along."

Joe sighed. "You're right. Let's go."

★ ★ ★

Apparently, when Jonah Steel showed up unannounced, the red carpet came out. Kyle and Shenkman, Attorneys at Law, couldn't have been more accommodating. But I wasn't interested in their Rocky Mountain spring water and freshly baked cookies. I wanted information.

Apparently we were here to see Cade Booker, an "of counsel" with the firm.

Damn.

Joe was right. Who knew who might be into the leather lifestyle? It wouldn't bother me, but apparently lifestylers preferred to keep their association private.

"Mr. Booker isn't in the office," the receptionist said to us. "We expect him back any minute. I'm sure he'll want to see you."

Had Joe been here before? Right, he had. The paperwork for Daphne Steel's commitment to the facility.

So why the big secret? Why hadn't he simply told me that Cade Booker had gotten him the name of the hacker? He could have left out the whole BDSM thing.

The receptionist led us to a separate waiting area, obviously for VIPs. Marble coffee tables held trays of French pastries, and a brass espresso urn graced a buffet. Books by renowned photographers sat in an array around the room, interspersed with complimentary charging stations for all types of devices.

I sat, my nerves skipping. Marjorie never left my mind. What if someone was hurting her? Violating her? I clasped my hands together, my knuckles white.

I should have never started a relationship when I couldn't protect her. Oh, she'd told me she didn't need protection, but she did.

I'd failed her.

Another young woman entered the room. "Mr. Steel?"

"Yes?"

"Mr. Booker has returned. He's waiting for you in his office."

We both rose.

"He wants to see only Mr. Steel," the woman said to me.

"No way," I said. "I'm coming along."

"Maybe you should wait here, Bryce," Joe said.

"Yeah. And maybe not. We came here together, and we're going to get to the truth together."

"Mr. Steel—"

Joe whisked past the employee. "It'll be okay. I'll explain everything to Cade."

"But—"

I followed Joe, whisking past the flabbergasted woman. Should I be sorry? Hell, no. I got that she was only doing her job, but Marjorie was everything to me. I had to get to the bottom of this, and if Cade Booker knew anything, I was going to find out.

Joe seemed to know exactly where he was going in this huge office. I followed him down the halls, people gasping when they saw us and edging out of our way quickly. Finally we came to a corner office. Joe knocked loudly.

"Come on in, Joe," a voice, presumably Cade Booker, said from inside.

Joe opened the door, and I followed him in.

"Have a sea—" Booker eyed me. "Who's this?"

"Bryce Simpson, a good friend of mine."

Booker eyed me. I recognized the look—the look that said, "You're Tom Simpson's son."

"Yeah," I said. "He was my father. But I'm not him. Got it?"

Cade Booker stood. He was tall, though not quite as tall as Joe and I were, and clearly in great shape. He wore his dark hair shaved at the sides and slightly longer on top—the kind of cut that didn't require any effort to maintain, except monthly haircuts. His suit was obviously tailored, and he wore two gold rings, one on each hand. All normal, except... He had a dark quality about him that went beyond his nearly black hair and tan skin. Something sinister seemed to exude from his pores. It was almost palpable in the room.

How had Joe not seen it? Or was it just my imagination?

I didn't trust him. But I did trust Joe.

"Have a seat, both of you. What's going on, Joe?"

"My mother has disappeared from Newhaven, and now Marj is missing as well."

"Your sister?"

"Yeah. May I speak freely?"

"Of course. This place is swept every evening for surveillance devices."

I stopped myself from widening my eyes. Why the hell would any place be swept *every* evening?

"The Spider hasn't answered us in days," Joe said.

Booker lifted one eyebrow, which gave him a sinister look. "Oh?"

"Bryce knows about the Spider. He's in this with me. He and I are the only ones who remember the kid. By the way, we remembered his last name. Valente. Justin Valente."

Booker's eyes fluttered slightly. A nervous habit?

"What was the last contact you had with the Spider?" he asked.

"He said he had information, and that he'd send it in a separate email. The email never came, and he hasn't responded to anything since. Plus, he seemed to be communicating with someone else on our encrypted account."

"I'll see if I can find him."

"He's the least of our worries," I said. "Marjorie and her mother come first."

"Of course."

"I understand you got Daphne into the facility," I said.

"I handled the paperwork for her commitment," Booker said. "My involvement doesn't go any further than that."

I looked to Joe, raising my brow. He didn't respond. He trusted this guy, clearly.

"Look," Joe said finally. "I know you need to keep your hands clean, and I respect that, but—"

"I can't help you," Booker said. "I'm pretty sure the Spider can't be involved in the disappearances. That's not how he works."

I shook my head. "Seriously? You like to keep your hands clean? What kind of person who keeps his hands clean has to have his office swept for bugs every night?"

"Bryce—"

"Come on, Joe. This guy isn't who you think he is."

"Look—" Booker began.

"Easy, Cade," Joe said. "Bryce's nerves are on edge."

"Yours should be as well," I said angrily. "I'll say it again. This guy isn't who you think he is."

Booker stood. "You're right. I'm not. And you need to leave. I'm armed."

"So am I," I said. "And I'd be willing to bet everything I own that Joe is too."

"Cade knows I don't go anywhere without Rosie," Joe said, eyeing his ankle.

"Tell us who the Spider is," I gritted out.

"That's not how I work," Booker said with equal grit. "I can't work with this hothead."

I was a hothead? Hardly. I'd spent half my life calming Joe down and keeping him from going off half-cocked.

"Cade," Joe said, "is there any other way to contact the Spider?"

"Not that I know of. Now you two are going to have to get the hell out of my office."

"Not until we get what we came for," I said.

"If he doesn't have any other way to contact—"

What would your clients think if they knew how you spent your free time? Oh, the words were on the tip of my tongue. But I had nothing against BDSM, and I appreciated his—and Joe's—need for privacy.

But I was pissed. Fucking pissed.

How could Joe not see right through this guy? Cade Booker was not on our side. Not at all.

CHAPTER SIX

Marjorie

"Your mother has been moved to a safe house," Dominic said.

My stomach dropped. "You said you didn't know anything about my mother."

"No. I said your mother wasn't here."

"Why does she need to be at a safe house?"

"The same reason you need to be. This is also a safe house."

"Where are we?"

"Outside the city limits. A mobile home park."

"Mobile homes are the most unsafe places ever," I said. "You'd better hope no tornadoes come rolling through."

"This is an abandoned mobile home park. These homes have been condemned."

"Great. Should I expect the roof to fall in on me at any moment?"

"Of course not. This place is completely safe. We've made sure of it. The rest of the places here, with a few exceptions, are unsafe. Because the park as a whole is condemned, no one comes here."

"I see." Though I didn't see at all. "Colin, are you following all of this?"

"Sort of," he said, still agitated. "Could you untie me, please?"

"Are you going to run?" Dave asked.

"Where would he go?" I said. "Clearly we're in the middle of nowhere."

"We're closer to things than you think," Dominic said.

"Who the hell are you? Was it simple coincidence that we met at the gym?"

"Of course not."

"It was you, wasn't it? You took the towel with my locker key pinned on it that day."

"Guilty."

"But you didn't steal anything."

"I needed to know everything I could about where I might be able to find you. Plus, I'm not a thief."

I scoffed. "Of course not. You only steal *people*."

"I've been paid very well to get you and Colin to safety."

"Yeah? The only people with the money to 'pay very well' are my brothers, and I know they aren't behind this."

"No, they're not."

"Who, then? Who would do—"

A cell phone buzzed. Dominic pulled a phone out of his pocket and spoke into it. "Yeah?"

Seconds seemed to stretch into hours as Dominic presumably listened to whoever was on the other end of the line.

"Could you untie my ankles now?" I asked Dave, adding a slight eye-batting for effect. "Please?"

He looked to Alex. She shook her head.

Obviously flirting wasn't going to work on her.

"Hanging in there, Colin?" I asked.

He nodded, though not convincingly. "My father is behind this. He has to be."

"If what Dominic says is true, that they're trying to keep us safe, it's probably not your father. Unless you're wrong about him."

"I'm not wrong about him. I'm just not sure these people are telling us the truth."

The thought had crossed my mind as well. But Dominic and the others hadn't hurt us. Other than knocking us out, tying us up, and abducting us, that was.

I had a lot more questions for Colin about his father, but I didn't want to say anything with Alex and Dave hovering over us.

Dominic finally ended his phone call. "That was CJ. Food's on its way."

"Thank God," Dave said. "I'm starved."

"How you eat the way you do and stay looking like a scarecrow is beyond me," Dominic said.

Dave did indeed resemble the scarecrow from *The Wizard of Oz*, right down to his straw-colored hair.

"All right," I said. "Someone paid you to take us. Who?"

"I'm not at liberty to say," Dominic said.

"Of course you're not," I said. "That would make this whole thing too easy. Whatever they're paying you, I can pay more. I'm Marjorie Steel, remember?"

"Not in this for the money," Alex said.

"Well, maybe a little," Dave offered.

"What my sister means is that we don't need the money. We're very well off."

"Why aren't you sitting on a beach in the Caribbean, then?" I said. "Kidnapping has its drawbacks. Number one, it's against the freaking law."

"We have talents others don't have."

"You kicked my ass as a trainer, so there's that. I suppose you're pretty good at kidnapping. Did I get all your talents?"

Alex stalked toward me. "Dom, I swear—"

"Let it go, Alex. She just doesn't understand yet."

"Yeah? Then make me understand. Why are you doing this? By whose orders were Colin, my mother, and I taken against our will?"

Dominic sighed, his dark eyes taking on a kindness I hadn't seen before. "Your father's."

CHAPTER SEVEN

Bryce

"You two need to leave," Booker said. "I don't know anything else."

"You know how to get in touch with the Spider."

"I already told you. He's not answering me either. I only have the one contact avenue, and it seems to be blocked."

"Blocked my ass," I said through clenched teeth.

"I'm sorry about your mom and your sister," he said to Joe, effectively ignoring me. "But I can't help you."

Joe nodded. "Let's go, Bryce."

"I don't believe him," I said.

"Doesn't really matter," Joe said. "He's not going to tell us anything. He's made that clear."

My father might have been a psycho, but I'd learned a lot from him, not the least of which was how to draw my weapon from a hidden holster in a flash.

Like lightning, I was on Cade Booker. "Start talking," I said in a low voice.

"Bryce . . ." Joe began.

"You may trust this guy, but I sure as hell don't. You know something, Booker—something you're not telling us. I'm not leaving this office until you've come clean."

"Bryce," Joe said again, "don't ruin your life here. He'll

have you arrested."

"No, he won't," I said. "Because I can make his lifestyle world news. Right, Booker?"

"You bastard," Booker said to Joe.

"Damn, Bryce," Joe said.

"Sorry, Joe. I believe in being trustworthy, and you of all people can vouch for that. But Marjorie's life is at stake here, and I'll do anything I have to in order to make sure she gets home safely. If that means telling the world that Cade Booker likes to dabble in bondage, so be it."

"There's nothing more I can tell you." Booker held his hands in front of him. "I'd help if I could. Joe, you *know* me."

"He's not lying to you, Bryce," Joe said.

"I don't believe him. If he has the Spider's information, then he knows who the guy is. And I want to know. Now."

The phone on Booker's desk buzzed.

"Don't fucking move," I said.

"If I don't answer, my secretary will get suspicious."

"Bullshit. If you don't answer, she'll think you're in the middle of an important meeting, which you are."

The phone buzzed twice more, and then sure enough, it stopped.

"Ready to talk?" I asked.

"Kill me if you want to," Booker said. "I'll go down fighting. I've been fighting my whole life."

Yeah, this guy was so not what he purported to be.

"I'm sorry for breaking your confidence about the club," Joe said quietly. "You can tell the whole world I used to be a member there if you want to. I don't give a shit if people know what kind of sex I like. But I'm beginning to think Bryce is right." He moved to the side of Booker and then quickly drew

Rosie out of his ankle holster. Then he looked around the office. "What kind of work do you do here, Cade, that you have to have your office swept for bugs daily?"

Booker opened his mouth but said nothing.

"I know you're armed," Joe went on, "but you can't take us both out at once. You try anything, you'll end up dead. So tell us what we want to know. Who the fuck is the Spider?"

"I told you. Go ahead and kill me. I've been dead for thirty years anyway."

"I thought you were a friend, Cade, and I trusted you—but when it comes down to you and Bryce, he'll win every time. Throw my mother and sister into the mix? It's no contest."

"I told you to kill me. Give it your best shot."

"Hold on, Joe," I said. "No one wants to die that badly. He's up to something."

Booker chuckled. "You'd better hope you're a good shot."

"The best," I said. "I learned from my psycho father. You want to try to take me on?"

"I learned from the best as well," Booker said. "And you seem a little psycho yourself from where I'm standing."

Rage welled inside me. "I'll hand it to you. You thought of exactly the right thing to say to piss me off even more." I cocked my gun. "I'm serious. Dead serious. You think I'm anything like my father? Even a little? Then you should be scared shitless right now."

My words produced a tiny—but still visible—shudder across Booker's body. I looked sideways at Joe. Yeah, he had noticed too.

"Hate to tell you this, Cade," Joe said, "but Tom Simpson taught *me* how to shoot as well. We're both crack shots, and fast as spit."

"I was trained by the FBI, in case you forgot," Booker said.

"Didn't forget," Joe said, "but Bryce and I have been handling guns since we were seven years old. I'd bet we're both more experienced than you."

"I wouldn't take that bet."

"Shut up and stand still." Joe walked toward Booker and frisked him. "Just as I thought. Two. Take off your shirt."

"Joe—"

"Now."

Booker removed his button-down, revealing a shoulder holster and pistol. Joe took the gun and slid it across the floor. Then he took the other weapon from Booker's ankle holster.

"Did you check his crotch?" I asked.

"I'd rather not."

"Do it. Or I will."

Unsurprisingly, he had a Beretta Pico hidden there. Joe relieved him of it quickly.

"Who the hell arms himself with three guns?" I said. "Who the fuck *are* you?"

"I think we're about to find out," Joe said. "You're not leaving this office, Cade, until we know everything you do."

"You think you two and your weapons scare me? Nothing scares me anymore."

"You're in good company, then," I said. "Joe and I have seen just about everything in this fucked-up world there is to see. You sure as hell don't scare us."

"Maybe I should."

"With three guns?" Joe said. "Maybe, if we're having a bad day. Unarmed, you're nothing, Cade. Not a fucking thing."

"You'd be wise not to underestimate me," Booker said. "Psycho Daddy might have taught you how to shoot like a pro, but you're forgetting who taught *me* how to shoot."

"The FBI?" I said. "I'd match Joe's and my skills against any rank-and-file agent any day."

Booker moved stealthily, easing his way around his desk. Joe and I moved as he did, staying the same distance from him.

"Hold still," Joe said, "or one of us will blow your big head off."

He smiled. The motherfucker smiled!

Joe's countenance remained stern. He wouldn't show weakness or worry, so neither would I.

Joe's firearm was aimed at Booker's head, so I lowered mine...aiming it at his crotch. "Whatever you think you're doing, stop it, unless you want to be dickless literally as well as figuratively."

"Bingo," he said, pushing his hand down.

"Wha—"

A white spray whooshed toward my chest.

I inhaled instinctively, arrows of flame hitting my mouth and throat. And my eyes. Blur. Blindness. Tears.

I gasped and choked. "Joe!"

But the word sounded only like a gasp.

I was vaguely aware of Joe beside me doubling over, coughing as well.

"Fuck! Damn!"

Again, the words were only gasps.

I was dying. I had to be dying. What the hell had he done?

My eyes and nose were on fire, and my throat full of acidic phlegm.

The blurred images disappeared into nothingness.

I was blind.

Choking, on fire, and blind.

CHAPTER EIGHT

Marjorie

If I'd been having any nice feelings toward Dominic, his last statement erased them. "Nice try. My father is dead. I watched him die with my own eyes."

"I didn't say your father was alive," he said.

"Last time I checked, dead people don't give orders, and I personally don't believe in ghosts."

"Your father was a client of ours for years," Dominic said. "He put plans in place to make sure his family was protected."

"Even if I believed you, which I don't, that would explain taking my mother and me, but not Colin. Besides, my father would never have us taken against our will. He wouldn't frighten us like that, especially not my mother. She's mentally ill, for God's sake."

"I never knew your father," Dominic said, "but I did know he was alive during the time you thought he was dead. There were few he trusted with that information."

His words hit me in the gut. My father clearly hadn't trusted *me* with that information. Or any of my brothers. He'd faked his death once we were all adults so he could care for our mother, who also, unbeknownst to us, was alive.

His reasoning had been simple. Our mother was not safe from Wendy Madigan, and as long as Wendy knew he was alive, she'd stop at nothing to torment him, using anything that made him vulnerable.

Our mother.

And all of us.

My father was dead.

Wasn't he?

Dominic hadn't said otherwise. But he hadn't said he was alive, either.

I had to stop torturing myself. The man was dead. I'd seen Wendy Madigan kill him so they could be together. I'd seen him double over. I'd seen the blood trickle from his wound. I'd fallen atop his immobile body, felt the life seep out of him...

Wendy had nearly killed Ryan as well, until Ruby shot her first.

That day was forever etched into my mind.

The scar on my thigh itched, and not in a good way. Not in a healing way.

No, it itched to be opened.

If I'd had my blade at this very moment, I'd be cutting my flesh to relieve the emotional torture swirling through me.

My father had so many facets that I'd never understand.

He was a man who could orchestrate his own death, purchase an island in the Caribbean. Hide himself and his mentally ill wife from the world.

From his children.

I forced myself out of my own head.

"You still haven't explained Colin," I said. "Why would my father care about protecting him?"

"We aren't given the reasons," Dominic said.

"So you're okay with taking people against their will? Without knowing why?"

"We know simply that it's for your protection. That's enough for us."

"That, and the money," Dave added.

"Zip it, Dave," Alex said.

"Hey, you two might not need the money, but I do."

"For God's sake," I said. "Tell us what Colin has to do—"

Dominic looked at his phone. "Food's here. Get it, will you, Dave?"

Dave feigned a bow and left the room.

My stomach gurgled as if on cue. How could I possibly be hungry with everything else going on? But I was.

Then it dawned on me. How long had I been gone? What time was it? Hell, what day was it?

"Are you going to let them eat at the table with us?" Alex asked.

"I don't know. Can you behave yourselves?" Dominic eyed me.

"I won't make any promises I can't keep," I said.

"I knew you were a spitfire when I first laid eyes on you," Dominic said. "I'd be lying if I said I didn't find you absolutely intoxicating."

Alex rolled her eyes. "Can you think with your *big* head, Dom? God. Every time there's a pretty girl involved..."

Alex's words struck me. I'd been going about this all wrong. I'd been fighting back the way I fought with my brothers—showing my strength and equality. Dominic's words creeped me out to the point I wanted to barf, but I needed to look at the bigger picture. He was attracted to me. I could take advantage of that.

Though God only knew what I looked like at the moment. But I had to try.

My mind was still a little fuzzy. Had I told him about Bryce?

Shit. Yeah, I had.

I could still flirt. The only problem? I wasn't a great actress, and right now I hated the son of a bitch. He hadn't convinced me that any of this was for my mother's or my own good. My brothers and Bryce would protect us both with their lives if they had to. And what about Colin? Why was he even here?

"We'll behave," I said sweetly. But not too sweetly. I didn't want to arouse suspicion. "What day is it, anyway? I don't know the last time I ate."

"It's still the same day," Dominic said. "Nearing evening."

Okay. I'd only missed lunch, then.

Colin finally spoke. "Why exactly am I here? I didn't even know Marj's dad."

"Like I said," Dominic said. "We just do as we're told. I'm going to untie your hands, both of you, and your feet, Colin. We'll eat at the table in the kitchen. Don't try to run away. You won't get far."

Stop threatening us.

The words hovered on the end of my tongue. I kept them inside. They wouldn't help my new plan of flirting with Dominic.

I wasn't a flirt by nature. I was anything but a girly girl. But I had to try. Nothing else was working.

"What are we having to eat?" I asked.

"Pizza," Alex said dryly.

"Pizza?" I said. "You're a personal trainer, Dominic."

"And I can't eat gluten," Colin added.

"Then you'll go hungry, won't you?" Alex said, untying

Colin's ankles, and not gently.

"Just eat the toppings, Colin," I said.

Dominic hadn't responded to my personal training comment. I tried again.

"Don't tell me you regularly eat pizza," I said to him. "Not with that body."

"Stop trying to suck up." Alex yanked me off the couch.

"Who's sucking up? Your brother's ripped. So are you." No lie there. Alex's muscles put some men I knew to shame. Not my brothers, though. And certainly not Bryce.

I looked over at Colin. He'd been a good-looking man with a great physique once. Tom Simpson had stolen all of that from him. Now he was thin and scarred. A shadow of his former self.

"Just come on. You too." She yanked Colin up by the arm.

"You're pretty rough with us for someone who's supposedly doing this to protect us," I couldn't help saying.

So much for trying to be nicer, though Dominic, not Alex, was my target.

"I can get rougher," she said. "Come on. The food's waiting."

I was no shrinking violet, but Alex had muscles on her muscles. She could most likely take me, especially since I wasn't at full capacity. I smiled—sort of—and followed her to the kitchen.

Dominic and Dave were already at the table.

"Help yourselves," Dominic said. "There's only water to drink. Sorry."

"Water is the best way to hydrate," I said sweetly. Sort of. "As a trainer, you should know that."

"It is, except when extra electrolytes are necessary," he

said. "You two should be fine with plain water, though."

"How did you get us here?" I asked. "My head doesn't hurt, so you couldn't have knocked me unconscious."

"A small injection in your neck," he said.

I trailed my fingers to my neck, feeling around. Sure enough, there was a tiny area of irritation. "You drugged us."

"Very safely," he said.

Again, I held back the words I wanted to spew at him. "What if one of us had had an allergy?"

"Unlikely," he said.

I inhaled. The pizza smelled good to me, and my stomach growled again.

Dominic chuckled. "Go on. I can tell you're hungry."

"I need a fork," Colin said. "I can't eat the crust."

Alex with the eye roll again. She opened a drawer and shoved a fork at Colin.

He grunted a thank-you.

I took a bite of pizza and nearly swallowed it whole. Run-of-the-mill pizza wasn't really my thing. When I made pizza, I did it with style and panache—prosciutto and provolone, or kalamata olives and goat cheese. But damn, regular old pizza—pepperoni and mozzarella—was totally hitting the spot.

I had downed one piece and half of another before I spoke again. "Why is it unlikely that we'd have an allergic reaction to whatever you stuck us with?"

"Because we're given detailed information on everyone we deal with."

"Deal with? Is that your nice way of saying 'kidnap'?"

So much for my flirting idea.

Dominic cleared his throat. "We're given detailed information, and neither of you had any drug allergies listed."

"Was Colin's gluten allergy listed?" I asked sarcastically.

Colin looked up. "It's not an actual allergy, and I don't have celiac disease, to my knowledge. I just can't eat it. Not since..."

"Tom?" I asked.

He nodded, looking down at the naked pizza crust on his plate. He'd eaten the toppings, as I'd suggested.

He didn't elaborate, and I didn't press it. I guessed he'd probably had only stale bread or something like that to eat, and now it didn't agree with him. Or maybe it was psychological. That was more likely.

Whatever it was, even the toppings didn't agree with him.

Colin retched, turning his head. At least he hit the floor instead of the table.

CHAPTER NINE

B r y c e

Dying.

Clearly, I was dying.

Tears poured from my eyes, and vision eluded me.

My sweet little son.

My mother.

Marjorie. Precious Marjorie.

I'd never see any of their faces again.

"Got you," a gruff voice said.

I was moving now, lying down and moving. Still coughing, choking, gasping.

Joe? Where was Joe?

Somehow I'd always known we'd die together. It was no less than we deserved for unwillingly letting a friend die and keeping a dirty secret for my father.

I deserved this . . .

I deserved death . . .

★ ★ ★

"Pepper spray," the blur in white said to me.

"Pepper spray?" I rasped out. But all that actually came out was a choking gasp.

"Don't try to talk, Mr. Simpson," the same voice said. "It'll take another hour or so for the effects to wear off, but nothing will be permanent. Your vision and voice will be normal again."

Pepper spray? That bastard attacked us with pepper spray?

Who the hell armed himself with three weapons and rigged his desk with streams of pepper spray? What other booby traps did he have hidden?

"Joe?" I said.

But it sounded like another gasp.

"Please," the man said.

Was he a doctor? A nurse? I had no idea.

I didn't care. Relief swept through me at the knowledge I'd recover. Pepper spray was considered innocuous. Didn't feel very innocuous at the moment.

Talon had been tased once. I remembered him telling his brothers and me about it. He'd been immobile, frightened, nearly lost control of his bladder and bowels.

I hadn't been tased, but I could relate. The sensation of not being able to breathe was something I didn't want to experience again anytime soon.

"Mr. Steel is in the next room," the person said. "He's recovering as well."

The bastard had gotten both of us. How many streams had he released? It probably didn't matter. One was probably enough to incapacitate us both.

We'd disarmed him.

He'd bested us anyway.

Who the hell was Cade Booker?

An ex-FBI agent.

An attorney in Grand Junction.

A man who was into BDSM.

Interesting, to say the least, but none were reasons to be so heavily armed.

Joe knew him, had trusted him. I trusted Joe. But I'd seen something dark in Cade Booker, something Joe hadn't seen. Maybe because everyone at a leather club exhibited a little darkness.

I tried to speak once more, but instead of words, gasps emerged.

"Rest, please, Mr. Simpson," the white blur said once more. "I've given you a mild sedative. When you wake up, you'll feel much better."

★ ★ ★

I jolted awake.

Where was I?

Panic set in. I opened—

Shit! My eyes wouldn't open. Damn it! They'd said my vision would return! Frantically I felt around for a call button. I found something at the side of the bed and pushed frantically.

Voices broke into my thoughts.

A television. I'd turned on a television. Quickly I moved my hand over the control, pressing every button. The voices became wretchedly loud.

Within seconds, I heard the door to the room open.

"Yes, Mr. Simpson?" said a female voice. She took the remote from me and turned off the TV.

"I can't see. What's going on?"

"Your eyes are swollen shut," she said. "Here. Let me help you."

A few seconds later, something cold and gelatinous

soothed my eyes. Heaven.

"It'll take about twenty-four hours for the swelling to go completely down. Right now they're crusted shut. I'm cleaning them out for you. This will only take a minute."

She could take forever, as far as I was concerned. The coolness on my eyes was nirvana.

"Okay. Try opening."

I forced my eyes open into slits. Her face was fuzzy in front of me. "Still blurry," I said.

"That's from the tears and mucus. It's your body healing the inflammation from the capsaicin. It will pass."

I nodded. What else could I do? "Joe?" I said.

"Mr. Steel refused the sedative," she said. "His wife is with him."

Of course. They would have called Melanie. I had no one for them to call. Marjorie was missing, and my mother and son were in Florida. I had no emergency contact.

No one had come for me.

I was isolated. Alone.

Just like always.

Joe and I were crack shots. We also knew how to fight like pros. And fucking pepper spray had taken us down.

Whoever Cade Booker was, I would personally destroy him.

After I destroyed whoever had stolen Marjorie from me.

I had a sneaking suspicion they might be one and the same.

CHAPTER TEN

Marjorie

"Seriously?" Alex scoffed. "Now I have to clean up vomit?"

"Stop your whining," Dave said. "I'll do it. Isn't that what I'm for, anyway? The grunt work?"

I touched Colin's arm. "You going to be okay?"

"Of course I'm not okay, Marj. I've been kidnapped again. I'm *not* going to be okay."

I nodded. What could I say? He was right.

"He needs something to soothe his stomach," I said to Dominic. "Do you have any Pepto Bismol? Peppermint tea?"

"Do we look like an apothecary?" Alex said snidely.

"Sorry," Dominic said. "We don't have any of that stuff."

"Yeah? What if one of us gets sick? Oh! Looks like that already happened."

"He probably had a reaction to the drug."

"No, he had a reaction to the fact that he was drugged and kidnapped for the second time in his young life."

"We haven't abused him."

"You don't think so? Drugging and kidnapping don't constitute abuse to you?"

"Hello?" Colin said. "I'm here. Don't talk about me like I'm a kid."

"Sorry, Colin." He was right. He was a grown man who'd

had some shit come down on him. I wasn't his mother.

"You haven't been abused," Dominic said.

I knew what he meant. This was nothing compared to what Colin had endured at Tom Simpson's hands. I was full of fire, though, and I didn't feel like playing nice.

So much for my catching-flies-with-honey idea. I just wasn't cut out for it.

At least Colin hadn't gotten any puke on his clothes. He'd aimed it all at the floor. Dave sopped it up with a towel and then sprayed disinfectant on the spot.

"I see you have disinfectant. But not an antiemetic?"

"For God's sake," Dominic said. "We're trying our best here."

"Try harder," I said through clenched teeth. "You can start by telling me why you think Colin and I needed to be kidnapped—which is a felony, by the way—for our own protection."

"I don't know. I'm only given the information I need."

"I don't believe you."

"That's your prerogative, but there's nothing more I can tell you. Look. You know me. You've had lunch with me."

"Yeah, I must be a shitty judge of character," I said. "Not once during lunch did I say to myself, 'hmm, I think this guy might be a kidnapper.'"

"We have more drugs, you know," Alex said. "I say let's knock her unconscious."

"I wasn't talking to you," I said. "You and I never had lunch."

She rolled her eyes. Again.

"What's up with her?" I asked Dominic.

"She's just being herself. It irks her that our clients don't appreciate what we do for them."

"Yeah, must be difficult, when your victims don't appreciate being drugged and abducted."

"That's exactly what pisses her off," Dominic said. "The way you're being. Right now. I know you don't get it, but what we do is a means to an end, and we're paid very well."

"I'd imagine someone would have to pay you well to break the law. And that someone is apparently my dead father."

"I have no idea if your father is dead or not."

"I do. I watched him get shot. It's a visual I'll never forget. He's very much dead."

"That information hasn't been shared with me."

"He *is*, Dominic. You don't forget something like that."

"Whether he is or isn't doesn't matter. He put plans in place."

"How? Who's calling the shots, then? Why are we in danger?"

"I already told you. I wasn't given those details."

I harrumphed and grabbed another slice of pizza. I'd better eat up. Who knew when we'd get food again.

"You feeling better?" I said to Colin with my mouth full of dough.

"Not really."

"You should try to eat again."

"Greasy cheese and pepperoni don't really sound good."

"Then try some of the crust."

"I can't eat glu—"

"Can't? Or don't want to?"

He looked away.

As I suspected. It was in his head. I tore the rim of crust off my piece of pizza and handed it to him. "Come on. It's only plain bread."

He winced, clearly disgusted.

"You have to eat, Colin. If you don't have an allergy or celiac, this won't make you sick."

Finally, he nodded and took the piece of crust and shoved it into his mouth.

Yeah, he was hungry.

"When will we eat next?" I asked, my mouth still full.

"In the morning," Dominic said. "Breakfast."

"We're going to be here all night?" No way.

"You'll be here until we hear otherwise."

"Meaning?"

"Meaning, until we receive instructions otherwise," he said, clearly irritated. "I say what I mean, Marjorie. You don't have to read between the lines."

"Right. You said exactly what you meant when we first met."

"I did. I told you I was a personal trainer, and I am."

"It's not your primary job."

"So? It wasn't a lie."

I grabbed another slice and ripped the crust off, handing it to Colin. Then I shoved a third of it into my mouth.

I was done being ladylike. It wasn't working anyway. I eyed Colin munching on the crust I'd given him. I pointed toward something with my eyes.

Dave had set something on the table next to Colin when he'd gotten a rag to clean up the vomit.

His cell phone.

CHAPTER ELEVEN

B r y c e

Once we were able, Joe and I gave statements to the police. It was nearly dark when Joe—who'd declined his sedative at the hospital—drove us home in Melanie's car. I was relegated to the back seat, but the Tesla Model X had more than enough room for my long legs.

Both of us still had swollen and bloodshot eyes, but our vision had cleared and was nearly back to normal. Normal enough for Joe to feel comfortable driving, anyway.

"Oh!" Melanie said suddenly.

"What? What's wrong?" Joe said frantically.

"It's nothing. A Braxton-Hicks contraction. They come on suddenly and happen more frequently during stressful times."

"I'm sorry, babe," Joe said. "I've added a load of stress to your life."

"None of this is your fault." She looked over her shoulder at me. "Or yours, before you say it is."

I nodded. Melanie was a good woman. She, Jade, and Ruby had married into a mess of problems—problems they'd all thought were over.

Until Joe and I had remembered Justin Valente.

This couldn't be easy on Melanie and Jade especially,

both being pregnant.

"This is a big one," Melanie said.

"Does it hurt?" Joe asked.

"No. It's not pleasant, but it's not crampy or anything. My whole belly just gets really hard."

"And you're sure it's normal?"

"That's what the doctor says. Plus, remember I'm also a doctor."

Joe nodded, his eyes still on the road. "I know, baby. But I worry about you, okay?"

"Trust me. These are noth— Oh!"

Joe swerved but quickly corrected it. "What? What is it?"

"I— I think my water just broke."

"Turn around," I said. "Get her to the hospital."

"That's ridiculous. We're almost home," Melanie said. "You can drop Bryce off. We need to be thinking of Marjorie and your mother."

"Right now I'm thinking of my wife. If your water broke, that means . . ."

"Yeah," Melanie said. "It means this baby is coming. But we have twenty-four hours before we have to worry about infection."

"Infection?" Joe said. "What about the fact that your due date isn't until— Shit!" He swerved to avoid a truck.

Fuck! Was it too soon? I didn't want to be the one to ask that question.

"Thirty-two weeks," Joe was saying, more to himself than to Melanie or me. "The baby will be okay. The baby *has* to be okay."

"Just stop and let me out," I said. "I can walk the mile to the guesthouse."

"That's silly," Melanie said. "We can take you home."

The few minutes to get home seemed like hours to me, so I could only imagine what it was like for Joe.

"Get her back to the hospital," I said when they dropped me off. "I'll call everyone and let them know what's going on."

"You find Marjorie and her mom," Melanie said. "We're counting on you, Bryce."

My eyes still swollen and slightly painful, I ran into the guesthouse. I quickly dialed Talon and then Ryan to let them know what was happening.

Joe.

My best friend.

His baby was early. Premature. I should be at the hospital with him and his wife.

But Marjorie...

Her mother...

Colin...

Someone needed to focus on them.

And that someone was me.

I'd be on pins and needles until I heard from Joe. Thirty-two weeks. Was that considered premature? I remembered from Henry's birth at thirty-eight weeks that the doctors liked a woman to make it to thirty-six. Plus, Melanie was nearly forty-one. She was hot and gorgeous, but old when it came to childbearing.

Damn! Damn! Damn!

Now what?

Cade Booker.

I had to figure out who the hell Cade Booker was and why he was keeping information from us. I had no idea if he could lead me to Marjorie, but at the moment, he was all I had. Now the police would be looking for him as well.

He'd probably gone on the run, anyway. A man couldn't just pepper spray a Steel and walk away unscathed.

There would have been questions.

Lots of questions.

Where was I supposed to begin?

I fired up my laptop and started searching for Cade Booker. His law firm came up first. His bio was no help. It extolled his virtues.

Right.

Why was I doing this when I had access to the best PIs in the business? I put in a call to Ruby. She didn't pick up, so I left her a message. She was probably out working on finding Marjorie and her mother.

Why hadn't I gotten the number for those PIs, Mills and Johnson, from Joe?

I tried the search engine again. Several of those companies offering arrest records surfaced. For a mere membership fee of twenty-nine ninety-five, I could get all the information they had on Cade Booker and anyone else.

I was desperate, so I succumbed. There went thirty bucks I'd never see again.

Cade Booker, age thirty-eight. Same age as Joe and me.

Relatives. Alessandra Booker, age twenty-four. Too old to be Cade's kid. Dominic Booker, age twenty-four. Richard Booker, deceased.

Dominic.

I'd heard that name recently.

Yeah, Marjorie's trainer. His name wasn't Booker, though. It was James.

I was going crazy. So Marjorie's trainer was named

Dominic. Who cared?

Cade Booker had an exemplary FBI record as far as I could tell, but he'd only been with the bureau for a couple years.

I needed a hacker.

The Spider.

He still hadn't responded to any of Joe's or my attempts to get in touch. I'd committed his information to memory. Why not use it? I certainly had no idea where else to turn.

I logged in to the account Joe had created to communicate with the Spider.

And jolted in surprise.

An email was waiting.

CHAPTER TWELVE

M a r j o r i e

I couldn't reach the phone, but I could create a diversion. I shoved the rest of the piece of pizza in my mouth and chewed ferociously. Then I made the best gagging sound I could and spat the contents onto the table in front of me.

"Are you freaking kidding me?" Alex spat out. "More puke?"

I kept choking and coughing, feigning gagging. I waved my hands around, clutching my throat. I said nothing, continued to gasp.

Someone had told me a long time ago that if you could ask for the Heimlich maneuver, you didn't need it. What I needed now was for them to *think* I needed it.

Dominic ran into the room. "Shit. What now?"

"The dumb bitch shoved a whole piece of pizza into her mouth and now she's choking."

"Help her!" Dominic yelled. "We need her!"

"I no longer care, Dom."

"I do." Dominic grabbed me around the chest.

I looked quickly at the table. The cell phone was gone. Colin had pocketed it. Before Dominic could break my ribs, I spat a chunk onto the floor and then inhaled a deep gasp. "I'm good. I'm good."

Dominic let me go. "Thank God."

I turned to Alex. "Thanks for your help."

Again the eye roll. What was up with her? Then I rolled my own eyes. Stupid question. She drugged and kidnapped people for a living. I really didn't need to know anything else to explain her behavior.

I looked quickly at Colin, and he nodded ever so slightly at me. Good. He had the phone. Now to figure out how to get alone and make a call.

First things first. "Thank you," I said to Dominic.

"She shoved a whole piece in her mouth, Dom. What was that about?"

"I'm hungry," I said. "How the heck do I know when we'll get food again?"

"I told you you'd get breakfast," Dominic said.

"Pardon me for not taking you at your word."

"I need to use the bathroom," Colin said.

"You didn't eat hardly anything," Alex said.

"I still have to piss," he said.

"I have to go too," I said. "Where's the can?"

"You want to go with him?"

"No thanks. I'll wait outside the door while he goes."

"I don't think so," Alex said. "Not happening."

"Fine. Whatever. But I might upchuck again."

"There can't possibly be anything left in you," she groused.

"I'll take him to the bathroom," Dominic said. "You stay here with her."

Colin would be alone with the phone. A good thing, but did he know the right number to text?

Yes! He might not have my brothers' numbers, but he did have Jade's.

Perfect.

He'd send a text— No, better yet, he should call and leave the line open so Jade could have it traced. Would he know to do that? We didn't have a lot of time. Dave could come back and realize his phone was missing any minute.

At least Colin would do *something*. I just wasn't sure what.

Damn. I should have gotten the phone from him somehow. But could I have? Dave had left it next to Colin, far from my reach.

I inhaled slowly and then let the air out. Trust. I had to trust Colin to do this right.

Each second he was gone in the bathroom felt like hours. Pretty soon, Dominic would be pounding on the door telling him to hurry. Colin was a nervous wreck as it was.

Please, please, Colin. Keep it together and get this done.

I looked at my watch, which, oddly, they hadn't taken from me. In fact, they hadn't taken anything, really. My purse was here somewhere. It had been next to me when they removed my blindfold on the couch in what appeared to be the living room.

I suppressed a surprised shudder.

My purse.

Had they gone through it?

I had no idea.

But in my purse . . .

My security blanket.

I hadn't gotten rid of the blade. It was still there, nestled in its zippered cavern, waiting for me. The little pouch was invisible unless you knew to look for it, and no one except Mel and now Bryce knew my secret.

Guilt had consumed me after I told them both I'd dumped

the blade for good. Thank God I'd kept it for a very good reason—a reason I hadn't known at the time.

Ten minutes had passed since Colin had entered the bathroom. Ten very long minutes. If he took much longer, Dominic would get suspicious.

Come on, Colin. Come on.

As if on cue, he walked back into the kitchen, Dominic following him. Alex leaned against the counter, looking as distrustful as ever. Dave hadn't returned for his phone.

So far so good.

If this didn't work, though, I had a backup plan.

"My turn." I rose. "I'm going to need my purse."

"Why?" Alex asked.

"My monthly friend is visiting," I lied.

"You're full of it," she said.

"You want to check?" I glared at her.

"Sure, you dum—"

"For God's sake, Alex," Dominic interrupted. "Get her purse."

I held back a smile. If I could depend on one thing always, it was the discomfort all men shared when it came to female body functions.

"She's lying," Alex said. "She would've had to go before now."

"Light flow," I said. "I'm on the pill." The second part was true, anyway.

Dominic and Colin had both turned the color of a red delicious apple.

Good. This was going well.

"Lighten up, Alex." Dominic left the room and came back holding my purse. "Here. And don't mention any of this again."

"Dom . . ."

"We've already been through her purse, Alex. We have her phone."

Ah. As I'd suspected. Thank goodness I always kept extra tampons in my purse, or they'd have had a lot of questions. Since he didn't mention the blade, he probably hadn't found it.

I wished for a psychic link to Colin. If only I knew if he'd gotten through to Jade . . . or whether he'd done anything at all. He could have easily chickened out, which was why I needed plan B.

I grabbed my purse and muttered a "thanks." Alex led me to the bathroom.

The room was tiny, since this was a mobile home, but I had enough elbow room to do what had to be done. I opened a tampon with as much commotion as I could, just in case she was listening, and I even inserted it, in case she wanted to check for the string. Not that I thought she would, but Alex was a question mark. I couldn't manipulate her the way I was manipulating Dominic.

Then I pawed through the contents of my purse, removing the bulkier items so I could access the hidden zippered pouch at the bottom.

Eureka!

I fingered the shiny blade.

The scar on my upper thigh began to tingle.

No time for that, though. I couldn't be bleeding while I tried to make someone else bleed.

These are my friends . . .

No, damn it. No!

Maybe just one little cut.

Just enough to relieve the tension.

No one would know.
No one would know.

CHAPTER THIRTEEN

B r y c e

Gotcha.

The entire contents of the email from the Spider.

Gotcha.

What the fuck?

We didn't know who the Spider was, and as far as we knew, he hadn't done anything—

Oh, shit.

Cade Booker had given us the information.

Cade Booker.

There was no Spider.

I pounded my fist on the kitchen table.

Who the hell was this Cade Booker? I needed information, and at this point, Joe would spill, even with the silent code of the BDSM club. The guy had attacked us with pepper spray. He'd been armed with three guns, for God's sake.

I grabbed the last known address from the file I'd gotten via the web and entered it into my GPS. Back to the city for me tonight.

I ignored my eyes. They were sore and tired. Closing them would be a godsend. But I couldn't. I wouldn't.

Marjorie never left my mind. What was happening to

her? I couldn't let myself consider any of the vile possibilities. No, she needed me whole. She believed in me, believed I was more than an empty shell.

I had to prove her right. I had to find her, and that meant focusing.

My phone buzzed.

"Talon?" I said. "What's up? Is Melanie all right?"

"I haven't heard anything about Melanie, and I'm not going to bother Joe with this. He needs to be with his wife right now. But Jade just got a text from a number she didn't recognize. It says it's from Colin. He's with Marj, Bryce. They're being held in a mobile home somewhere."

"Oh my God. Anything else?"

"Yeah. After he sent the text, Colin called Jade and left the line open. We're tracing it now."

"We've got to move quickly. I'll be right over."

"We're already on our way," Talon said. "Ryan and Ruby are with me. We're going after our sister."

I marched into my bedroom and retrieved my alternate pistol, as the one I'd been carrying earlier had been taken when I was at the hospital, and I hadn't thought to get it back. I was armed again.

Armed and ready.

★ ★ ★

"Two hours away," Talon said when I got into the passenger seat of his truck. "Fucking two hours away."

"Could be a trick," Ruby said. "In fact, it's probable. The best way to keep us off the trail is to *send* us off the trail."

"We have to try," Ryan said. "You know that."

"Of course I know that. Why do you think I'm with you? You need me. I'd do anything for this family. Everybody armed?"

"Always," I said, echoing Joe's response I'd heard so many times.

Talon had been in the military, and Ruby had been a police detective. Clearly, they could shoot. Joe said he had taught Ryan, but was he any good? Did he carry a gun?

"Yeah," Ryan replied.

That answered that question.

"Of course," was Talon's response.

"I still think we should tell Joe what we're up to," Ryan said.

Talon shook his head. "He has enough on his mind. Let him become a dad. He deserves it."

"I agree," I said. "We can handle this. Everyone in this car loves Marj just as much as Joe does. Plus, his baby is premature. He needs to have his head in that game right now."

"I talked to Melanie," Ruby said. "There's a good chance the baby will be fine without incubation. Babies have survived that are born at twenty weeks. Everything will likely go well, so I agree with Bryce. Let them have this time together."

"Joe will be pissed," Ryan said.

"Oh, yeah," I said. "He will. But after he gets over his hotheadedness, he'll realize we did what was best."

"He needs to be with Melanie," Talon agreed. "Besides, we don't know what we're getting into. This could be dangerous."

"Said the new father of almost three," Ryan reminded him.

"I've gone into many a battle," Talon said, "and I've come out of all of them, even when I didn't want to."

Silence after that.

We all knew Talon's story, how he'd tried to get himself killed in Iraq. Seemed life had other plans for him. Plans with a wife and kids.

Talon would come out of this alive.

We all would.

Including Marj.

She would.

She had to.

I needed her.

We drove in silence for another half hour, when all of our phones dinged with a text simultaneously.

From Joe.

He's here. Four pounds even. Tiny but breathing on his own. Strong as an ox and gorgeous like his mom. He'll be in NICU for a week or so. Expected to do fine.

We all sighed in relief.

"Won't he be expecting us at the hospital?" I asked.

"It's late. I'm sure he'll expect that we'll come see the baby tomorrow," Talon said.

Joe was a father.

Wow.

Being a father was something that had enriched my life in so many ways. It would be great to watch my best friend enjoy those things for the first time.

"What's his name?" I said.

"The text doesn't say," Ruby said. "You know, it's funny. Melanie and I talk all the time, and she never mentioned any names they were considering. The few times I brought it up, she said they hadn't decided."

"We'll know soon enough," Ryan said. "He can't be nameless forever."

"Melanie was worried for so much of this pregnancy," Ruby went on, "because of her age. I wonder if she was just trying not to get too attached to the baby, you know?"

"You *have* been spending a lot of time with Melanie," Talon said. "That sounds exactly like something she would say."

"Her pregnancy has been textbook easy," Ryan said. "Nothing like Jade's."

Talon visibly stiffened in the driver's seat. "Jade's doing a lot better. She's been feeling pretty good since that scare."

Silence again.

Then, "Shouldn't one of us text him back?" Ryan said. "Or call?"

"I'm driving," Talon replied. "Jade will text him for us."

I hurriedly tapped into my phone. "Wonderful! Congratulations! Welcome to fatherhood. Your life is about to change drastically, but you'll love it. Love you, bro."

"Text sent," I said.

"Yeah, me too," Ryan said. "I feel like we should call him."

Talon kept his eyes on the road. "He's busy. We'll call him when we're done with this."

When we're done with this.

Interesting choice of words.

This could very well be leading us to nowhere good.

CHAPTER FOURTEEN

Marjorie

No one would know.

Slowly I lowered the blade to the scar of my flesh. Tingles shot through me at the chill of the sharp blade against my skin.

Just a little cut...

Just a little, to relieve all this tension—

"What the hell is taking you so long?" Alex banged on the door.

Reality set in with a brick to my gut.

What was I doing? This was no time for my ridiculous self-indulgence. I had a job to do, especially if Colin had failed.

"Give me a break," I said. "Haven't you ever had a period before?"

"Yeah. And I take care of it quickly. You've got two more minutes before I knock this fucking door down."

Shit. Okay.

The blade burned hot against my fingers.

Alex on the other side of the door, ready to pound her way in...

My friend.

Almost no thought in my head as I cut a centimeter incision into my scar.

The pinch of pain flowed through me, calming me.

Yes, and I could make this work. I opened another tampon, sopped up the blood, and then threw it in the wastebasket next to the toilet. I'd flush the extra wrapper.

Ha! Let Alex check the trash. She'd find what she needed to find, and I got the pleasant calming of the pain in my thigh. I tore the wrapper off a bandage and taped up the cut. Wrapper from the bandage went in the toilet as well.

Later, I'd berate myself for succumbing.

Later, when I had to think about what I'd done.

For now, I had a job to do—get Colin and myself out of here.

What to do with the blade? I was wearing sweats with no pockets, a sports bra, and a workout shirt. My bra seemed the safest place. I carefully placed it on top of my left breast, taking care not to scratch my skin. Then I adjusted my sweatpants and flushed the toilet. Yes! The mobile home toilet had handled the extra stuff. I washed my hands before opening the door.

"Took you long enough," Alex said, frowning.

Actually, had I ever seen her smile? Nope. The frown was a permanent fixture on her face. I smiled sweetly... which took a lot of effort. "Thanks. I feel better now."

No truer words.

She scowled at me and led me back into the kitchen.

Dave still hadn't returned for his cell phone, which was making me nervous. How did a person not know his cell phone was missing? Especially someone in the business of crime?

Thoughts filled my head. Did he have two phones? Was the cell phone a plant? Were they setting us up?

Maybe. I had no idea. All I knew was that I had a plan, and I'd stick to it. What else could I do?

The blade prickled against my breast. It was only my

imagination. The chill from the cool metal had warmed almost instantly.

No, this was the tingling I was used to. The vibration I felt whenever I held it. Held *my friend*.

I had to ignore it.

So I had the blade. What next? If they tied us up again, I wouldn't be able to access it. I needed a plan. Colin still sat at the table, white as a sheet. I assumed he still had Dave's phone hidden . . . somewhere. Most likely in his crotch, the place he figured Dominic and Alex wouldn't look.

Now what?

Might as well ask.

"What now?" I asked Dominic. I was tempted to ask where Dave had gone, but I didn't want to bring attention to him or his phone.

"You'll be comfortable here for the night. Alex will stay here with you. Dave and I have other things to attend to."

Dave wasn't coming back. Shit. He'd eventually realize his phone was missing.

Crap. What if Dominic tried to call Dave and the phone rang in Colin's crotch?

Had he thought to put the phone on silent? I wasn't sure, because the thought hadn't occurred to me until this very moment.

Trust. Again, I had to trust Colin. He was a smart man, even though he'd been through horrific times. Horrific times didn't erase intelligence and cunning. It hadn't for Talon. I had to believe it hadn't for Colin.

If Dave was gone for the evening, Dominic and Alex would have no reason to call him.

Right?

Nothing I could do about it, at any rate.

"You two will have to share a room," Dominic said. "There's a bed, and everything is clean and comfortable. It's connected to Alex's by a door. That's the only way out. The windows are barred, so you'll have to get past Alex if you're thinking about running."

"Let's just tie them up and be done with it," Alex said.

"No. Our orders are to keep them comfortable here."

"Fuck the orders," Alex said.

"You're getting more like our brother every day," Dominic said. "You want to switch sides? Say the word."

"No. I don't want to switch sides," she said with sarcasm. "I'm just tired of dealing with these privileged little fucks."

Privileged?

I was a Steel, and Colin came from a privileged background as well. After all we'd both been through, though, I had a hard time thinking of either of us as privileged.

Whatever.

"I'll need access to a bathroom," I said.

"Alex will take you if you need to go," Dominic said.

"So I'm reduced to being a babysitter. Taking the little toddlers to go pee pee."

"Alex ..."

She sighed. "Sorry."

I held back a scoff. Bitch wasn't sorry at all. If she hated this line of work so much, why was she in it? Why did she let Dominic run the show? She put on a tough act, but maybe she wasn't so tough after all.

I intended to find out.

"All right," Dominic said. "I'm out of here. I'll be back in the morning with your breakfast. Dave might get here before me, if he finishes—"

"Shouldn't we have heard from him by now?" Alex interrupted.

Dominic looked at his watch. "I'll call him from the road."

Alex nodded, and relief swept through me. Now Colin would have time to silence the phone if he hadn't already—assuming he could do so without being seen.

"You two behave yourselves," Dominic said to us.

"Sure, Dad," I said dryly.

Colin said nothing.

Dominic left, and I sat, my nerves jittering, waiting for the phone to ring in his crotch, or wherever it was. After a few minutes, I allowed myself to stop worrying. A little.

"Come on," Alex said.

We followed her into what I assumed was a bedroom. It looked as if an extra wall and a door had been installed to make a nursery or something. "You two are in here."

"Uh . . . there's only one bed in here," I said.

"Then you'll be cozy. Shut the fuck up." She walked through the door. "This stays open, by the way."

I didn't dare speak to Colin until I hadn't heard anything come from Alex's room for about ten minutes.

"Phone?" I mouthed.

"Died," he mouthed back in a light whisper. "Battery was almost dead, but I managed to send a text and keep the line open."

I gave him a thumbs-up. Hopefully its juice had held out long enough for Jade and Talon to trace the call.

"Take the bed," Colin whispered. "I don't mind the floor."

I held a finger to my lips, urging him to be quiet. It didn't really matter who took the bed. If we came up with a plan, we wouldn't be here long.

Then I pointed to my left breast. I lifted my shirt and showed him the blade secured in my bra. I still didn't know what I'd do with it.

"If the phone's dead," I whispered, "just tuck it somewhere. Dave will think he left it behind."

He nodded. "When we go."

"Plan?" I mouthed.

"Slit her throat," he mouthed back.

CHAPTER FIFTEEN

Bryce

Roughly an hour and a half later, we drove into what appeared to be a deserted mobile home park. Trailers sat in ruins.

"They can't possibly be in here anywhere," Ryan said.

"You'd be surprised," Ruby said. "In my day, I busted a lot of drug rings that were run out of places like this. They could very well be here."

"You said it could be a setup," Ryan said.

"It still could be. I don't know, Ry. But this is a den for criminal activity, I can tell you that much. I feel it in my bones."

"What's that supposed to mean?" her husband gibed her.

"It means after a decade on the force, you learn to follow your instincts."

"No lights anywhere," I said. "If they're here, it'll be like looking for a needle in a haystack. We'll have to check each of these trailers."

"Not necessarily," Ruby said. "We look for other things. Tire tracks, for instance. Footprints."

Ryan kissed her cheek. "That, right there, is why I married you."

"It's dark, though," I said. "Did anyone bring a flashlight?"

"Of course," Talon and Ruby said in unison.

Of course. The military man and the cop. They'd think of that. Why I hadn't, I wasn't sure. It was certainly logical.

Easy. They'd been trained to focus when in dire straits. I hadn't been. My only thought had been getting to Marj. I was armed because I was almost always armed. My father had made sure I'd gotten my concealed carry permit as soon as I turned twenty-one. Joe, as well. It was pretty much part of getting dressed, as far as I was concerned.

Right now, I was thankful for that lesson learned, even if it *had* come from my father.

Talon pulled his truck into a secluded spot. "We should do this on foot. Damn. This feels familiar, doesn't it, Ry?"

"Yeah," Ryan agreed.

"What do you mean?" I asked.

"When we were on that island, looking for Ruby," Ryan answered. "Tal and I were alone and armed, with no idea where we were going."

"You found what you were looking for that time," I said.

"We did. Plus a lot more. Our mother, for one," Talon said.

"*Your* mother," Ryan said tersely.

"Come on, Ryan," Ruby said. "She was your mother too. In every way that counts."

Ryan didn't respond, and I didn't look into the back seat to see his reaction. None of my business. Plus, we had more important things to attend to.

"Let's go," Talon said. "We should split up. Ryan and Ruby, you go together. I'll go with Bryce."

"Makes sense," Ruby said. "Everyone got their phones on?"

We all nodded. We had temporarily retired our normal phones and started using burner phones to stay in contact with each other. It had been sheer luck that Jade and Melanie were still using their original phones. Thank God. Otherwise, we wouldn't have gotten the text from Colin.

Talon and I headed toward the first run-down trailer to the north of the truck, while Ryan and Ruby headed south.

Talon had his light on the dimmest setting. "I don't see any tire tracks or anything around here. You want to go in and check it out?"

"I don't think we should leave anything to chance," I said. "What if someone walked back and covered the tracks?"

"It's possible. All right. Let's go in."

I walked up the cracked concrete stoop and tried the door. It was locked, but I easily executed a side kick and knocked it in.

"Bryce," Talon said. "That's not exactly being quiet."

"You got a better idea?"

He shook his head, and we both walked inside.

"Marjorie?" I yelled. No need to be quiet after kicking in a door. "Are you here?"

Nothing.

I followed Talon, who had the light, as we searched every inch of the unit.

Nothing.

On to the next one.

Nothing in the next four units, either.

Finally, we came across what looked like tire tracks and footprints.

"This could be the one," Talon whispered.

This door was padlocked and had been recently replaced. Not a great chance that I'd be able to kick it in. I tried, though, and got a nasty charley horse in my thigh.

"Maybe both of us together," Talon said.

We kicked on three. Nothing.

"No one's there, apparently, or they'd have heard us kicking," Talon said.

"We still have to try," I said. "What if she's in there? Tied up and gagged?"

I could hardly bear the thought.

Talon nodded. "Let's check the windows."

We walked the perimeter of the unit, Talon shining the light in each window. "A-ha," he said. "Beakers and Bunsen burners. This is a meth lab."

"So that's why it's locked up, and why there are tire tracks. Still, what if Marj is in there? She could have easily been taken by meth heads."

"We'd have gotten a ransom demand if that were the case," Talon said. "My gut tells me she's not here. We shouldn't waste the time."

"We can't take the chance. We have to know for sure."

He nodded. "You're right." He pushed his flashlight through a window, breaking the glass. "Give me a boost."

"You need a cloth. What if a shard gets you?"

"I've been through worse than a cut from broken glass," he said.

I nodded and made a scoop with my hands. He pulled himself up to the window.

"You stay here and keep watch," he said. "I won't be long."

"Roger."

I heard faint noises of Talon tussling around inside, looking for clues. A minute passed. Then another. Then ten more, until—

Crash!

Shit! I hoisted myself up quickly and landed, not gracefully, on the floor of what appeared to be the kitchen. I didn't have a flashlight, but my eyes adjusted quickly. This was a meth lab, all right, but it had long since been abandoned.

I followed the noises Talon was making, my weapon drawn. "Talon! I'm coming."

"This way," he said.

Soon I came upon him. His light was shining on a skinny sandy-haired man. He held his gun aimed at the man's heart.

"He came in the back way after I got in," Talon said.

I moved to Talon's right to cover the guy from the back. I aimed my gun at his brain.

"Start talking," Talon said.

"You better have a good reason for breaking and entering," the man said.

"And you better have a good reason for having a meth lab in your kitchen," I retorted.

"It's not mine," the man said.

"Sell it to someone else." Talon cocked his gun. "We're looking for three people. An older woman with brown hair and eyes, a younger one, same coloring with long hair, and a young man with light brown hair and hazel eyes. Hair's real short."

"Don't know what you're talking about," he said. "Put those guns down, please."

"Not on your life," I said through clenched teeth. "You're holed up in a meth lab. Even if you don't know where—"

A slight movement to the man's right.

Then, a woman's voice.

"Brad? Is that you?"

CHAPTER SIXTEEN

Marjorie

Slit her throat.

The words rang in my head.

Could I? Was I capable of doing harm to another human being?

I was certainly capable of harming myself. With the slight thought, my fresh cut itched and tingled, and the steel blade grew hot against my breast.

My friend...

Would I get in trouble? I'd been kidnapped. Taken against my will. Surely this would be a case of self-defense.

If only Jade were here. She was an attorney. She could tell me for sure.

Alex rustled around in the other room. Until she fell asleep, we couldn't do anything anyway.

Still, the blade burned against my flesh, as if it were branding me.

"What now?" Colin mouthed to me.

"We wait, I guess," I mouthed back.

We should be exhausted, but energy rolled through me. My heart beat rapidly, keeping me on edge. No way would I be able to sleep. No way.

I just hoped Alex could. Apparently, she was used to doing

these sorts of things for a living. If so, she should be able to sleep through anything by now. Or she slept lightly. I prayed it was the former.

Come on! Fall asleep, damn it!

Still, she rustled around, sounding as if she was having a difficult time getting comfortable. Served her right, though I wanted her comfortable at the moment.

I wanted her damned comfortable, dreaming about pink clouds and unicorns and sleeping like a baby.

I lay down on the bed. "Lie down," I said barely audibly to Colin. "In case she comes in here."

He nodded and took his place on the floor.

Normally I'd have resisted lying down, afraid I'd fall asleep. Not tonight. My beating heart wouldn't let me succumb to slumber anytime soon.

* * *

I sat up in bed and checked my watch. Shit! Forty-five minutes had passed in the span of two. So much for not falling asleep. On the floor next to me, Colin had succumbed as well. Maybe this had been a good thing. If Alex thought we were asleep . . .

I moved slowly, cringing every time the stupid bed made a creak. I didn't want to wake Colin. Not yet. The less sound, the better.

I tiptoed to the door and peered into the other room. I squinted to try to see better. Alex was a dark lump on the bed, her chest rising and falling in a regular rhythm. Did that mean she was asleep?

So far, she hadn't heard me. Did I dare actually walk into the room?

No.

I had to wake Colin first. But how to do that without alarming him? He might cry out, and that would wake up Alex.

I walked back to where Colin lay on the floor. I nudged him gently.

He opened his eyes. "It's okay. I'm awake," he said, mouthing more than saying the words.

Relief swept through me. "I think she's asleep," I mouthed back.

He nodded and sat up. "Let's do it."

Again, the blade burned against my flesh. *Take it out of your bra, Marj. You need to have it in your hand.*

I drew in a deep breath, gathering my courage.

I was about to wound—perhaps mortally—another person.

"You have no choice," Colin whispered.

Had I said those thoughts out loud? Or could he just read the tormented expression I probably had on my face?

Didn't matter. He knew. And he understood. He'd been through a hundred times worse than what we were going through now.

Once more, I gathered my courage, my cut itching and throbbing. I reached into my shirt and pulled the blade out from my bra.

My friend . . .

Tingles shot through me, and my fingers itched to descend to the bandage on my thigh. I could easily sweep my sweatpants over my hips and slice into myself again.

Easily.

So easily.

"Ready?" Colin said.

"Thank you," I mouthed.

He cocked his head at me. He had no idea why I was thanking him, of course. He was my focal point. He was keeping me focused, and I was eternally grateful.

I suppressed the shivers that threatened to overtake me as I walked as quietly as I could out the door and toward the lump on the bed that was Alex.

The blade flamed between my fingers, growing hotter, hotter the closer I got to its target.

Did Alex feel the tingles, the thrilling sensation? The torturous pleasure at knowing she was about to be cut into?

I didn't.

Seemed I only got that when I was about to cut into myself.

Instead, jitters tormented me—jitters, and shivers, and shakes.

Closer. I walked closer. Her chest rose and fell, rose and fell, rose and fell . . .

Colin was behind me. I motioned for him to escape, get out the door.

Still, he stayed next to me.

A nice gesture. He didn't want me to be alone while I potentially ended another human life. Gentlemanly of him. I'd have felt better, though, if he'd have just gotten away. He could run and find help.

Again, I motioned for him to leave.

Again, he didn't.

These are my friends . . .

Do it. Do it. Do it.

I moved closer to Alex, my hand hovering above her.

CHAPTER SEVENTEEN

Bryce

"Brad, is that you?"

For an instant, Talon lost his focus, and the thin man lunged toward him. I aimed to graze the bastard's ankle and shot.

He cried out as he fell to the floor.

Talon went running toward the voice, while I dealt with the asshole on the ground. "Who else is here?"

No response.

"It's a scratch. Answer, damn it, or the next bullet will go between your eyes."

"No one. Just me and the old lady."

The old lady.

Brad, is that you?

Brad Steel. Shit! We'd just found Daphne Steel!

"Where's Marjorie?" I said through clenched teeth.

"I need medical help here!"

"You're fine. If I'd wanted to kill you, I would have. Trust me."

"Please. Call 9-1-1. Please."

"You'll get nothing until you tell me where Marjorie Steel is." I grabbed his shirt collar. "I don't give a shit if you bleed to death right here in this trash heap, got it? I only care about

Marjorie, so start talking."

"Down the road," he gasped. "Next block over. Mobile ... home ..." His eyes fluttered closed.

What a fucking wuss. An ankle graze hurt like hell, for sure, but he wasn't going to bleed out. I hadn't hit an artery, for God's sake. "Dude," I said out loud, "you're in the wrong business if you're fainting from this."

No response, but I couldn't take the chance he was bluffing. I continued to hold my gun on him. "Tal! What do you have in there?"

"My mother. She passed out. I'm bringing her out."

He emerged, carrying Daphne Steel as if she weighed no more than a child. In her arms, she clutched a realistic-looking doll. Marjorie had told me about the doll she called Angela, which had been Marj's name at birth.

"Is she okay?" I asked.

"She's far from okay. She's messed up. But she's alive. She was in a room that looked ..." He shook his head. "This isn't a meth lab at all. Her room was a replica of her room at the facility, right down to the bassinet for her doll. The abandoned meth lab is a cover. Fuck. I need to get her out of here."

"We can't go yet. Marjorie."

"Ryan and Ruby are still on it. They can help you. I have to see to my mother."

Marjorie was first on my mind, so I had a hard time understanding. But I'd do just about anything for my own mother, so I nodded. "Call them and tell them to meet me a block over. Dickless here says that's where Marj is. He might be bluffing, for all I know."

"He's out cold," Talon said.

"Maybe. I don't trust him."

"Looks out to me. I've got my mother. You go find Marj."
He tossed me the flashlight without so much as letting his
mother drop.

I caught it easily. "Count on it."

Talon carried his mother out of the room and then out
of the mobile home. He'd have to carry her all the way to his
truck, which was several blocks away by this time. He could do
it. Talon had carried many wounded soldiers out of harm's way
in Iraq. He'd returned as a hero because of his actions.

I hurried back to the thin man, who was still passed out on
the floor. "For God's sake." I quickly unbuttoned his shirt and
removed it, ripping it into strips. I bandaged his wound. I'd call
9-1-1 on the way to Marjorie.

I hurried out. Next block over, he'd said. What the fuck
did that mean?

Didn't matter. I had to find Marjorie. I had to.

And I would.

Or I'd die trying.

CHAPTER EIGHTEEN

Marjorie

I trembled, my heart pounding.

These are my friends.

Do it! Do it! Do it!

Then I jerked.

Alex had moved ever so slightly.

"Easy," Colin said quietly behind me.

I slowly brought my hand—

No. This blade. This friend. This friend who had seen me through some of the most difficult times in my life was not my friend.

It was all a lie.

Using this blade on myself didn't make me stronger. It had made me weaker. Now I needed strength. I needed the strength to save myself, but the blade didn't give me that.

Still, I had to.

Had to . . .

Alex jerked upward. "Fuck! What's going on?"

Do it. Do it. Do it.

But I froze. I fucking froze.

Only seconds before Alex would get her bearings. *Do it! Do it! Do it!*

But the blade was no longer in my hand. Colin had yanked

it from me, slicing his own fingers in the process. "It's okay," he said to me. "Go."

Then he lunged at Alex and jammed the blade into her throat.

Her scream rang through the air like a shrieking storm.

Still, I stood, immobile.

My friend.

No longer *my* friend.

Colin's friend now, and though it had made me weak, this friend gave *him* strength. The strength to do what was necessary.

"Go!" Colin commanded again. "Go!"

I ran for the door, nearly stumbling over a bulge in the carpeting at the doorway. Was Colin behind me? I had no idea. I cared . . . but at the same time I didn't.

One thought and one thought only permeated every membrane of my body.

Get. The. Hell. Out. Of. Here.

And that was what I did.

I ran.

I ran back through the kitchen.

Through the living area where I'd been when I'd woken up here.

Out the door.

Into the darkness.

I opened my mouth to scream, but nothing came out.

Still I ran.

And ran.

And—

Until the breath was knocked out of me by the force of a mountain in my way.

"No!" I yelled.

Massive arms wrapped around me, forcing me to stop in my tracks.

"Let me go! Let me go!" Tears welled in my eyes as I drummed my fist against the hardness of the mountain holding me. "Let me go! Let me go!"

"Easy, honey." Strong fingers stroked my hair. "Easy. It's me."

I inhaled.

The sweet scent of familiarity.

The sweet scent of the man I loved.

All the tears I'd held back since I'd been taken gushed out of me. Crying was for girls, I'd always said, growing up with three older brothers.

I used tears sparingly.

Not this time. This time, I let them out. Let them flow. Let them flow onto Bryce's chest and shoulders.

He kissed the top of my head. "Thank God," he murmured. "Thank God."

I let myself weep for several minutes unchecked.

Bryce held me. Simply held me and let me break down. I reveled in it for these few minutes, let myself go, until I knew it was time to gain my composure. I didn't know where Colin was, and Alex was inside the mobile home bleeding to death.

I gulped down my last sob and wiped my face on Bryce's shirt. "It's you. It's really you."

"I'll always come after you," he said, stroking my hair, which had to be a ratty mess by now. "Always."

A few more seconds of gentleness passed.

"You okay?" he asked.

What a loaded question. I was far from okay. I'd been

drugged and abducted. But I hadn't been beaten or raped. I nodded into his chest.

"Hey," Bryce said.

I moved my head to look around. Colin was behind me.

"They didn't hurt us," he said. "Other than drugging us and taking us. They actually fed us and everything."

Colin seemed coolly fine for someone who'd just slit a woman's throat. Not that Alex didn't deserve it, but still.

Or had he just recaptured his confidence? Done something to help himself when earlier he hadn't been able to?

"The woman inside needs medical help," he said to Bryce.

I nodded. I didn't want to see Colin charged with involuntary manslaughter or anything. Was that possible? Jade would know.

"I already called 9-1-1 for a guy in another trailer. They're on their way." He stroked my cheek. "We found your mom."

Sweet relief swept through me. "Is she okay?"

"She passed out. Talon got her to the truck."

"Tal is here?"

"Yeah. Plus Ruby and Ryan." Bryce tossed his phone to Colin. "Call 9-1-1 and tell them about the woman."

Colin caught the phone easily—confidently—and made the call.

"I want to know everything," Bryce said. "Every detail. But first we're going to get you to a hospital. Both of you."

"We're okay," I said.

"Not good enough. I want you checked out."

"Bryce—"

"Nonnegotiable. Your brothers will agree with me."

I nodded numbly. He was right. I had no idea what Dominic had injected me with. I'd go to the hospital.

Then I wanted to go home.

And put an end to this madness once and for all.

"By the way," Bryce said, "you have a new nephew."

I jerked. "What?"

"Melanie's water broke earlier today. The baby's small but doing well. He's expected to be fine."

"It's my fault," I said. "All the stress from my being taken must have made her go into labor."

"Don't take this on," he said soothingly. "You didn't ask for this, and the baby is doing fine."

"Joe doesn't know about you being here, does he?"

"He knows you were missing, but no. He doesn't know about Colin's message to Jade."

"Thank God it worked." I sighed.

Bryce gripped my shoulders and pushed me away slightly, meeting my gaze. The moonlight slid over his features. He looked both beautiful and insanely mad at the same time.

"Thank God," he echoed. "I'm never letting you out of my sight again."

CHAPTER NINETEEN

Bryce

Marjorie.

I held on to her, relishing her body melded against mine. We fit together so perfectly, almost divinely, even like this.

I hadn't let the fear overtake me while I searched for her, hadn't let myself give in to the fear that threatened to consume me. No, I'd had to focus—focus enough to be able to use every bit of my muscle to kick in doors. For her.

But now? Holding her like this, letting her cry into me . . .

All the fear flew through me in retrospect.

I couldn't let her go. Didn't want to let her go. If I let her move away from my body, would I be able to protect her?

I'd meant what I said. I wanted her and Colin to go to a hospital to get checked out. Talon was probably already on the road with his mother. Had he checked in with Ryan and Ruby?

Colin still had my phone.

Even if I had it, I wasn't sure I'd have let go of Marj to text them.

I wasn't ready to let go just yet.

I might never be.

"All good," Colin said. "They're on their way."

I nodded.

"Now what?" he asked.

"Go to my contacts. It's a short list on this burner phone. Text Ry and Ruby and let them know I have you and Marj. Tell them Tal has Daphne as well. I'm not sure if he texted them."

Colin nodded and began pecking at my phone.

And still I held on to Marj.

"I'm never letting you out of my sight again," I said echoing myself. "Never again."

I expected her spitfire personality to emerge and fight my words. But she didn't. She just leaned into me. She was no longer bawling, only a sniffle now and then.

We stood, and even though clothing separated us, I felt like we were one body. Like we'd always be one body.

Ryan and Ruby found us, and though I spoke to them, told them what had occurred, it didn't seem like me talking. The real me was glued to Marjorie.

Time moved slowly, and it seemed like hours before the police and ambulance showed up. Ruby took the lead with the police, and the paramedics brought the woman inside the unit out on a stretcher.

"Is she alive?" I heard Colin ask.

"She'll be okay," one of the medics said. "We got here in time. The other guy just has a flesh wound on his lower leg."

Colin said nothing more. At least he wouldn't be responsible for taking a life, though he'd certainly had good reason to attack. I selfishly wished I'd been the one to slit the woman's throat. I'd have liked to kill with my bare hands everyone involved with Marj's disappearance.

The police didn't make Marj and Colin tell their stories yet. Instead, they drove us all to the hospital where Talon had taken his mother.

After the doctors had given Marjorie and Colin a clean

bill of health, the police took them into a secluded room to tell their stories.

I still didn't know everything that had gone on.

I sat next to Talon in the waiting area. "How's Daphne?"

"Physically, she's fine. They didn't do anything to her. Apparently she walked right out of Newhaven with someone she thought was my father."

"I thought whoever signed her out used Joe's name."

"He did. He wouldn't use my father's name. Everyone knows he's dead. Did you get any information out of Marj?"

I shook my head. "I just held her. Didn't want to let her go."

He nodded.

Ruby had been let in with the officers doing the questioning as a courtesy because she was an ex-cop, and Ryan had gone somewhere. I wasn't sure where. To get food maybe. It was the middle of the night. I'd wanted to call Jade so Marj and Colin would have an attorney, but Marj and Talon both nixed that idea.

"Who do you suppose is behind this?" Talon asked. "It couldn't be Ted Morse. He's Colin's father."

"I'm not sure that makes a difference," I said. "I guess Marj didn't get a chance to tell you what Colin told her right before she was taken."

Of course she hadn't. She'd been taken while she was on the phone with Joe and me.

"What's that?"

"Colin thinks his father actually sold him to my father." I couldn't hold back a shudder. Every time I let myself think about what my father had been capable of, I reacted physically. I couldn't help it.

"What?" Talon said.

"You heard me. I don't know what kind of proof Colin has. I'm sure he'll share it with us once he gets over this most recent setback. This must have been horrible for him, being taken again. At least it doesn't look like he was tortured this time."

"Man, I hate to feel sorry for that guy, after what he did to Jade, but..." Talon shook his head. "Seems he saved the day here, though."

"I know, man. I get your ambivalence, and I agree. He saved Marj. Plus, he didn't deserve what my father did to him." This time I shook my head. "No one did."

"No," Talon agreed. "No one did."

I felt like an idiot. Talon was so strong and seemed so together. Sometimes I forgot that he had been among my father's first victims.

"Sorry, man."

"It's okay. Sometimes I don't think about it for days. My life is great now, you know? Then, times like this, it comes back in vivid images."

I nodded. "You were alone all that time, right?"

"Yeah."

"You never saw another kid?"

"I saw Luke. He was already dead."

Nausea swept up my throat, and I grimaced.

"Sorry," he said.

"Hey, no worries. I'm the one who asked. You never saw someone else? A kid my age, maybe?"

"You're wondering about the kid you and Joe knew. Justin."

I nodded.

"Sorry. I only saw Luke. And like I said, he was already dead."

"Got it."

It had been worth a shot. Justin Valente had to figure into this whole thing. I just had no idea how. Hell, I didn't even know if he was dead or alive.

Though my instinct told me he was alive. Alive and in contact with Ted Morse.

But was my instinct worth anything? I wasn't a detective like Ruby. She had honed her instincts over a decade of police work. I was a finance guy. I had good instincts about money and investments. Why would I trust my instinct about anything else? Especially something that had happened thirty years ago that I hardly remembered?

I needed to talk to Joe.

But that wouldn't happen. Not until we all decided to tell him what was going on. He had Melanie and his new son to think of.

I knew Jonah Steel, though. Probably even better than his brothers or wife did. He would *not* be happy to have been left out of all of this. He'd understand why we did it, but he'd be pissed as hell.

Joe pissed as hell wasn't a pretty picture.

"Anyone here for Alessandra Booker?" a doctor asked.

Alessandra Booker? The name sounded familiar. Right. Cade Booker. Alessandra Booker. Dominic Booker. Marj, or maybe it was Colin, had said the woman whose throat Colin had slit was named Alex. Was her real name Alessandra?

"I am," I lied.

"And you are . . . ?"

"A friend."

"I need a family member."

"Oh."

Well, I'd tried.

"Was she the one who came in with the slit throat?" I asked.

"I'm not at liberty to say." The doctor walked away.

A few minutes later, Ruby and Marjorie emerged from the room where they'd been talking to the police. Marjorie's eyes were sunken and rimmed with dark circles. My poor baby.

I took her into my arms and kissed her forehead.

"They're not arresting Colin," Ruby said. "They're calling it self-defense for now."

"It *was* self-defense," Marj said adamantly. "Where *is* Colin?"

"Wasn't he in there with you?" I asked.

"For a while. Then they took him to question him separately."

I nodded. Though I was grateful to him, Colin was the least of my worries at the moment. "How are you holding up?" I asked the woman I loved.

"Okay, I guess."

"You must be exhausted."

"I'm sure we all are." She turned to Talon. "How's Mom?"

"Confused, but that's nothing new. Physically she's fine. She keeps talking about Dad, though. Keeps saying he picked her up and took her and the baby somewhere."

"I'm not sure what to think about Dad." Marj rubbed her temples.

"What do you mean?" Talon said. "He's gone. We both witnessed it."

"I don't know," Ruby said. "Sometimes our eyes can deceive us."

CHAPTER TWENTY

Marjorie

Ruby's words rang in my ears.

Did I think my father was truly alive? No, I didn't, and I certainly didn't expect my brothers to think it either.

"The fact remains, though," I said, after briefing them on what Dominic had told Colin and me, "that according to Dominic—"

"Dominic?" Bryce asked.

"Yeah. Dominic my trainer. He's Alex's brother, apparently. He's the one—"

"I'll fucking kill him," Bryce said, his voice a dark monotone.

"You'll have to find him first," Ruby said. "The cops are looking for him, but the guy you shot"—she eyed Bryce—"isn't talking, and his sister can't talk at the moment."

Ryan turned to me. "According to Dominic . . . what?"

"He was acting on orders from Dad." I rubbed my eyes, and then I noticed Bryce's.

"He's blowing smoke up your ass," Ryan said. "I watched my nutty mother kill him. I saw the blood on his chest."

"I saw it all too," Ruby said. "But there are ways to fake a death, and your father had all the money in the world to figure out how."

"What happened to your eyes?" I asked Bryce.

"Pepper spray."

"Are you okay?"

"Yeah. It's a long story and I'll tell you later."

I sighed. I loved this man with all my heart. Who had harmed him? When was this all going to end? "My father wouldn't fake his death twice," I said. "He just wouldn't."

"Look," Ruby said. "I never knew your father. I get that. All of you *did* know him, including you, Bryce. You say he wouldn't fake his death twice. Okay. Let's go with that for a minute. But let me ask you this. Did any of you think he would fake his death *once*?"

She paused. Was she waiting for us to say something?

"Because he did," she continued. "We know that for a fact."

Talon, Ryan, and I said nothing. What was there to say? She made a valid point. I would have bet the entire Steel fortune that my father would *never* fake his own death, leave his children, leave his business.

But he had.

Why would he do it again? It didn't make sense. Wendy Madigan was dead. Ruby had killed her. Tom Simpson, Larry Wade, and Theodore Mathias were all dead. We had proof of this. Joe had witnessed Tom kill himself, Larry had been killed in prison, and Wendy had killed Mathias when he tried to save Ruby, his daughter.

All of the people from whom he was protecting his mentally ill wife—whose death he'd also faked—were gone.

Except they weren't.

Someone had taken my mother from her facility—the best facility available that supposedly had top-notch security.

If Dominic was to be believed, it was for her own protection, which meant someone out there meant her harm. Meant *me* harm.

Even if this had something to do with Ted Morse or Bryce's childhood friend Justin Valente, why would either of them care about a mentally ill woman? Ted might have had a beef with Tom Simpson, or he might have sold his son to him. Either way, it had nothing to do with our father. Nothing to do with our mother.

And Justin Valente? If he was indeed still alive, his beef would also be with Tom, who was dead. He couldn't seek revenge against a dead person.

But if Justin was alive, if he'd somehow survived whatever Tom had done to him that weekend three decades ago, he might blame the two people who'd invited him to that camping trip.

My brother Joe.

And the man I loved. Bryce.

Joe and Bryce.

Who were their Achilles' heels? For Joe, his pregnant wife. For Bryce, his son.

But one person was a weakness for both of them.

Me.

I'd be the first target if Justin wanted to hit Joe and Bryce at the same time and avoid harming a pregnant woman or a little boy.

Bryce had been right to send Henry away. He didn't yet know *how* right.

Had there been truth to Dominic's ravings about the order coming from my father? He hadn't said my father was alive. He'd only said a system had been put in place. My father didn't need to be alive for a system to work in his absence. But if Dominic had been telling the truth, my father had known there were still threats beyond Madigan, Simpson, Wade, and Mathias.

He *knew*.

For a moment, I allowed myself to have a smidgeon of hope that my daddy was still alive. That he hadn't been killed by his crazy ex-lover, Wendy Madigan, right in front of my eyes.

But he had been.

Ruby said eyes can deceive, but I'd know if my father hadn't died that day. I'd run to him, thrown myself over his body. His body had still been warm. The blood had been warm. It had covered my fingers.

Joe had tugged me away, made me leave the room. I'd kicked and screamed and cried in protest, but still he'd dragged me out. "For your own good," he'd said.

The police had come, and we'd made arrangements for our father's cremation. The last time any of us had seen the body was in Talon's office that day. That horrible, hellish day.

Ruby hadn't asked her question again, and no one else had spoken.

Which meant only one thing.

Talon and Ryan were most likely struggling with the same thoughts.

Perhaps even Bryce was, although he hadn't been with us when our father died.

Finally—

"No." From Talon.

"Not twice." From Ryan.

"He wouldn't do that to us again," I agreed.

Ruby nodded. "If you say so. I didn't know the man."

I had a hunch she had more to say, but she kept her mouth shut. Maybe later, when we were home.

Or maybe not.

He wouldn't do that to us again.

Did I believe my own words?

Bryce hugged me to him, and though his strong arms gave me warmth and love, a niggling chill swept over me.

The chill wasn't fear so much as it was foreboding.

CHAPTER TWENTY-ONE

Bryce

I brought my sweet Marjorie home to the guesthouse and ran a warm bath for her. "Take your time," I said, "and holler if you need me."

She smiled weakly. "I'll be fine. I just need to get the grunge off me, and then I want to sleep in a nice warm bed."

"I can handle that," I said. "It's nearing morning."

She yawned. "I want to go see Mel and the baby."

"We will. After you rest."

"No," she said adamantly. "I want to see them as soon as possible. In the morning."

"It *is* morning, honey."

Another yawn split her face. "I just need to wash my hair and clean up a little. Then rest for a few hours. Please, Bryce. I have to see my brother's baby. And I want him to know I'm okay."

I nodded. But was she okay? She'd been through a traumatic ordeal. Thank God no one had touched her inappropriately. I'd have been on a warpath. As it was, I still was on a warpath.

Talon and Ryan planned to go into the city around nine. We'd go as well. Marj could probably get a couple hours' sleep at least.

"All right," I relented. "I'll check on you in a few minutes."

"I'm okay. Really."

I smiled and closed the door to give her some privacy. I wanted to believe she told the truth. I did, in that I believed she *thought* she was okay. Marjorie Steel was as strong a woman as I'd ever met. But she was also a woman who'd succumbed to pain in the past.

That damned blade.

I couldn't help a smile. That blade might have saved her and Colin. They might not have been able to escape otherwise. Alessandra Booker had been armed, and I'd approached the unit alone because Talon had been dealing with his mother.

If Colin hadn't cut their captor, she might have heard me coming.

I could be dead right now.

And I wasn't.

Because Marj had succumbed to her weakness and hadn't destroyed that blade like Mel and I had asked.

I could hardly be angry with her. That razor might have saved her life. And mine and Colin's, though according to Dominic, their lives hadn't been in danger.

What to believe?

I walked to the kitchen and put the tea kettle on the stove. My mother swore by chamomile tea for relaxation. Maybe it would help Marj.

A few minutes later, armed with a cup of steaming herb tea, I walked back through the bedroom to the bathroom to check on Marjorie.

I knocked lightly.

"Come in," she said softly.

She sat in the tub, frothy lather bubbling around her. Her

dark hair was wet and plastered to her shoulders and breasts. She looked like a shining angel.

"I thought you might like some tea."

"That was sweet of you. Thanks."

"I'll set it here on the counter."

She nodded and stood. Water dripped in rivulets off her wet body.

My groin responded.

She was so beautiful, so tempting . . . but the last thing she needed was me all over her.

Or perhaps I was wrong.

Her gaze dropped to my crotch.

"Please," she whispered.

"Anything, my love. Anything."

"Make love to me. Now, Bryce. I'm not asking for the earth to move. Just something soft and wonderful. Help me remember what's beautiful in the world."

She stepped out of the tub, and I handed her a towel. She squeezed the wetness from her long hair and then wrapped it into a turban while I encased her in another warm towel. Then I pulled her into my arms and held her close. Her body was warm from the bath, and it permeated into me, infusing me, saturating me.

Thank God.

Thank God.

Thank God.

My Marjorie was home.

I kissed the top of her head and held her tightly.

"Please," she said again, her whisper more of a hum against my neck.

I didn't reply, simply helped her dry the last of the water

from her body and left the two towels in a heap on the floor. Then I led her into the bedroom and set her gently on the bed that I'd already turned down.

My cock was already pulsing, ready for me to thrust into her.

But she'd asked for soft.

No matter how much I wanted to get rough—to fuck her thoroughly and mark her, never let anyone take her from me again—I couldn't. I needed to be there for her now, see to *her* needs, not my own.

I undressed slowly, easing each garment from my body in what seemed like slow motion, even though I wanted to tear the clothes into shreds and get inside Marjorie.

Her gaze never left me, those warm brown eyes searing into me and making me even hotter.

My cock was hard and ready, but I was determined to go slowly.

I lay down on the bed and gathered her into my arms. "I love you so much," I whispered.

"I love you too."

Her words warmed me, made me want to protect her and keep her from all harm.

I'd already failed at that quest.

I would *not* fail again.

I tilted her chin upward and pressed my lips to hers in the softest of kisses. Her sweet lips were parted, and I longed to force my tongue between them, take her in a firm and drugging kiss that would lead us to everything I desired.

Instead, I gave her another light kiss on her full pink lips.

This time, though, she took the lead. She trailed her tongue over my lower lip and then swept it inside my mouth.

I responded with all my pent-up passion.

This was the kiss I wanted. The marking kiss. The kiss that would imprint on her psyche and make her mine forever.

Our lips slid together.

And then hands. Hers on my cheek and then my shoulder. Over my hip and clasped onto my ass. Mine in her silky wet hair, pulling and tugging, sliding over the top of her breast and then to the fleshy indent of her waist, all the way to that jewel between her legs.

She was wet. She was so wet.

She broke away from me, panting. "Fuck what I said, Bryce. I don't want soft. I want hard. Fuck me. Fuck me now."

CHAPTER TWENTY-TWO

Marjorie

Bryce flattened me on my back and hovered above me, sweat dripping from his brow. "You sure?" he panted.

I bit my lip. "God, yes. Get inside me."

And then I was full, so complete, his cock so deep that he touched the edge of my soul.

No more emptiness. No more fear. No more need.

Everything was full. My body, my heart, my spirit.

Everything.

He touched a part of me so fathomless that I knew I'd never be lost again as long as this man was in my life. Perhaps I'd never need that blade again.

I lifted my hips to meet every precious thrust. And I rose, slowly, each tug on my clit emanating out to the farthest reaches of my body . . . until it all snapped into one ferocious climax that burst inside me like a thousand twinkling diamonds.

That feeling, that feeling of being one with the man I loved and one with the universe at the exact same time . . .

"Bryce!" I cried out. "I love you so much, Bryce."

He plunged into me again and again, panting, gasping. "I"—*thrust*—"love"—*thrust*—"you"—*thrust*—"too!"

And he tunneled so far into me that my climax began again as he released.

We soared together for timeless moments until we both lay panting in each other's arms, recovering from our orgasms.

He rolled off me and sighed heavily. "I can't lose you, Marjorie. I can't ever lose you."

I snuggled into his chest. "I'm not going anywhere."

"I've never been so scared in my life. When you disappeared..."

"Shh. I'm okay. They didn't hurt me."

He tensed beneath me. "I'll kill anyone who hurts you. I swear it."

His words both warmed me and sent a chill through me.

"You'll never have to," I said, hoping the words were true.

Then I breathed in his spicy warm scent—the scent that gave me comfort above all else—and closed my eyes.

★ ★ ★

I awoke to the sun's rays streaming into the bedroom.

"Bryce?"

He was gone.

I reached for the clock on the nightstand. "Noon!"

I scrambled out of bed and grabbed the closest thing I could find. Bryce's shirt he'd been wearing the night before.

"Bryce?" I walked out of the bedroom to the kitchen. "Bryce!"

"In the office," came his voice.

I hurried toward the extra bedroom he'd put into use for a home office. He sat at the makeshift desk, his laptop open.

"It's noon," I said.

"Yeah, it is."

"You were supposed to wake me. We were going to the hospital."

"I talked to Tal, Ryan, and Joe. They all agreed—"

"My brothers don't dictate my life!" I clenched my hands into fists.

"Calm down, honey. We all just thought—"

"You all just thought!" Ire ripped through me.

"Baby..."

"Damn it! I'm so tired of everyone else in the world thinking they know what's best for me. If you're going to turn out to be just another Steel brother, Bryce Simpson, I swear, I—"

"Hey." He stood and gathered me in his arms. "We just wanted you to get some sleep. Melanie and the baby are fine. Melanie wanted to make sure you got some rest."

"So now Mel is making my decisions for me too?"

"She's a doctor, Marj. We all take what she says seriously."

I was overreacting. I knew I was. My brothers would all take a bullet for me. So would Bryce. I was used to their overbearing behavior. I usually gave it right back to them. Why was it angering me so much now?

Take a deep breath, Mel would have said.

Take a deep breath and let it go.

I drew in lungs full of air, held it for a few seconds, and let it out slowly.

I was still pissed.

I pulled away slightly from Bryce and met his sparkling blue gaze. "You should have woken me up."

"I'm not going to be sorry for letting you get some much-needed sleep."

"God! You're acting like my brothers."

"Your brothers love you, Marj. And you know what? I love you more than they do. More than anyone has ever loved you and ever will. I failed you, yesterday, damn it. Do you have any idea what that does to me? Knowing I couldn't keep you safe? That someone tried to take you away from me?"

I was still pissed, but I was starting to see his reasoning. He thought I needed sleep. He was probably right. He wanted to protect me from not getting the sleep he knew I needed.

"You can't protect me every minute," I said gently. "That would drive us both crazy."

"You want to know what crazy is?" he said. "Crazy is not knowing where the woman you love is. Crazy is imagining some degenerate doing all kinds of horrible things to her. None of this is your fault, honey. None of it. But I'll be damned if I'm not going to do everything I can to protect you, whether you like it or not, and that includes making sure you get a good night's sleep after what you've been through."

I opened my mouth, but I was all yelled out. He was right, of course. I had needed to sleep, and I was just getting angry to get angry. I'd spent my entire life fighting against my controlling brothers, and now I was fighting against a controlling boyfriend. Except he didn't want to control me.

He just wanted to protect me. Make sure I had everything I needed, including a few extra hours of sleep.

My temper finally settled down. "I love you," I said. "So much."

"I love you too. You hungry?"

"I am. But let's just pick something up on the way to the city, okay? I want to see my nephew."

CHAPTER TWENTY-THREE

Bryce

I couldn't deny her anything. Besides, I wanted to see Joe and his kid too.

I kissed her cheek. "You'll have to put on something besides my shirt, then."

"Okay. And don't you follow me, or we'll never leave the house." She smiled and left the room.

She was right about that. I was already hard for her. I always was, and I always would be.

I'd been in a virtual meeting with my staff most of the morning. Even though I needed to sleep, I still had work to do, and this particular meeting couldn't wait. I didn't want to leave Marj alone in the house, though, so luckily I'd been able to do it remotely.

Talon and Ryan had already gone to the hospital. They were the big bosses and could move around as they pleased. They'd told me I could as well, but they were the Steels, and I wasn't. I was determined to earn my keep around here.

I texted Joe quickly to let him know Marj was awake and we'd be on our way soon.

Then I fingered the business card I'd pulled out of my wallet earlier.

Dominic James, personal trainer.

He'd kicked my ass that day at the gym. He knew his stuff. He also apparently kidnapped people for a living.

He hadn't hurt any of them—other than drugging them and taking them against their will. That in itself was hurtful. But as far as the torturous, violating hurt that my father had inflicted on Colin Morse? Dominic and his cohorts hadn't done any of that. Still, he'd hurt the woman I loved, and she might suffer long-lasting trauma because of it. Now he was missing. But I'd find him. I'd find him and make him pay.

Dominic James was most likely Dominic Booker, some relation to Cade Booker and Alessandra Booker.

The mobile number on his business card had an Iowa area code.

The phone calls Joe and I had received had also come from Iowa area codes. Different numbers, though, and no word from Mills and Johnson on their origins.

Couldn't be all coincidental, though. Could it?

I picked up my cell phone and dialed Dominic's number. I didn't expect to get an answer, and I didn't.

This is Dominic James, personal trainer. Please leave your name and number, and I'll get back to you as soon as I can.

"This is Bryce Simpson," I said into the phone, carefully regulating my voice. I'd never get what I wanted if I threatened to tear him limb from limb. "You and I need to talk. I have information you need."

I set my phone down and stared at it for a moment. I was bluffing. I had no information he needed.

Or did I?

I knew of his affiliation with Cade Booker, who had disappeared from his law firm the day he'd pepper-sprayed Joe and me. Did his law firm even know about the mafia-style setup in his office? Did they know he regularly armed himself with three weapons? No one had heard anything from him since then. Only a little more than a day had passed. My eyes were still slightly irritated, though I'd forgotten all about it while I was in search of Marjorie. Some things were more important than physical pain.

Marjorie peered into the room, now dressed in one of my T-shirts and the sweats she'd been wearing earlier.

"Do you want to stop at the main house and get something else to wear?" I asked.

She shook her head. "I want to get to the hospital. I've been kept out of this loop long enough."

I wasn't about to argue with her.

★ ★ ★

"He's beautiful." Marjorie cuddled her newborn nephew in the NICU.

The baby was breathing well on his own. Sometimes, when he forgot to breathe, either Joe or Melanie or a nurse tapped his little heel and he started up again. This would get less frequent as he got older, everyone said, and he'd remember to breathe.

"Good job, man," I said to Joe.

Despite everything else going on, Joe couldn't stop smiling. He was so proud to be a father.

"If I'd known being a dad was this amazing, I might have done it before now," he said.

"It's the most rewarding thing ever," I agreed, missing my little son horribly. Knowing he was safe, though—that was worth everything. I'd called my mother earlier and talked to

Henry. He babbled in my ear about nothing in particular.

He was safe. Safe and happy.

Melanie was still in her hospital room but was being released later. The baby would stay for at least a week, perhaps more, until he'd gained a pound or two and his breathing had completely normalized.

"She wants to stay here with him," Joe said. "I booked her a suite at the Carlton."

"You staying with her?" I asked.

"I want to, but she insists I get back and figure out what's going on." He sighed. "It breaks my heart to leave them, but she's right."

Marj looked up then. "When are you going to give this little guy a name?"

Joe sighed again. "I don't know. We were going to name him Brad, after Dad, but now? Knowing he might have faked his death yet again? I don't know."

"He's still your dad, no matter what. He meant a lot to you. What's wrong with naming your son after him?" I stroked the baby's soft cheek.

"I don't know, man. It just doesn't feel right."

"What does Mel think?" Marj asked.

"She thinks I need to get over myself." Joe chuckled.

"You should listen to your wife," Marj said.

"I usually do," Joe said. Then, to me, "Remember our first son pact?"

★ ★ ★

"I feel bad for kids with only one dad," I said, making the last fold on my paper airplane.

"Some kids don't have a dad at all." Joe added a pinstripe to the wing on his.

"Our dads are the best." I shot the plane into the air.

Brad Steel had taught me how to make a perfect paper airplane. He'd taught me to work the land, to do an honest day's work.

My own father had taught me how to pitch a tent, how to fish for my own food, how to shoot a gun.

"I'm going to name my first kid after your dad," I said.

"Then I'll name mine after yours. And mine. Thomas Bradford Steel."

"Bradford Thomas Simpson," I said.

Joe spit on his hand. "Let's shake on it."

I spit, and we shook. "Deal."

★ ★ ★

"Damn," I said. "I'd actually forgotten about that."

"So you don't mind if I break it?"

"Of course not. I already have. I guess Henry should have been Bradford Thomas. Instead he's Henry Thomas. Frankie wanted to name him after an uncle she admired. I'm going to change his middle name once all this blows over. I don't want him bearing that bastard's name."

"Obviously I wasn't going to stick to it either," Joe said. "Not after . . ."

He didn't need to finish. Not after he found out who my father actually was.

"Why not name him Bradley instead of Bradford?" Marj suggested. "Then you can call him Brad, so he's sort of named after Dad, but he also has his own name."

Joe lifted his brow. "I actually really like that idea. You think Mel will go for it?"

"I think Mel will be fine with it," Marjorie said. "Plus, Bradley Steel is a great name."

"What will his middle name be?" I asked.

"Melanie wants Jonah, after me."

"Then let Mel have her way," Marj said. "Bradley Jonah Steel. Sounds perfect to me."

"I don't know. This might be the only kid we have. I want him to have his own name."

"First of all," Marj said. "Melanie got through this pregnancy with no issues at all."

"Except preterm labor," Joe reminded her.

"Most likely brought on by stress. Does she want to have more children?"

"We both would," Joe said.

"You're acting like she's an old lady. She's forty, for God's sake, and she looks ten years younger."

"Forty is old for having kids," Joe said. "We both understand that."

"No reason why you can't try again. Heck, you got pregnant this time without even trying."

Joe laughed. "It's that Steel sperm. It gets through no matter what."

I punched Joe's arm. "God, you Steels are a pain in the ass."

"We're the gift that keeps on giving," he said.

Marj made a retching sound. "You're not going to be like that, are you?" she cooed to baby Brad.

"The hell he's not," Joe said. "That's prime Steel stock right there."

Marjorie rolled her eyes. "You and Mel can always adopt too. Talon and Jade did." She handed the baby to the nurse who entered.

"Time for him to eat," the nurse said. "Let's take you to Mama."

CHAPTER TWENTY-FOUR

Marjorie

"He's latching on really well," Melanie said, nursing the baby. "That's unusual for a preemie. And it's a great sign."

"He's going to do fine," I said. "He's so beautiful. Look at that head of dark hair!"

"Steel hair for sure," Melanie said.

"You never know," I said. "That hair will fall out, and he might be blond like you."

"Maybe." She smiled.

"Whatever his coloring, he'll be gorgeous. No doubt." I swallowed. Joe had most likely told Mel everything that had happened . . . including the fact that Colin had cut Alex with a blade. Mel would know where that blade had come from.

Joe and Bryce had gone to get some coffee, and Melanie and I were alone in her private room while she nursed baby Brad.

"Mel . . ." I began.

"It's okay," she said. "I understand."

"You don't even know what I was going to say."

"The blade, Marj. I understand."

"But I lied to you. Again. And to Bryce."

"I'm not going to condone lying. Not to your therapist and especially not to your significant other. But the fact is you had the blade when you needed it. Something held you back, and it turned out your instinct was on the nose."

"But that's not why—"

"It's okay. Really. Maybe I was wrong to insist you get rid of it. Therapists aren't always right, you know. We do make mistakes sometimes."

"You didn't make any mistakes with Talon."

"Childhood trauma is my specialty," she said. "But that doesn't mean I didn't make mistakes with your brother. Just because his outcome was great doesn't mean I did everything perfectly. Perfection isn't possible, Marj."

Perfection isn't possible.

No truer words.

Was that my issue? I wanted perfection in my life? No, not really. I wasn't ever consumed with perfection...until I started cutting.

It had been my outlet, my way to stay sane when thinking about what my conception had cost my middle brother. Now, I wanted desperately to stop. Go cold turkey. Be strong enough not to need the security blanket.

Yes, I wanted perfection.

I wanted to be able to *not* need that stupid blade.

"You're berating yourself," Melanie said. "I can see it on your face."

I couldn't help a soft laugh. "You're good."

The nurse came in before Mel could respond. "How did he do?"

"Hard to say," Mel said, "but he latched on well. I sure felt that."

"You'll get used to that. It's painful for the first couple days. Right now, you're only producing colostrum. Wait until your milk comes in. Then he'll be feasting." She took the baby into her arms. "Better get him back to NICU."

Melanie simply smiled. "Thank you."

Once the nurse had left, I said, "You're a doctor. You know all about colostrum, right?"

"Yeah, I do."

"Does it bug you when medical professionals tell you things you already know?"

"Not really. They're just doing their jobs."

"That would drive me nuts," I said.

"That's because your brothers constantly do that to you." Melanie laughed.

I joined in her laughter. "You really *are* good."

"I just know the Steel men," she said. "I know how they treat you. But they truly do it out of love, Marj."

"I know. It's still annoying, though. Sometimes they talk about me like I'm not even in the same room."

"I'd like to say they're going to change . . ."

"But you don't want to lie to me."

"No." She laughed again. "I don't."

I sighed. "I love them all. I do."

"I know. And they adore you. Why do you think they're so protective? Jonah was mad as a rabid dog when he found out they'd gone after you without him even knowing."

"They knew he'd want to be here with you."

"I know. And he would've been, but he still wanted to know what was going on."

"Freaking Steel men," I said.

"They are forces to be reckoned with," she agreed, "but they're also the best men I know."

"Yeah, me too," I said. "Plus Bryce. Who treats me the

same way, of course."

"He's as close to a Steel man as anyone except for the actual Steels. And he loves you very much."

I smiled. "He does. In truth, I don't want him to change a bit."

"That's true love, then. I wouldn't change Jonah, either."

"Good thing," I said, "because not one of my brothers will ever change who they are."

"That's why we love them," Melanie replied.

Again, the woman was good. She spoke the utter truth.

★ ★ ★

Driving back to the guesthouse, Bryce filled me in on his and Joe's visit to Cade Booker and how they ended up pepper-sprayed.

"Apparently Cade is related to a Dominic Booker and an Alessandra Booker," he said. "We think Dominic James's real name is Booker."

"He did say Alex was his twin," I said. "And they called her Booker at the hospital."

"She's going to make a full recovery," Bryce said.

"That's good for Colin."

"Yeah. It is."

"Bryce . . ."

"Yeah, baby?"

"I . . . I was supposed to be the one to cut Alex's throat. It was my blade."

"Oh?"

"But I couldn't. I froze. And then she woke up, and still I couldn't, so . . ."

"Colin did it."

"Yeah. He moved so quickly. Just grabbed the blade from me and sliced his finger open. Then jabbed it into her throat like he didn't even need to think about it."

"It's a good thing he did."

"Yeah. It is. But why couldn't *I* do it?"

"Marj, it's not a bad thing that you couldn't harm another human being. That's a *good* quality."

"But this bitch had it coming."

"She did. Still, don't punish yourself."

"I had already motioned for Colin to escape before Alex woke up. But he didn't. He stayed with me. What if he'd done as I asked? What if—"

"He didn't. He stayed with you, and he took care of business. That's a good thing. Don't torment yourself with the 'what if' game. Trust me. I know it well, and it doesn't lead to anything good."

I nodded. Bryce had spent the last few months torturing himself over his father.

We didn't speak again during the drive.

CHAPTER TWENTY-FIVE

Bryce

Marjorie stopped at the main house to change clothes and see Jade, so I went to the office building to put in a few more hours of work.

At about seven p.m., I decided to head home just as my phone buzzed from the number I'd called earlier.

I couldn't believe he had the nerve to return my call.

"Hello, Dominic," I said into the phone. "Dominic *Booker*."

No response.

"You called. You must have something to say."

"You need to keep Marjorie safe," he finally said.

"Yeah, I do. Safe from people who drug her and kidnap her."

"I didn't lie to her. I was under an order from her father."

"Her dead father."

"I'm not privy to that information."

"You didn't talk directly to Brad Steel, then."

"No. I never talk directly to a client."

"Do you do this for others?"

Silence.

"You going to answer me?"

"Not on the phone. Meet me."

"Where?"

"I'll text you the address. Bring your friend. Jonah Steel."
The line went dead.

I could smell a setup a mile away, and this was definitely a setup. Still, I was going. There was never any doubt of that. And bring Joe along? The guy clearly didn't know Joe's wife had just given birth to a premature baby. No way would I be bringing him. He was still in Grand Junction.

I could bring the next best thing, though. Joe's brothers. I quickly texted Talon and Ryan. Once I got their responses and gave them the meeting place, I trashed the phone. Time to pick up a new one.

★ ★ ★

"You think he'll show?" Talon sipped a rotgut bourbon at the little bar in the next county. He'd ordered a Peach Street, and the barkeep had erupted in a gale of laughter.

"Someone will," I said. "Whether it's him or a band of goons who try to take us out, I have no idea."

"They can give it their best shot," Ryan said. "Does Marj know where you are?"

I shook my head. "She's spending the evening with Jade."

"Yeah," Talon said. "The two of them were in a hen session when I left. The boys were doing homework. I just said I was going out for a while."

"And they bought it?"

"Hell, no. But that's what I said."

"Shit. Marj will figure it out. If she shows up here..." I took a sip of bourbon. Seemed like a bourbon kind of night, for some reason. Oddly, I'd been drinking a lot of bourbon lately, and so had Joe. He was usually a martini man, and I normally preferred a beer.

"How can she? She doesn't know where we are."

"She followed Joe and me to my father's cabin in the middle of the night."

"She's been through a traumatic experience," Ryan said. "She's not going to go out looking for trouble."

I scoffed. "You really believe that?"

Ryan laughed. "Hell, no."

"The fact remains," Talon said, "that she doesn't know where we are. So she won't show up."

"I hope not." I set my drink down and looked toward the doorway. "Ah. The guest of honor."

Dominic strolled toward us. "I told you to bring Jonah."

"Jonah's unavailable. These are the other two Steel brothers, Talon and Ryan."

"Yeah." Dominic waved his hand. "I know who they are."

"You're lucky we don't have you arrested for kidnapping," Ryan said. "Bryce here convinced us to listen to you first."

"Why would you do that?"

"Only because Marjorie said you didn't hurt her. In fact, she said you defended her against your sister, who, by the way, *is* in police custody."

"Alex will be fine. Once she leaves the hospital, arrangements will be made for her bail and a plea bargain. And thanks for your concern, by the way."

"The two of you kidnapped our sister," Ryan said. "Spare us the guilt over concern."

"Alex sometimes goes a little overboard," Dominic said.

"I'd say you both do," I said. "We're here because Marjorie would want us to hear you out, but the minute you take a wrong step, we'll turn you in."

"We're all armed," Ryan said, "just so you know."

"And you think I'm not?"

"Still," I said, "it's three against one. I don't see any backup."

"I don't need backup," Dominic said. "I was trained by the best."

"Yeah? I was trained by my psycho father, so don't get any ideas." I took a sip of bourbon.

Dominic didn't miss a beat. "I was trained by my psycho brother."

I nodded. "Cade. Cade Booker is your brother."

"Half brother, actually." Dominic signaled the bartender. "Draft, please."

"What does Cade Booker have to do with any of this?" Ryan asked.

"He's the psycho who pepper-sprayed Joe and me and then went on the run," I said. "He's an attorney in the city, former FBI guy. Ruby probably knows of him. Maybe we should have her meet us here."

"Are you nuts? I'm not dragging my wife into this."

"Your wife would want to be dragged into this," Talon said. "She's probably better with a gun than you are."

Dominic raised an eyebrow.

"Don't get any ideas," I said. "Ruby's an ex-cop, but I guarantee you *I'm* every bit as good with a piece as she is, and I've been shooting way longer."

"Slow down," Talon said. "Seems you and Joe have been keeping things from us, Bryce."

Dominic chuckled.

"I wouldn't be laughing if I were you," I said. "We can still have you dragged out of here in cuffs."

"You haven't yet."

"We've explained why. I also warned you not to push me."

"I told you I was working on orders from your father," Dominic said, nodding to Talon and Ryan, "and that's the God's honest truth. I'm not the enemy here. But I know who is."

"Your brother."

Dominic scanned the bar. "Let's get a table. You said you have information for me."

Of course. He was calling my bluff.

"I'd say you have information for *us*," I said. "I'm not telling you a damned thing until you spill every detail about your half brother and anything else you know."

CHAPTER TWENTY-SIX

Marjorie

My blade was gone. It was sealed in an evidence bag somewhere, even though no charges had been filed against Colin.

My friend.

My friend was gone.

Forever.

I could still feel its phantom brand against the top of my breast where it sat between my flesh and the fabric of my bra, just waiting to be plunged into Alex's neck.

But though it *had* been plunged into Alex's neck, I had not been wielding it. That blade—that *friend* that had been my go-to problem solver when confronted with the guilt of being inadvertently responsible for my brother's abduction and torture—had failed me when I needed it to harm another human being.

What did that say about me?

About the blade?

Jade had gone in to check on the boys. Dale was doing much better. Helping Ruby investigate the hoodie-wearing guy he'd seen at the playground at school had done wonders for him. He felt more involved now, more like part of the family. In another couple weeks, when we went to court, he'd be an official Steel. Talon and Jade had allowed the boys to choose new middle names. Dale had chosen Robertson, his original last name, in memory of his mother. Donny—whose full name was Donovan—had chosen Talon, after his new father.

Jade looked so beautiful now that she was finally feeling better. She'd entered her second trimester, and the nausea had finally eased up. Plus, she hadn't had any more spotting, and the pregnancy was progressing normally.

"I can't wait to see the baby," she said, bringing us both glasses of water.

"He's gorgeous," I said.

"I was going to go with Talon this morning, but I had a meeting at the boys' school."

"Everything okay?"

"Yeah, just a parent-teacher thing. I insisted Talon go see his nephew, that I could handle it."

"How are the boys doing?" I asked.

"Donny's thriving, of course. Grades are great, and he gets along well with everyone. Dale's grades aren't quite as good, but his teacher says he's doing better, and also he's finally starting to make a few friends."

"Do their teachers know . . ."

She shook her head. "They know they've been through an abusive situation, but we didn't fill them in on the details. Talon felt it was important that their teachers not hold their situation against them."

"Why would any teacher do that?"

"They wouldn't, at least not on purpose. Talon thinks they might subconsciously either be easier or harder on them."

"Harder?"

"I know. It doesn't make sense to me either, but it does to

Talon and to Melanie. And they're the experts."

I took a sip of my water. "I should call Bryce."

"He's not home."

I jerked. "Oh?"

"Talon went to meet him and Ryan somewhere."

"Where?"

"I asked. He didn't say."

"You didn't insist on knowing?"

"If Talon wanted to tell me, he'd have told me. I can't push Talon. I learned that the hard way in the beginning. You push Talon, and he shrinks away."

"But he's come so far."

"He has, but every once in a while he's still that little boy who had his innocence shredded way too early."

I nodded, gulping quietly.

My security blanket was gone.

My brother's innocence had been shredded because *I'd* come into existence. It wasn't my fault, but still... Knowing my blade was hidden securely in my purse would have helped.

But it was gone now.

My friend was gone.

"Marj?"

I jerked. "Yeah?"

"You okay? You seemed lost in space for a minute."

I smiled weakly. "I'm okay."

"You sure? You've been through—"

"I've been through nothing," I stormed. "Nothing compared to what Talon and Colin have been through."

"Marj, I—"

"I'm sorry, okay? Yeah, I was drugged and taken against my will. But no one hit me. No one raped me. No one starved me. It was nothing, Jade. Fucking nothing."

"It wasn't nothing."

Anger seethed through me. "Excuse me, but you weren't there. I was. It was nothing compared to what happened to my brother, to Dale and Donny, to Juliet and Lisa, to Ruby even. To *all* of them. It was *nothing*."

Jade regarded me, her lips trembling slightly.

I'm sorry.

The words were lodged in my throat.

She hadn't deserved to be the target of my outburst, but damn it, I'd been through *nothing*.

Where was my fucking friend?

Just knowing my blade was waiting for me in my purse would help this angst.

But it wasn't there.

It wasn't there.

I walked to the kitchen quickly and opened the refrigerator. The cold air chilled my skin.

Jade didn't follow me. Why would she? I still lived here. I did a lot of cooking. Opening the refrigerator wouldn't be an odd thing for me to do.

She didn't know why I was doing it, though.

I breathed in the coldness, let it flow through me, begging it to take away my troubles.

Because in truth, I didn't have any troubles. I'd been taken against my will, and yes, I'd been frightened.

But ultimately, I hadn't been harmed.

Not like all those other innocent souls.

I inhaled, exhaled, inhaled, exhaled . . .

But still the need pulsed within me. The scar on my upper thigh burned and itched.

Burned and itched.

Burned and itched.

Until—

"Marj?"

Jade's voice. From behind me.

"Are you looking for something?"

I suppressed the urge to snap at her. She was my best friend, and she was pregnant. I was being self-indulgent.

I'd promised myself I'd stop this ridiculous self-absorption.

Why wasn't I strong enough?

Why?

I closed the refrigerator door. "I need to talk to you."

She nodded. "I know." She led me down to the family room and sat next to me on the leather couch.

She didn't push me, didn't insist I start talking. She just sat with me, waiting.

I didn't owe her any explanation. I didn't owe anyone, other than Mel and Bryce, both of whom I'd lied to.

Finally, she said, "The razor blade."

I didn't respond, simply nodded.

"It was yours."

Again, I nodded.

"It's okay," she said. "Anyone would—"

"I'm not anyone," I said adamantly. "My brothers would have been stronger. Look at all of them, what they've been through."

"Talon tried to get himself offed in Iraq," Jade said. "Ryan nearly drove his car off a cliff when he found out about Wendy being his mother. Joe has the hottest head of all three of them, and he almost took a gun into the police station to shoot Ted

Morse. Yeah, they're strong, but they're not invincible. They've had their own issues, and they've all nearly gone off the deep end at one time or another."

"But—"

"I don't blame you for idolizing them. They're amazing, all three of them, especially the one I'm married to. I love him more than anything, but even I know when not to push him."

"So you're pushing me instead." A statement, not a question.

"I'm not pushing you. I'm sitting here with you, giving you time. But if you think I can't tell when something's bothering my best friend, think again. I know you as well as you know yourself, Marj."

"Not true," I said.

"Bull."

I chuckled. "Not true. You actually know me better than I know myself. I was trying to think what I've been through doesn't matter because it was so tame compared to what Talon and the boys have been through. But you're right. It *was* traumatic."

"I know it was."

"What you don't know is . . ."

"What?"

I shook my head. I couldn't tell her. Couldn't.

"You can tell me."

"The blade . . ."

She grabbed my arm. "I know."

I arched my eyebrows.

"No one told me, Marj. I just know, okay? I've seen the scar when you have your suit on to go hot tubbing."

"Only two others know," I said.

"Bryce."

"Yeah. And Melanie. She's been helping me."

"You can trust me. I haven't told anyone. Not even Talon."

"Please don't tell Talon. If my brothers knew—"

"They'd move heaven and earth to help you," she finished for me.

I smiled. "That's not what I was going to say."

"I know, but it's the truth. They'd do anything for you. They adore you."

"But—"

"He doesn't blame you, Marj. He never did."

No, Talon didn't blame me.

"In fact," she continued, "if it weren't for you, Talon and I wouldn't have met."

I nodded again. That much was true, and Jade had changed Talon's life. He was happy. He was complete. He was a father.

" . . . all because of you," Jade was saying.

I choked back a sob. Crying was for girls.

"He's happy," Jade continued. "He wants you to be happy too."

"I am," I said. "I have everything, Jade. I have Bryce. I have you, Mel, my brothers. I *am* happy."

"Marjorie"—she looked me straight in the eye—"happy people don't carry razor blades around in their purse."

CHAPTER TWENTY-SEVEN

Bryce

"My half brother has been obsessed with the Steels for years," Dominic said. "He was my mother's son from her first marriage. He appeared when Alex and I were teens. Our mom had just died. Anyway, he had nowhere else to go, so my dad took him in, and he changed his last name to Booker."

"Where had he been, if he wasn't with your mom?"

"She never talked about him. She only told us that we had an older brother but he died when he was young."

A brick hit my gut.

"And he's obsessed with the Steels?" I said.

"The Steels, yeah, mostly Jonah. And your father. Tom Simpson."

"My dad's dead."

"I know."

"If he has a beef with a dead man, I don't know what to tell you."

"If he has a beef with a dead man, you know why," Dominic said. "We all know who your father was."

Chills crawled up my spine. Oh, yeah, I knew all right. But damn it, *I* was not my father.

"I'm not responsible for what my father did to anyone, and neither are the Steels."

"I know that," Dominic said, "but my brother isn't quite as logical as I am. He tends to think with his emotions, which are out of whack."

"You called him psycho," I said.

"Yeah, and I stand by that assessment."

"I do too. Only a psycho would arm himself with three guns and booby-trap his office with pepper spray."

"Agreed," Dominic said.

"Look," I said. "I don't know what my father did to your brother, but I know it can't be pretty. Your brother was far from the only one."

Dominic nodded. "I know that, man, but that thought never helped my brother and probably not any of the others."

Talon visibly tensed. His story had gone public when all hell broke loose months ago. Dominic probably knew Talon had been among my father's victims. That wasn't for me to say, though.

"You're saying your brother is a danger to the Steels? And to Colin? That's why you acted on orders to protect them?"

"That's right. But thanks to you all, they're no longer protected."

"You need to look no further than to us to protect our mother and sister," Talon said through clenched teeth. "You'd better keep your hands off them and every other Steel from now on."

I turned to Talon and Ryan. "Did you guys ever find the file of news clippings from the kids who disappeared around the same time as Luke?"

"Not yet. Joe was going to look for them," Ryan said.

"Any chance a little kid named Cade disappeared?" I asked.

"I was too young to remember," Ryan said.

"And I just remember Luke," Talon said. "And . . ."

And . . . himself. He didn't finish the sentence.

"What was Cade's father's name?" I asked.

"I don't know," Dominic said. "My mom never talked about him. Like I said, she told us Cade was dead."

"And she never mentioned his father?"

"Not once. It was like he never existed. She wouldn't talk about it. We always figured he'd been really abusive."

"What happened to him?"

"She never said."

"And you never asked?"

"We were young," he said. "We didn't think about it. Then she died."

"Of what?" Ryan asked.

"Drive-by shooting in our little Iowa town. The first and only. No one was ever caught."

"Right before Cade showed up," Talon said. "Seems a little incriminating."

I nodded. "And more than a little convenient."

"You think Cade shot his own mother?" Dominic asked.

"You said yourself he was psycho. Do you mean this never occurred to you?"

"Cade acted all broken up about it," Dominic said. "So no, I didn't think about it."

"Your father took Cade in, let him take his name."

"Yeah. My dad was a good man."

"Was?" Talon asked.

Dominic nodded. "He died last year. Cancer."

"Okay." At least we knew Cade hadn't offed his stepdad. Even the biggest psycho in the world couldn't force cancer on someone.

"Fast-forward," I said. "How did you start working for Brad Steel?"

"Cade kind of took Alex and me under his wing. He taught us how to handle guns, and he was good, man. Really good. I didn't think much about it at the time, but right around the time Alex and I finished high school, he got a little weirder than usual. Like I said, he was obsessed with your father and the Steels. He asked Alex and me to go in with him, help us avenge him. We didn't know what he was talking about, and he wouldn't elaborate, but I could tell he was thinking about doing something terrible. Alex and I declined, and a few days later, we got a phone call from someone claiming to represent Brad Steel, asking if we wanted to work for him. He offered us some outrageous money, so we took it."

"Was Cade already with the FBI when he showed up?" I asked.

"He'd left the bureau and was setting up a law practice. Like I said, Alex and I were teens. He offered to teach us how to shoot like the FBI had taught him. Our dad was okay with it. We thought it was great at the time."

"So somehow, between the time your mother *thought* he allegedly died and the time he came back, he worked for the FBI and managed to go to law school and pass the bar?"

"Apparently," Dominic said.

"I smell a rat a mile away," Ryan said. "I wish Ruby were here to listen to this. She'd have called bullshit a half hour ago."

"You can easily check records to see where he went to law school and whether he was with the FBI," Dominic said.

"Records can be forged," Talon said.

"Federal records?" Dominic shook his head.

"Kid," Talon began.

"Kid?"

"Yeah, kid. What are you? Twenty-five?"

"I'm no kid."

"Whatever. The right amount of money can buy anything. Trust us. We've seen it."

"You're saying my brother never went to law school?"

"It's possible."

"But he's been practicing law."

"So?"

"He's good at it."

"Doesn't mean he didn't go about it illicitly. I'm not saying he didn't go to law school, but I'm not saying he did either. We've seen people wearing aliases like different color shirts this past year."

"True," I said. "What was Cade's original last name? Do you know?"

"I'm not sure he ever told us."

"And you didn't think to ask?" I said.

"I was sixteen. I didn't think past tomorrow."

"What about your sister?"

"Same."

"Marjorie says she wasn't as nice as you were."

"I told you. Alex comes on strong sometimes. She's got one big chip on her shoulder."

"Why is that? You said your dad was kind."

"He was. You think a person has to be abused to have a chip on her shoulder? It doesn't work that way."

I couldn't fault Dominic's observation. Joe Steel had one massive chip on his shoulder, and as far as I knew, he hadn't been abused.

Who the hell *was* Cade Booker?

"Can you find out his original last name?" I asked.

"I can try. My dad would have known, but he's dead."

"Check his records. Did he leave any files?"

"I can look, but wouldn't it be easier to check the state records? Aren't name changes a matter of record?"

"Yeah," I said. "If your brother actually changed his name legally. Some people just start using aliases."

"Why would he choose to use our father's name as an alias?"

"Kid"—this time I said it. I felt like I'd aged a generation in the past several months—"if I knew why a psycho did anything, I'd have figured out my father way before now. You can't use logic to figure this out. Trust me. But we need to know his original name if we have a chance of tracing him."

Dominic sighed. "I'll see what I can do."

"Do more than see," Ryan said. "Don't forget we can have you arrested for what you did to Marj, Colin, and Daphne Steel."

Dominic nodded. He seemed oddly unconcerned about being arrested, seemed to think Alex would be getting off easily. I almost mentioned it, but then thought better of it. Dominic turned.

"Just a minute," I said. "I need to speak to him alone for a minute."

Talon and Ryan nodded.

I walked out of the bar with Dominic. "It's no coincidence that you ended up as Marjorie's trainer at the gym, is it?"

"No. My brother's been watching her, and I've been watching him, all while waiting for the order to get her to safety."

"I see. And when I came into the gym?"

"That's when I realized the situation was dire," he said.

I lifted my brow, trying to appear less surprised than I was. "How so?"

Dominic dug his wallet out of his pocket, opened it, and pulled out a white card. "This." He handed it to me.

The card I'd lost, with the account set up for the Spider.

"It's my brother's calling card," he said.

CHAPTER TWENTY-EIGHT

Marjorie

Happy people don't carry razor blades around in their purse.

Jade's words rang in my mind as I contemplated how to respond to them.

Maybe if I just didn't respond—

"You going to answer me?" she said.

"You didn't ask a question." True enough.

"Let me rephrase, then. Why did you have a razor blade in your purse?"

I bit my lower lip, silently gulping.

"I get it. It's personal. But this is me, Marj. Your best friend. We don't have secrets."

"It's a security blanket," I said.

"Why would a sharp blade be security? Do you mean for self-defense?"

"Yeah. Sure." Even I could hear the lie in those words.

"Try again," she said.

"It's over, okay? I just needed some relief from the pain, you know? The fact that I was conceived is why Talon was taken. Gave me a little bit of a complex, which I'm thinking might be normal under the circumstances."

"That's very normal," Jade said. "What's not normal is cutting yourself."

I sighed. "It's over, like I said."

"All right. Just know you can talk to me if you need to. You know I'd never break a confidence."

"I know."

"I won't ask about it again."

"You don't have to. The blade is evidence now. It's gone."

"Doesn't mean you can't get another."

"It doesn't work that way," I said.

True words. That blade was my friend, and my friend was now gone.

"Miss Jade?" Donny interrupted us.

"Yeah, sweetie?" Jade said.

"I need a glass of water."

"Okay, coming."

While Jade took care of Donny, I went to my room and packed a few things to take to the guesthouse. I wanted to be with Bryce when he got home. He might need me. And if he didn't? I needed him.

I quickly said goodbye to Jade and Donny and headed over to the guesthouse.

I let myself in using the key I'd had for ages and put my stuff in Bryce's bedroom.

Then I walked to the kitchen to make myself a snack. The table was spread with papers. I glanced over them. They were the files Bryce had found at the cabin.

Curiosity got the best of me. I sat down and began sifting through the papers.

Nothing stood out to me. A lot of invoices for farm equipment, not that Tom Simpson had ever owned a farm that I knew of. Then again, there was still a lot I didn't know about Tom Simpson.

I grabbed an unopened manila folder and peeked inside.

And nearly slid out of my chair.

A document stared me in the face—a document that Bryce clearly hadn't seen yet.

It was a bill of sale for unspecified merchandise.

Tom Simpson had paid one million dollars for unspecified merchandise nearly thirty years ago.

To a man named Bertram Valente.

CHAPTER TWENTY-NINE

Bryce

I stopped myself from jolting in surprise. "Excuse me?"

"Cade. He likes to call himself the Spider."

"The Spider isn't some hacker he knows?" Though I already knew the answer.

Dominic guffawed. "Is that what he told you?"

"Then why..."

I couldn't say anything more without telling Dominic how Joe knew Cade in the first place, and I'd promised Joe. Still, I wanted, needed, to know more.

"Why what?" Dominic asked.

"Nothing. But you need to tell me everything about your brother and his so-called Spider alias." I grabbed his collar. "Don't leave out one fucking detail, or I'll have your ass in prison so fast—"

"Easy, Simpson. Shit."

I loosened my hold. "This isn't a damned joke."

"I never said it was."

"Start talking. I want to know everything about your brother and the Spider."

"They're the same person."

"We were told the Spider was a high-priced hacker who could find someone for us."

"Cade's a pretty good hacker, from what I know," Dominic said.

"So he's the Spider?"

"Yes and no."

"You'd better get real clear real fast," I said through clenched teeth.

"It's a name he's used ever since I can remember. I don't know why."

"You're telling me there is no separate Spider who's a hacker. I've been communicating with Cade."

Gotcha.

As I'd suspected, Cade had been playing us.

But why? What the hell did Cade have against us?

A former FBI guy, an attorney in the city, a guy into BDSM, a hacker. What did it all mean?

And now he had disappeared.

What was he up to?

And what did he have against Joe and me? Against all the Steels?

Something to do with my father . . .

"Not that I know of," Dominic said, "but there's a lot about my brother I don't know."

"What *do* you know about him?"

"Not much. We don't have a lot in common, other than a love of baseball. He's messed up."

"You're telling me."

"Look. I can't tell you anything more. I only know he's obsessed with your father and the Steels. How do you even know about the Spider? Where did you get that card?"

I couldn't say anything more. I'd already violated Joe's trust by telling Marjorie about Justin Valente when I'd promised not to. Granted, he'd also told his wife, but still. I wouldn't violate his trust again.

"None of your business," was my answer.

"If you want me to help you figure this out, it *is* my business."

"No, it's not. I do want your help, but there are some things I can't discuss."

"Have it your way," he said. "You know how to reach me."

I headed back into the bar.

"What was that all about?" Talon asked.

"I wanted to know how he'd come to be Marj's trainer. Whether it was part of the whole thing."

"And?" Talon said.

"It was. He's been watching her for a while because Cade has. Probably watching all of us."

"But only Marj and our mom were his targets for safety?" Talon said. "And Colin? How does that make any sense?"

"I don't know." I shook my head. "If your dad is—"

"He's not," Ryan said, cutting me off. "He's dead. I watched my psycho mother put a bullet in his heart."

"I watched it too, Ry," Talon said, "but he's come back to life before."

"Not possible." Ryan took a long drink from his glass of wine. "He's dead. Just like I would be if Ruby hadn't saved me."

I nodded. No use arguing the point. Brad Steel *was* most likely dead. If he wasn't, we'd find out eventually.

"What do you think?" Ryan asked me.

"About what?"

"Dominic." Apparently he'd put the issue of his father possibly being alive to rest.

"I don't get the sense that he's lying," I said.

"Me neither. I really should have brought Ruby along. She can sniff out a liar a mile away."

"I don't think he's lying either," Talon said, "but I also don't think he's volunteering any information."

"I need to talk to Joe," I said.

Both of the Steels nodded.

What they didn't know was that I needed to speak to Joe alone. The whole family might know all about Justin Valente and Colin Morse and my father's involvement with each, but they didn't know their brother was acquainted with Cade Booker because of his membership in a leather club.

I wasn't about to divulge that tidbit.

My phone buzzed with a number I didn't recognize. Since we changed phones every twenty-four hours, I'd learned to pay attention to all callers.

"Yeah?" I said into the phone.

"Bryce," Marjorie said. "You need to come home. Now."

CHAPTER THIRTY

Marjorie

Bryce stared at the document I'd handed to him as soon as he walked through the door.

"It's a payoff," I said. "It has to be. This Bert Valente must have been Justin's dad. Your dad paid him off to keep quiet about Justin's murder."

Bryce didn't glance up from the document. "I'm not so sure," he said.

"What do you think it is, then?"

"It says unspecified merchandise."

"So? What merchandise could he be talking about? It's just code. He paid Justin's dad off not to turn him in for murder."

"I can't believe I'm saying this, but you have to think like my father."

"Uh...okay."

"He was a trafficker. To him, people were merchandise."

My stomach dropped. "You think..."

"You said Colin thinks his father sold him to my father, right? Does he have any proof of that?"

"He must, or he wouldn't have said it. I guess I forgot to ask him while we were being held captive." I hadn't meant to sound sarcastic, but I did.

"Honey, I'm not blaming you for anything. We need to talk to him. Find out why he thinks that. But right here I think is documentation not of a payoff but of a purchase."

"You think Justin is alive."

"I think he was alive then. I don't know about now."

"But you said—"

"The memories are fuzzy. I know that. But his lips and skin weren't blue when we found him by the river. And then he and his family just disappeared."

Nausea welled in my throat. Bryce's dad had truly been evil. Not that I'd ever doubted it, but to buy a kid? And what the hell kind of parent would sell a kid?

Ted Morse.

This guy. Bert Valente.

I shook my head slowly. "I don't understand."

"Be glad you don't," Bryce said. "I am. Every day."

I opened my mouth to respond, but he grabbed me and crushed his lips to mine.

But almost as quickly, he pulled back and pushed me away. I lifted my eyebrows.

"Too much in my head," he said.

"Let me help, then. Let me be your escape." I cupped his cheeks and pulled his lips down to mine, opening for him, urging him.

His tongue invaded my mouth, filling me with a raw need. He was taking, escaping—I could feel it in the way he kissed me, as if I were a drug he needed for survival, a salve to take away a crushing pain, a knowledge he wished he could erase from his mind.

I kissed him back, showing him how much I needed him in return. We needed each other.

When would this vicious cycle end? When would we each be free from the ghosts of our past?

Even now, as I reveled in Bryce's kiss, the scar on my upper thigh itched. Just the thought of the blade hidden in my purse would have calmed it.

But the blade was no longer in my possession. Would never again be in my possession.

Bryce didn't need a blade to relieve his guilt. He was using my body instead, so I'd do the same.

More. I needed more. More kisses. More Bryce. More everything that only he could give me. If I didn't have my blade, I still had the most important person in the world to me, the man who was kissing me right now as if his life depended on it.

He deepened the kiss, backing me against the refrigerator where the buzz of its motor vibrated against my back. His cock was hard, and he ground the bulge into my vulva. My pussy throbbed, aching for him to fill me as only he could. We kept kissing, though, grinding against each other, panting and groaning, until he broke the kiss and inhaled sharply.

Bed, I expected him to say. *Bed. Now.*

Instead, he crushed our mouths together once more. Each kiss was rawer than the last, more feral, more primal, until it was only instinct that guided us, as if we were two animals in a dark forest coming together from a sheer urge.

Still fully clothed, we continued to grind against each other, bringing our aching need to a pulsing point. My heart fired rapidly, my skin full of chilly tingles. My core on fire, and my pussy wet and swollen. Already the wetness was soaking me.

Bryce's hands were everywhere. First on my cheeks, then my shoulders, then one gripping my ass and pulling me tighter against his erection. One cupped a breast, thumbed a nipple. Another pulled one of my thighs upward, giving him a better angle against my denim-clad pussy.

I undulated against him, my body erupting in flames. Could I come fully clothed, just from the friction—

"Oh!" I gasped, my body humming as a climax rolled through me.

My nipples poked hard through the fabric of my bra and shirt, and my pussy contracted around nothing, longing for a cock or a finger inside to help milk more from it. I ground against Bryce furiously, letting the orgasm collide into me.

I was constricted. Wholly constricted by my clothing, yet still I came. I came against this man I loved more than anything, needed more than anything. Wanted more than anything.

He broke our kiss once more and drew in a deep breath. "You're so hot, baby. That's it. Come for me. Only for me."

His words made the climax draw out further, but still . . . I needed to undress. Be naked. Roll around with Bryce and feel his huge cock inside me.

"Please," I rasped. "Bed. Naked. Please."

He pulled me into his arms and carried me to his bedroom. We undressed each other quickly, clothes flying everywhere and landing in wrinkled puddles on the floor.

Naked at last, we fell onto the bed, and within another second—

"God!"

He was inside me, his huge dick penetrating the depths of my pussy, sliding in with ease as I was already dripping wet. My nipples longed for his attention, my skin ached for his touch, but for now, we fucked.

We fucked like the animals we were, as if we were under

a full moon in the dark woods, answering nature's call to copulate, to preserve our line.

It was a good fuck.

A damned good fuck.

The *friend* we both needed.

When Bryce released into me, I grabbed his ass, trying to push him farther and farther into me as he grunted and bit at my neck.

"Never enough," he grunted. "Never enough with you."

God, no. Never enough. I'd never have enough of Bryce Simpson. And as far as I was concerned, this night was just getting started.

CHAPTER THIRTY-ONE

Bryce

I found solace within her body, peace within her heart and soul. No matter what outside forces—memories of my father's heinous crimes, haunting recall of things long buried—tried to consume me, Marjorie could give me peace.

I could never let her go.

I had to learn to be the man she deserved, the man worthy of her uniqueness, her beauty, her passion.

Her love.

I wasn't that man yet, but I would be, when I laid the ashes of my father's crimes to rest once and for all.

I'd released inside her body. We'd had a good fuck, a fuck we both needed. An escape.

Now I wanted to make love to my woman.

We rested together for a few timeless moments, and then Marjorie rose and brought back two glasses of water and two apples. Rehydration and carbo-loading. Always a good idea. I quickly polished off my apple and downed all the water.

Marj lay down next to me and snuggled into my shoulder. She wasn't ready to stop, was she?

Then I smiled as she nibbled at my jawline. No, she wasn't ready to stop, and neither was I.

She trailed her soft lips over my cheek and then around

the shell of my ear, flicking her tongue and driving me slowly crazy. Her breasts swept over my chest, making my nipples come alive.

I banished all thoughts of our current situation from my mind. I was going to enjoy this. I *deserved* to enjoy this, and so did she. Her lips made a pathway from my earlobe down my neck to my chest. When she flicked her tongue over one nipple, I shuddered. No woman had paid this much attention to my nipples, and it drove me insane. Anything Marjorie did with her lips and tongue drove me insane.

I moaned as she teased me with her lips and tongue, nibbling at my nipple and then sucking it between her lips. So good. So fucking good.

She traveled downward to my belly and then to my cock that had hardened again in anticipation.

When she flicked her tongue onto my head, I breathed in sharply, holding back the pulsating that threatened to erupt. I wanted to savor this. Savor what she had in mind for me.

Slowly she wrapped her lips around the head of my cock, humming a slow vibration that I felt all the way to my toes.

"Baby, go easy," I said, clenching my teeth. "I want this to last."

She met my gaze but didn't smile with her mouth full of my dick. But she arched her brows slightly.

Yeah. I was in for it.

She gently slid her lips down the length of my cock about three-quarters of the way, and then she moved backward. I tensed my body, my legs and my feet coiled and ready to spring. How could I take this blissful torture without grabbing her, turning her around, and pounding into her again?

But I was determined.

This would last. This would last all fucking night.

Marjorie let my cock drop and nibbled on my inner thighs and then my balls. They were already tightly scrunched toward my body, and her tiny nips made them coil up even more. When she moved me over onto my side and slid her tongue between my ass cheeks, I thought I might burst.

Her sweet little tongue probed my asshole.

Oh. My. God.

This was new for me. New . . . and really fucking thrilling.

No wonder women loved anal stimulation. This was heaven. I shivered and fisted my dick, holding it at the base to try to settle it down. I wasn't going to come. Not yet.

She gave little bites to my ass and thighs while she continued her passionate assault.

Then the flat of her finger rubbed against my asshole.

And I thought I might explode.

No, don't penetrate me.

But God, please penetrate me.

She didn't.

Just rubbed the surface of the hole with her finger, and it felt really, really good.

I'd longed to take her sweet little ass before, something I'd never done. I'd hoped we could be the first and only for each other, but her attention to mine had me wondering . . . Had she done this before?

I opened my mouth to voice the thought when she rolled me back onto my back and began kissing my upper thighs.

My cock stood at attention, aching for more of her licks and nips, aching even more for her to take me to the back of her throat, balls deep.

But no, I'd savor this. Savor every second of attention she

was giving my body.

"Mmm, I love your legs," she said against my skin. "They're so muscular."

She licked down one leg, tickling me as she kissed my knee, and then smoothed her mouth over my calf to my foot. She licked my toes. Seriously sucked them.

And God, it was heavenly.

She worked her way back up my other leg until she came to my still rock-hard cock.

"Please," I said, clenching my teeth. "Suck me, baby. Please."

She gave the head a quick nip but passed on the sucking, moving up my belly to my chest once more.

"Fuck!" I fisted the comforter. "You're driving me insane. Totally insane."

"That is my plan," she said naughtily. "I want you so on edge that you're ready to pop at the slightest touch."

"I'm. Already. There."

"You *think* you're already there," she teased. "Trust me. You're not. Not yet."

Then she clamped her lips around my nipple and sucked.

My cock throbbed, and I moved my hips upward, searching for something to fill. Her sweet cunt. Her hot little ass. Her beautiful, warm mouth.

Nothing. I was screwing air.

She continued her attack on my nipple. Damn. Women always loved having their nipples sucked, but it had never occurred to me how good it might feel to me as well.

She had the touch. She knew my body better than I did.

"Baby, please," I begged. "I need to get inside you. Please."

She had worked her way up to my head, and she pressed

her lips to mine in a soft kiss. "Tit for tat," she said teasingly. Then she turned around, positioning her pussy over my lips.

Eat her? No problem. I could suck on her sweetness for hours, especially if it meant she put her warm mouth back on my cock.

I groaned when she took me inside her warmth, tonguing me gently as she blew me.

Her swollen pussy beckoned in its aromatic beauty. I inhaled, and then again, saturating myself with her musky fragrance. Then I dived in.

Her folds were silky under my tongue and coated with her juices. I sucked at them, lapped up her cream, eating my fill.

She squirmed on top of me, taking me deeper the more ferociously I ate her.

So I ate her more ferociously, enjoying every single minute of it.

I licked her hard clit and then forced my tongue into her wetness. Then I moved upward and flicked over her cute pink asshole. She'd played with mine, and now it was my turn. How I longed to fuck her in this virgin hole. I would. Someday.

For now, I licked it, and when it was good and lubed up, I stroked it with a finger as I continued to lick her sweet pussy. She was amazing, so responsive to my every touch.

God, I loved this woman. This beautiful woman.

When she began moving more rapidly, I thrust two fingers into her tight cunt and massaged her G-spot. She came at once with an explosion, and without warning, I eased one finger into her tight little asshole.

She squealed onto my cock, driving me to the brink. I released, shooting into her warm sweet mouth as I fucked both her holes with my fingers.

Her pussy pulsated around my fingers, and I continued fucking her furiously, both holes in tandem, as she released again and again.

CHAPTER THIRTY-TWO

Marjorie

Muddled.

My mind was muddled. Lusty incoherent thoughts blended together in psychedelic visions of color and movement.

This climax rolled through me like crashing waves against sandy shores.

Penetration.

Such pure and lovely penetration.

Not just in my pussy, but in . . .

Waves and waves and waves . . .

Pure joy. Pure rapture. Pure euphoria.

Bryce's voice, so soothing and hot and sexy all at the same time. His words? Didn't matter what he said. Just the sound waves of his sexy rumble rang in my ears, taking me further . . . further . . .

I ground against his lips, his chin, his sandy stubble scraping me and making me hotter.

My whole world was my pussy, my whole world was this moment.

And I wanted it to last . . . last . . . last . . .

Baby. Honey. Come for me. That's it. Yes. Enjoy it, sweetheart. You're so hot. So beautiful.

I love you so much.

All the words. All the words from his throat in his deep husky timbre.

All ... the ... words ...

I soared even higher, his tongue vibrating against my clit, his fingers plunging in and out of me, stroking me, giving me more and more pleasure with each silky thrust.

Heaven. Pure, raw heaven.

I continued grinding, determined to take it all ...

Until the pleasure grew so intense, so lusty, so perfect ...

One perfect implosion, bringing every cell of my body together in humming joy.

One.

Perfect.

Implosion.

Words poured out of my mouth, but I couldn't say what they were.

Words of passion, joy.

Words of love for this man bringing me the ultimate pleasure.

Words not from my body or even my heart.

Words from my soul.

He slowed his fingers as I came down from my high.

Down, down, down ... until my hips stopped grinding and I lay on top of him, his hard cock against my cheek, perspiration dripping from my forehead, from my breasts.

My breath came in rapid puffs against his thigh.

Bliss.

Pure joy.

The climax settled, and the contractions of my body grew slower and less frequent until they disappeared altogether, leaving me in a peaceful harmony I'd never experienced.

I could fall asleep here, against his hard thigh, his cock smooth and hard against my cheek.

So easy. It would be so easy...

My eyes closed of their own accord.

Marj. Baby. Honey.

His voice? Or my imagination? I didn't know at this point.

"Marj. Baby. Honey."

I opened my eyes. "Hmm?"

"I love you so much. That was so hot."

"Mmm," was all I could muster.

"Here," he said. "Let me move you over so you're comfortable."

"Perfectly comfortable," I murmured, closing my eyes again.

Still, he gently moved me so that my body was cradled by the silky sheet and the soft mattress. I held my arms out to him.

He smiled above me, his eyes heavy-lidded. "I can wait."

No. I needed him to release, to experience the miracle I'd experienced. "Please," I said softly. "Make love to me. Please."

He smiled again, his chin and cheeks glistening with my wetness. Then he slowly pushed his cock into me.

"God. So tight."

Yeah, I was tight. Tight as a drum after that plentiful orgasm. His big cock tunneled into me, burning through and making me want to come again. I wasn't sure I could after that amazing climax, but damn, that slow burn...

"Can't. Need to fuck you."

Bryce increased his pace, thrusting...thrusting... thrusting...

The burn turned to flames within me, and the pressure built, until—

"God, honey." He plunged into me balls deep.

And I shattered with him.

A glorious climax in tandem. Nothing like the last one, but no less spectacular.

We flew together, our bodies joined in the ultimate clasp, our sweat mingling, his lips pressed to my neck.

I love you. I love you. I love you.

The words swirled around us, sometimes in his voice, sometimes in mine. Sometimes simply vibrating in the air between us.

Whole. Complete. Never alone again.

Never.

Never alone again.

★ ★ ★

Morning came sooner than I wanted it to. I woke next to Bryce when the alarm on his phone went off at seven a.m. I stretched my arms languidly above my head, letting the sunlight stream from the window onto my still naked body.

Bryce opened his eyes and fumbled for the phone. "Sorry about that."

"It's okay. We've both got to get up anyway."

He smiled. "Last night was amazing."

"It was perfect," I said.

He sighed. "But now back to reality."

"Afraid so." I kissed his lips lightly. "Unless you've got time for another round?"

He pulled me into his embrace. "I always have time for that." He pushed my long hair out of my eyes. "I've never been so afraid in my life as I was when you were missing. I don't know what I'd do if I lost you, Marjorie."

I kissed him again. "You won't lose me."

"I can't." He inhaled and let it out slowly. "I want you to go to Paris."

"We've been through this. I'm not leaving until Jade has the baby. And right now, I can't leave. Not until all this is settled."

"I miss Henry like crazy," he said, "but at least I know he's safe. I text my mom hourly. I'm sure she thinks I'm nuts."

"She thinks you love your son, and you do." I kissed his forehead, his hair tickling my lips.

"I'll miss you like crazy too, and I'll text you all the time. I just can't go through not knowing where you are again, what's happening to you."

"Nothing happened to me. Nothing horrible, anyway."

"But it could have. What if it hadn't been Dominic who took you? What if it had been that psycho brother of his?"

"It wasn't. He was busy trying to take on you and Joe. How do you think I feel? You got pepper-sprayed, but something much worse could have happened."

He shook his head. "We were ready for him to be armed. We took care of that."

"But you weren't ready for the pepper spray."

"How could we be? It's a pro move. We're lucky it wasn't something lethal."

"It didn't have to be. It took you out for the time required for him to get away."

He chuckled. "I'd like to say you were wrong, but—"

"You can't," I finished for him.

"Fucker had his office booby trapped. It's not a bad idea, actually."

"Don't you start booby-trapping your office. Or this house. I don't want to live that way, Bryce."

"We won't," he promised. "But I have to figure out this whole thing first. Cade Booker and Ted Morse and how they all tie in to Justin Valente and my father. I need to talk to Joe."

"Yeah, we all do. He's busy with the new baby."

"I know. I hate to bother him, but he knows Booker better than the rest of us."

"He does?"

"Yeah. I can't say how, but he does."

"You can't keep secrets from me, Bryce."

"I don't want to, but this is Joe's story to tell, not mine. Talon and Ryan don't know either."

Curiosity pounded through me. "Bryce . . ."

"I can't. I've already violated Joe's trust once, and I won't do it again. You wouldn't do it to Jade, would you?"

Shit. He had me there. "No," I said reluctantly.

He threaded his fingers through my disheveled hair. "Thank you. For understanding."

"I do understand. I don't like it, though."

"I don't like it either. I promise a day will come when there are no secrets between us."

"Just not today," I said.

"Not today. But I can give you something else today." He pulled me to him and kissed me thoroughly.

And a moment later, I forgot all about my oldest brother and his secrets.

CHAPTER THIRTY-THREE

Bryce

Her mouth was warm and inviting, as always, and I hardened instantly.

Would we always want each other like this? I couldn't imagine not wanting Marjorie. Not craving her. Not aching for her touch, her lips on mine, her body gloving me.

I hovered over her and slowly entered her, and then I wrapped her in my arms and rolled us to our sides, so we were facing each other.

I met her gaze, our eyes locking. "I love you so much," I whispered.

"I love you too." She cast her gaze downward. "Watch. Watch as you go in and out of me. It's so beautiful, isn't it?"

I followed her gaze to our joining. As I slid in and out of her sweet, tight body, I did as she asked.

I watched.

Mesmerized.

Entranced.

Had I ever seen anything more perfect?

We always ended up fucking in a passionate frenzy, but this morning...this was lovemaking in all its truth. In all its perfection.

Slow. Sweet. And with the perfect partner.

Our lips met tenderly, our tongues twirled, and our mouths melded into one.

And I made love to my wonderful woman.

★ ★ ★

At the office later, Joe showed up.

"Hey," I said. "How are Melanie and the baby?"

"They're good. She's set up in her hotel suite but spends most of her time at the hospital with little Brad so he can get regular breast feedings. He should be good to come home in a week or two."

"That's great news."

He nodded. "I'm not sure I'll ever forgive you guys for going after Marj and my mother without me."

"You had to stay with Melanie and the baby."

"I know, but you could have at least told me."

"Your attention needed to be focused on your wife and child, Joe. We all agreed."

"We all agreed? I didn't get a vote in there."

"We all thought—"

He stopped me with a gesture. "Fine. I get it. I probably would have done the same thing if it had been Tal with Jade giving birth. Still..."

"You didn't like being left out."

"Nope. It doesn't sit well with me."

"It's over now. We got Marj and your mom back. But there's still a lot—"

He nodded. "I know. Let's go outside."

I followed him outside the office building until we were about a hundred yards away.

"You still think we're being spied on?" I said.

"I can't prove it, but damn, I feel like someone's watching me."

"We're doing everything we can. Changing our cell phones, watching what we say anywhere inside. What else can we do?"

He didn't reply.

"Joe," I said, "you're going to need to be straight with me about something."

"What's that?"

"Booker. Cade Booker. I know you don't want to tell me anything more about how you know him, but I'm going to ask you to do it anyway. You both went to the same underground leather club."

He nodded.

"I need more information if I'm going to help you figure this out. What else can you tell me about him?"

"Nothing." Joe was adamant.

"Please." I quickly filled him in on our discussion with Dominic last night. "His own brother says he's a psycho."

"Hell, I agree. Who else but a psycho is armed with three guns and has his office rigged with pepper spray?"

"Not a psycho, maybe. Someone who's very afraid of something. Someone who is overly cautious. That's why I'm asking. What else do you know about this guy?"

"Just because he's into—"

"Damn it, Joe, you know that's not what I mean. What you do in the bedroom is your own thing, and whether you like to do it at some club doesn't bother me one bit. But Booker's the issue here, and you've seen him in a way others haven't."

"What he likes doesn't matter."

"Maybe it doesn't. But maybe it does."

"I can't, Bryce. It's a gentleman's code."

"The man attacked us. I think the code is broken."

"What if he makes it public that I used to go there?"

"You ashamed of it?"

"Hell, no. But it's not something I want my mother and sister to know, for God's sake."

"Your mother is out of it. She won't have a clue. As for your sister—"

"Don't even. I don't want to hear about any of my sister's kinks."

I chuckled. "I wasn't going to give you anything like that. Trust me."

"God. You mean there *are* kinks?"

I shook my head. "Let's not get into Marj's kinks or yours, okay? I'm only interested in Booker's, and certainly not from a sexual standpoint. Just from the standpoint of learning more about him."

Joe stayed quiet for a minute.

He'd tell me, though. I needed to know, so I could help him. He knew that.

"He's a switch," Joe finally said.

"Say what?"

"A top-bottom switch. Sometimes he likes to dominate, other times he likes to submit."

"O . . . kay."

"You don't know the jargon," Joe said. "I get it. But here's the thing. Most men are Dominants, and most women are submissives, at least at this club. We had a few female Dommes and a few male subs, but it's usually the other way around at a place like this. Switches, though, are even less common than male subs and female Dommes."

"So he's got an uncommon kink."

"These aren't really kinks. Maybe they are. You've got to understand. When you like this stuff, it seems normal."

"I've got nothing against any kind of alternative lifestyle—"

"What I'm saying is that it doesn't seem alternative to us. I'll be honest with you. It's not a whole life thing for me. I like to be dominant in the bedroom."

That was hardly a surprise. I'd known this guy my whole life. If there was ever a born Dominant, it was Jonah Steel.

"But I don't take it into real life. I don't even always do it in the bedroom. Most of the people at the club were like me. It was just a place where we could play out scenes with willing partners."

"You had partners?"

"Duh, Bryce. You think you can dominate thin air?"

"No. I mean, you were with that one woman. Karen, was it?"

"Kerry. Kerry Ross. Yeah, she was my sub for a while, but she was never my slave outside the club, though she wanted to be."

"Slave?"

"That's a sub who's submissive in all aspects of life, not just the bedroom. Not my thing. I never wanted a slave. I wanted an equal." He raked his fingers through his hair. "I can't believe I'm telling you this."

"It's all safe with me. You have to know that."

"Right. It's still weird. This part of me has always been very private."

"If it helps, you don't need to tell me about you at all. Just about Booker."

"You need to know about the other stuff to understand. Booker was a male switch, the only one at the club."

"And that's unusual?"

"Switches are unusual, yeah. Usually you're one or the other, dominant or submissive. But a switch is a different kind of personality."

"Doesn't seem that weird," I said. "Okay, it's all a little weird to me, but why wouldn't you want to experience both sides of the coin?"

"He wasn't just a switch. He was a bisexual switch. He played with both men and women, and he topped and bottomed for both."

"Topped?"

"Top means taking the dominant role. Bottom is submissive."

"Okay, not my cup of tea, or yours apparently. But surely being a bisexual switch isn't altogether unusual."

"I suppose it isn't, but he was the only one at our club."

"Anything else?"

"That's it. I'm not a voyeur, so I never watched him in action."

"You mean others . . ."

"Yeah, every club has a certain number of voyeurs and exhibitionists. Those who go to watch and be watched. I didn't fall into either category. No one watched me. I had a private suite."

Of course a Steel would have a private suite at an underground leather club. This was so much TMI.

"That's a shame."

"A shame I had a private suite?"

"No, not that. A shame you never watched Booker. You

might have some insight if you had."

"Dude, you just gave me a visual I didn't want."

I couldn't help a laugh. "Sorry."

That got a chuckle out of him.

"Can you ask Melanie? About whether a switch has any psychological issues?"

"I already have. She says like any other kink, it can be perfectly normal behavior. It's not the preference that's ever the issue. It's the person."

"And doing it with both men and women?"

"Also normal."

"Maybe his sexual behavior is normal, but Booker is anything but."

"Knowing what I know now," Joe said, "I agree with you."

CHAPTER THIRTY-FOUR

Marjorie

Bertram Valente was dead.

I'd scoured the obits and found several Bertram Valentes, but only one in Colorado. The ages matched up. He could easily have been Justin Valente's father.

So where was Justin's mother?

I had no idea, and nowhere to turn...other than to my best friend, who was also the City Attorney.

I walked to the main house and found her relaxing in a recliner in the family room with a glass of juice.

"Hey," she said when she saw me.

"Hey. I hate to ask you this, but are you still up to checking the city's databases for Justin Valente?"

"Yeah. Of course. I want to help. But Talon—"

I stopped her with a gesture. "We're all in this together. You have a resource, and we should be using it."

She nodded. "I wholeheartedly agree. Problem is, I can't access the server from here. Only from the office. That's part of the security stuff I had installed. We'll have to go into town."

"What about Mary?"

"I'm still the boss."

"I know, but if she sees us snooping around..."

"She won't. We'll use my office."

"She's not using it?"

"No, she's using the other office. The one I used when Larry was City Attorney."

★ ★ ★

An hour later, we were in Jade's office. Mary had taken off for her lunch break, so we wouldn't have any interruptions.

"I just had a thought," I said. "What if someone got into the databases and made changes again, like before?"

"They shouldn't be able to. Not after the safety upgrades I had installed."

"I know, but these people, Jade. They get away with everything. Someone walked into a mental health facility and took my disabled mother away . . . and no one seemed the wiser."

"Well," Jade said, "we'll soon find out. I'm going in."

She tapped on the computer and went through screen after screen. Wow. She really had put in top-notch security.

"The city of Snow Creek really paid for all this?" I said, flabbergasted.

"Oh, no. I didn't even ask. Talon gave me the money to have this done."

I nodded. I should have known. Maybe this security would hold after all.

"Bingo," Jade said, coming to a screen. "Here he is. Justin C. Valente. Father Bertram Valente. Mother Cadence Russo Valente. Last known address just outside of town. He would have been bused to school."

"With your brothers?"

"No. Looks like he lived east of town."

"So we check out the house?"

"We can, but I'm sure they've been gone forever. I can check the property records." She tapped furiously. "Looks like they rented a small place on someone's farm."

"Did he have any brothers or sisters?"

"No, not that it says. The school records don't show any siblings. Looks like an only child."

"Okay. My research shows that Bertram Valente is dead. Died ten years ago, shot at a convenience store."

"Yeah." She tapped. "Just substantiating that."

"Did they ever catch who did it?" I asked.

"Doesn't look like it. It's an unsolved case in Denver."

"So Bertram Valente left Snow Creek, went to Denver."

"Looks like it. He bought a— Wow!"

"What?"

"He bought a freaking mansion nearly thirty years ago in Cherry Hills. That's *posh* Denver."

"And his wife?"

"Let me check. They divorced about a year later. It's all here. Public records."

"What happened to her?" I asked.

"Looks like she remarried . . . Let me get the name." Then she swallowed and turned pale.

"What? What is it?"

"She married a man named Booker. Richard Booker."

Chills rattled my flesh. "Booker? As in Cade Booker? Dominic and Alessandra Booker?" Thoughts whirled in my head. "Justin C. Valente. Cade must be his middle name. Cade, Cadence. After his mother."

Jade typed frantically. "Here are the birth certificates. Dominic James Booker and Alessandra Cadence Booker.

Father is Richard Booker, mother is Cadence Russo. Shit. The. Fucking. Bed."

"Dominic James. That's the name he uses for training."

"Is he even a trainer?"

"He claims he went to UCLA and studied... Oh, hell. I don't even know. Does it matter? Is he really any better than his half brother? He claims he's acting on orders to keep me safe, but he still drugged me and took me against my will."

Jade was still staring at her computer screen. "They can't be the same person. Justin died, right? He's dead. Tom Simpson killed him."

"No," I said quietly. "Tom Simpson drugged him, and then Tom Simpson *bought* him."

CHAPTER THIRTY-FIVE

Bryce

"Now we just have to find the bastard." Joe shuffled through all the records Jade had printed out.

We were at the main house, outside as usual. Marjorie had grilled burgers, but none of us were particularly hungry. The food sat uneaten on platters in the center of the table.

I swallowed, trying to dislodge the apple-sized lump in my throat. *Now we just have to find the bastard.*

I couldn't fault Joe's words, but if Cade Booker was indeed a bastard, Joe and I had something to do with it.

We'd taken him camping. We'd given my father access to him.

"Don't do this to yourself." Marjorie rubbed my forearm. "This isn't your fault. You're not the one who sold your son."

Just the thought made anger rage within me. I was a father, for God's sake, and I'd do anything—*anything*—to protect my son. This motherfucker, this Bertram Valente.

Still, if we hadn't taken Justin camping...

"Please. Stop," Marjorie said softly.

The others were talking, but the words jumbled in my head. Only the warmth of Marjorie's hand helped keep me sane.

Because I knew the truth.

This *was* our fault. Joe's and mine, and more mine, because *my* father had taken us camping. We'd had no intention to harm him, but that didn't negate the fact that, but for us, my father would have never known Justin Valente.

Justin hadn't died after all, and his father had given him up and been quieted by my father's money.

Then what had happened? So far, we knew only that he'd "returned" after his mother had remarried Richard Booker and Dominic and Alessandra were in their teens. He changed his name to Cade and took the last name Booker. Had he truly trained with the FBI? That could have been totally fabricated. My father could have taught him to handle weapons as well or better than the FBI. Cade's law degree could be fabricated, as well.

Where had he been during those lost years? Dominic was twenty-four now and had been sixteen when Cade returned. That was only eight years ago.

We knew absolutely nothing.

"...probably trained as a slave," Ruby was saying. "That's what they did to the rest of the kids. Those who were trouble were killed, and some probably died from the training. Whatever happened to Cade, we know he didn't die."

I eyed Joe. He shook his head at me slightly.

I suppressed the bit of anger that threatened to emerge. I'd never spill the beans about the leather club. But Cade knew who Joe was. He'd clearly been watching Joe through the club, and the rest of us through... I didn't know. Dominic had said his brother was obsessed with the Steels and with my father.

My father was now dead, and I was the substitute. Or perhaps I'd never been the substitute. After all, I was the one who'd invited him camping.

Marjorie's hand never left my arm, though she did join in the conversation.

"Alex was a lot more hotheaded than Dominic," she said. "She didn't have a lot of patience with Colin or me, didn't seem to understand that we didn't like being taken against our will, and if we didn't want her protection, we could just leave. She even said she wanted to crush my skull at one point."

I'll crush your damned skull.

I moved my arm from her touch. "Say that again."

"What? Alex didn't have any patience."

"No. The last thing. She said she wanted to crush your skull?"

This time Joe took note as well, his brow rising.

"Yeah. I think those are the words she used. Big deal. She thought she was tougher than she was."

"It *is* a big deal," I said. "Joe and I used to use that phrase when we were kids, didn't we?"

Joe nodded. "And we must have heard it somewhere."

"Not from here," Talon said. "I don't remember Dad ever saying it, and I didn't even hear that in the military—and believe me, I heard a lot of shit there I don't want to repeat."

I cleared my throat. "I don't remember"—*true*—"but we must have heard it from my father."

"And Alex probably heard it from Cade," Joe said, "who probably heard it from . . ."

"My father," I mumbled.

Marjorie lifted her hand to touch my forearm once more, but I moved it away from her. I didn't want comfort at the moment.

I didn't deserve it.

"Not your fault," she mouthed.

She was right.

I'd been nine years old. Nine fucking years old.

"You guys are missing something really important here," Jade was saying. "Cade may have been abused, but he got away."

"He's a mess, though," Ryan said.

"But he's alive. He didn't die there, wherever *there* was. He just needs help."

"He's not the one who kidnapped Mom and me," Marjorie said. "That was his half brother and sister." She held up her hand. "I know. You're going to say—if Dominic is to be believed—that he did it for our protection. Protection from Cade. But the reality of the situation is that Cade didn't do anything to us."

"He did to Bryce and me," Joe said. "My eyes still don't feel quite right."

"We were holding him at gunpoint," I interjected.

"Assault with a deadly weapon," Jade said.

"We didn't assault him," Joe said.

"Doesn't matter. Assault doesn't actually require anything physical. The legal definition is simply the threat of physical violence. Technically you both *did* assault him."

"Are you kidding me?" Joe said.

"Easy," Talon said.

"Maybe we did," I said. "He had it coming. I'm sorry for whatever he endured at the hands of my father or anyone else, but he's been fucking with us for a long time now. We know that."

"What?" Ryan said. "A long time now?"

Shit. Joe eyed me once more. The rest of them didn't know about his association with Cade at the club, and I'd just shot off my mouth.

"Seems like a long time, anyway," I said.

That seemed to appease them.

"His mother died in a drive-by shooting," Joe said. "In a tiny town in Iowa, right before Cade returned. Don't tell me that doesn't stink."

I nodded. Joe was right. "I'm guessing Cade was involved. Offing his mother for selling him—"

"Wait," Marj said. "How would Cade know what his father did? And do we even know his mother was in on it?"

"Whether Cade knew or not," Talon said, "he could easily have blamed his parents for everything. For letting him go camping. For not finding him. A million different reasons. You have to understand. When you're in that situation . . ." He shook his head. "You'll blame just about anyone or anything."

"He needs help," Jade said. "We should get Melanie's opinion."

"Leave Melanie out of this," Joe said. "She has her hands full in the city with the baby. I've got bodyguards on them as it is. I don't want her bothered with anything else."

"Do we know how Cade's father died?" Ryan asked.

"Shot in a convenience store nine years ago," Marj said. "Jade and I found the records."

"Timing is just about right," I said. "What do you bet Cade knocked off his old man and his mom both?"

"If he did, who can blame him?" Marj said. "His father sold him like goods to be tortured and abused."

"We don't actually know what he went through," Joe said.

"Joe, come on," Marjorie said. "We *know*."

"Actually," I said, "there's a lot we don't know. Where he was taken. What he went through. How he got out. Whether he was really trained by the FBI. Whether he actually went to law school. And there's only one way to find all this out. We have to find *him*."

CHAPTER THIRTY-SIX

Marjorie

I looked to Talon. His gaze was glassy.

I knew the look.

He was remembering.

My scar on my thigh began to tingle and itch.

But for my conception...

No. Can't go there. Not now. Not when we have all this other stuff to figure out.

Damn it!

No more self-indulgence. How many times had I said that to myself? How many fucking times?

My phone buzzed. A text.

From Colin Morse.

My cufflinks are gone.

Shocking.

When was the last time you saw them?

I have no idea. Years. I never wore them.
I just assumed they were in the bottom of
my dresser drawer like they always were.

I cleared my throat. "I just got a text from Colin. His cufflinks are indeed missing."

"Can he look at the one we found?" Ruby asked. "Tell if it's a match?"

"Plus the one we found at my father's cabin," Bryce said.

"He's in Denver right now," I said. "We can send him a photo."

Ruby nodded. "The cufflink, the baseball card—"

"Shit," I said. "Why didn't I think of this before? Dominic said he coaches baseball. That he had a scholarship to play but had to quit because of an injury."

"You're thinking Dominic might be the bad guy here?" Ruby said.

"Not necessarily. Not that drugging people isn't a bad thing. But if he was interested in baseball and was talented at it, it's possible his older brother was as well."

"They have different fathers," Ryan said.

"So? You're a lot like Talon and Joe and you have diff—" I stopped abruptly. "I'm sorry, Ry."

"No, it's okay. You're right. You're right."

Ruby laid her hand over Ryan's.

"The scholarship thing could be fabricated," Bryce said, "but Dominic did mention that he and Cade shared a love of baseball."

Ruby squeezed Ryan's hand. "We also have the cigarette butt and polished rock that Dale found. Any ideas?"

"Is Cade a smoker?" I asked. "Dominic isn't, at least not that I've ever seen."

"What about Alex?" Ruby asked.

"Not that I saw," I said again.

"Cade is a smoker," Joe said quietly.

"How do you know?" I asked.

"I just know," he said.

"Yeah," Bryce said. "He was smoking the other day, when he pepper-sprayed us."

"In a city office building?" Ruby said. "That's not—"

"The guy isn't exactly a law-abiding citizen," Joe said stiffly. "He was smoking. Bryce is right."

Joe and Bryce exchanged a look that I couldn't quite read.

"What about Dale's rock collection?" Ruby asked Jade and Talon. "You never found it?"

"We got everything at the house," Talon said. "It was gone."

"Probably just misplaced," Ruby said. "If Cade was indeed taken and abused as a child, he wouldn't go after a little boy who'd been through the same."

"Then you don't think he was the guy on the playground?" Talon asked.

Ruby sighed. "I just don't know. This is strange. There are things that don't add up. When you're dealing with a psychopath, there are certain things you can usually depend on, certain ways their minds work. Melanie and I have talked about this many times. Look at my father and yours, Bryce. They were both psychopaths, but there was a certain sense to how they operated. With this Cade Booker?" She shook her head. "I'm a little lost."

"If Mel were here," I said, "she'd tell us that we have to look at his actions through the lens of what he's been through."

"But we don't know—"

"We do," Talon said. "We know exactly what he's been through. Rather, *I* know."

Silence.

No one could respond to that.

"Then, Tal," I finally said, "tell us why he's doing these things."

CHAPTER THIRTY-SEVEN

B r y c e

Sometimes, when I looked at Talon Steel, I saw him as a ten-year-old boy. I saw my father behind him, breathing on his neck, doing unspeakable acts to him.

Then, before I hurled, I had to erase the uninvited image from my mind.

But I couldn't erase the truth.

It *had* happened. My father had raped Talon Steel when he was ten years old. My father had tortured him, starved him, beaten him.

The truth will set you free.

Whoever said that was an idiot.

I'd never be free. Never be free of the knowledge of what my father had been, what my father had done.

Never.

"He's blaming anyone and everyone," Talon was saying. "He needs help."

"If he killed his mother and father," I said, "he's going to prison for a long time."

"They're unsolved crimes from years ago," Ruby said. "So that's doubtful."

"Ruby's right," Jade agreed. "The trail is long cold."

"What about DNA?" I asked.

"Unlikely," Ruby said. "But I'll get in touch with some people on the force. Maybe there's still some stuff in evidence we could test."

"One thing I don't get," Marj said. "Why would Cade Booker be watching Dale on the playground? And why would Dale think he recognized him? Cade has been away from that island for almost ten years."

"Just one more thing that doesn't make sense," Ruby said. "See what I mean? Most psychos can be tracked once you figure out their mind-set. This one doesn't have any"—air quotes—"*logic* behind it."

"Cade's gone now," Joe said. "Maybe he hasn't been back this whole time after all. Maybe he went back to that island on occasion, although why he'd want to is beyond me."

"We can check with his firm," Jade said. "See if he's taken leaves of absence."

"I'm on that," Ruby said. "I planned to question everyone there anyway."

"I'll go with you," Jade said.

"No, you won't." Talon shook his head adamantly. "In your cond—"

"Women have been making babies forever," Jade said. "I'm finally feeling good. I want to help. I'm an attorney. I know how to talk to other attorneys."

"She *would* be a big help," Ruby agreed.

"No—"

"For God's sake, Tal," Marj said. "You don't *own* her."

Talon's face reddened. "Of course I don't own her. I'm trying to protect her and our unborn child."

Marj had woken a beast. I could see it in Talon's eyes. He'd been enslaved for two months of his young life. Marj had hit a nerve.

She seemed to sense it, thank God. "I didn't mean it that way. I'm sorry for my poor choice of words."

Talon nodded.

"I won't go if it means that much to you," Jade said, "but I want to be part of this. I want to help."

"I know you do," Talon said. "Go, if you think you can help."

Jade smiled at him, her blue eyes sparkling. She was good for him. I hoped all my father's victims, even including Cade Booker, found the peace Talon had found with Jade.

They all deserved that much.

★ ★ ★

Later, after I'd called my mother and Henry, I sat on the guesthouse deck with a glass of iced tea. Marjorie had said she'd come over as soon as she could. She wanted to help Jade make sure the boys got their homework finished and got to bed.

Were we right? Was Cade Booker Justin Valente? It sure all added up. I took out my phone and logged on to Joe's and my secret account with the Spider, who apparently had never existed.

Nothing. Not even another *Gotcha*.

Not that I expected to find anything.

My mind flew to the encrypted emails I'd found in the trash bin several days ago. Someone had been communicating with Cade on this account . . . and it hadn't been Joe or me.

The trash bin was now empty.

My phone dinged with a text, an Iowa number.

*This is Dominic. Can you meet me in
town? We need to talk. Come alone.*

CHAPTER THIRTY-EIGHT

Marjorie

I was packing up an overnight bag to take to the guesthouse when my phone dinged with a text from Colin again, responding to the photos of the cufflinks I'd sent.

Not sure if they're mine, honestly.
I haven't looked at them in years.

> *When are you coming*
> *back to Snow Creek?*

I have business with my father.

> *Are you going to ask him about . . . ?*

Not sure.

> *If you're staying in his house,*
> *you need to take care of this.*

I'm not. I'm heading to our condo

*in Glenwood Springs. Looking
for a place. And a job.*

*Good for you, but we need you to
help us figure this whole thing out.*

Silence for a while, until he finally responded.

*I can't do this anymore. I have to heal.
I have to face the reality of my life now.
I can't help you.*

My fingers hovered over the tiny keyboard as I thought about how to respond. I could hardly blame him for wanting out. After all, our fight wasn't his fight. His beef was with his father. Well, his father and Tom Simpson, but Simpson was dead.

Thanks for looking for the cufflinks.

*No problem. Give Jade my best.
And tell her I'm sorry.*

For what?

Everything.

I threw the phone on my bed just as it dinged with another text.

This time from Bryce.

I have to go into town for a while.
I'll text you when I'm home.

Oh, hell, no.

What for?

Not sure yet. Dominic wants to meet me.

Then I'm coming with you.

He said to come alone.

Do you think I care?

Let me do this. I'm armed, and I can take
care of myself. We'll be in a public place.

I was in a public place when
he drugged me, remember?

A few seconds before the dots began moving.
Then—

*Let me do this. I'll get
back as soon as I can.*

I sighed.

> *Fine. But I'm pissed.*

I know. I love you. Trust me.

> *I love you too.*

God, I did. I just hoped he wasn't walking into some kind of trap.

My first instinct was to call Joe, but he was heading into Grand Junction to see the baby and spend the night with Melanie at the hotel suite. Talon and Jade had the boys to consider. That left Ryan and Ruby. Would they know what to do?

I was poised and ready to hit Ryan's number when Bryce's words struck me.

Trust me.

Did I trust him?

Yes, I did.

I wasn't sure I trusted Dominic, though.

But Dominic hadn't hurt me.

Still, had I been able to defend myself, I'd have gotten away.

My brothers all knew how to shoot a gun, and they were good at it. Especially Joe and Talon. I needed to learn. The idea scared me more than a little, but it was something I needed to do.

But ask my brothers to teach me?

No way. They wouldn't do it, anyway, and even if they did, I'd have to deal with all their Alpha bullshit.

I had a sister-in-law who was a former police detective and a crack shot. I'd ask Ruby.

I sent her a quick text.

She texted back.

As it happens, I'm going to the shooting range tomorrow. You can come with me, and I'll show you the basics.

I smiled.

It's a date.

CHAPTER THIRTY-NINE

Bryce

I insisted on meeting in the park. That it was the place where he'd taken Marj was no coincidence. I also frisked him, even checking his crotch, which wasn't fun, but his brother had been carrying there. Dominic was armed, of course, and I insisted he remove his gun and set it down on the bench. I did the same.

"All right, then," I said. "What do you want?"

"There's someone who wants to meet you."

"Who?"

"I can't tell you who, but he's only a text away. Are you willing?"

"You're nuts." I picked up my gun and placed it back in the ankle holster. "You said *we* needed to talk. Not that I needed to talk to anyone else."

"I'm not here to make any trouble," he said. "I'm being well paid to ask you if you'll talk to this person."

"I won't talk to anyone unless you tell me who it is."

"I can't do that. Not yet."

"Why the hell not?" I was tempted to sic my gun on him, but what good would that do? His weapon was sitting right next to him, and I was no killer.

"That's all I can say."

"Where's Cade?" I demanded.

"I don't know. It might surprise you that he doesn't tell me when he disappears."

"Then he's disappeared before?"

"Lots of times. His law partners put up with it because he funds the firm."

"Hold on. He *funds* the firm? With what?"

"His father was loaded. He died intestate, and Cade was his next of kin."

I wasn't sure why I hadn't considered this fact. Of course Cade's father had been loaded. My father had paid him off. Bert Valente had bought real estate that had increased in value, and who knew what else he had invested in?

"Right," I said. "He got shot at a convenience store."

"How did you know that?"

"I have my ways. Do you know how Cade's father got his money?"

Dominic shook his head.

"He sold his son. He sold Cade. To my psycho father."

Dominic shuddered slightly. If it weren't night, I was sure I'd see his tan face turning white.

"How do you know this?"

"I found documentation hidden in my father's things." I wasn't about to tell Dominic the whole story—that Joe and I had been responsible for my father even knowing about Cade.

"He's right," a low voice said.

I jerked around, looking for the source of the sound. "Who's there?"

"The person who wants to talk to you."

"Get out here, then," I said harshly. "Show yourself."

A figure approached, a black mask covering his face. He was tall, easily as tall as I was, possibly taller.

"I don't talk to you unless I know who you are," I said.

"I'm the person who's trying to protect Marjorie and her mother."

His voice was laced with familiarity. Depth and familiarity. It was a voice I'd once loved, I'd once respected.

"You're not..."

"Brad Steel?" The figure sighed and slowly pulled off his mask.

Bradford fucking Steel stood before me. His hair was still dark, as I remembered, though it was speckled with silver that shone in the light from the moon. Though I'd felt the ghost of my father more than once, this was no ghost. This man was alive. Alive and well.

"Fuck it all," I said. "You're supposed to be dead."

No response.

"And weren't you dying of cancer? Pancreatic, I think?"

"No. That was a lie. If Wendy hadn't tried to kill me, I needed another reason to die."

"You did this to your kids again. You're a fucking freak of nature, Brad."

"I have my reasons. I meant to stay covered, but once I saw you, I knew it wouldn't work. You recognized my voice, didn't you?"

I nodded.

"I'm counting on your discretion, Bryce. I love my children more than anything. You know that. You were an honorary child of mine, and I loved you nearly as much."

"But how...?"

"Pretty simple, actually. A bulletproof vest equipped with blood pellets. Then a payment to the coroner ahead of time who pronounced me dead and disposed of the body."

"Marjorie said you were cremated."

"Someone was. It wasn't me."

"They never saw your body again..."

"No, they didn't have to. They identified it at the scene. Everything was in order long before Wendy shot me."

"No one checked you for a pulse?"

"Would you want to touch a dead body? Marjorie fell on me, but her brothers pulled her off."

"How did you know what would go down?"

"I knew Wendy. Once I was back in Colorado, I knew she'd come for me and for Ryan. If Ruby hadn't killed her first, I had plans in place for Wendy before she could harm my son."

"I don't believe it. Marj told me what happened. It happened so fast she hardly remembers, yet she describes it as almost being in slow motion."

"Trust me when I say I'm sorry to have put my children through any of this. But they're strong, and my first duty is to their mother. My children can take care of themselves. My wife can't."

"So *you* took her from the facility using Joe's name."

"I did."

"You wrote Joe Steel instead of Jonah Steel."

"Did I? I was thinking only of getting Daphne out of harm's way."

"Does he work for you?" I gestured to Dominic.

"He does. He's well paid. And well trained."

"You never went to UCLA, huh?" I said.

"No. That's my cover. I'm a hell of a trainer, though. I kicked your ass during that sample session."

I couldn't deny it.

"An associate of mine approached Dominic and Alex

when they turned eighteen," Brad said. "I knew about their brother's return, and my first inclination was to teach them how to protect themselves from him. As it turned out, Cade had already taught them both how to expertly handle weapons. As for the rest, they were both quick studies and had enormous potential. Now they work for me."

"So you don't coach baseball."

"Not currently," Dominic said. "But I love the game, and I'm good at it."

"Do you collect baseball cards?"

"Some. Why?"

How much of this was I allowed to say? I had no idea. "No reason," I said, and then I turned back to Brad Steel.

"How long have you known about my father?"

"I've known for a long time that some of his activity was criminal, but I only found out about the trafficking, and what he did to his victims, after Talon was taken."

"Right about the same time you stopped letting Joe go on our camping trips."

He nodded. "Do you blame me?"

"No. But you have to know. My father never touched me or Joe."

"I believe you, Bryce. He touched a lot of others, though, including one of my sons. I'll never forgive him."

"Neither will I. And you don't have to anyway. He's dead. There was no faking that one."

"All three of Talon's captors are dead. I've double- and triple-checked it all."

"Yet you're still here."

"I am."

"Why stay away again? Wendy's gone. My father, Wade,

and Mathias are gone. The threat to your children is gone."

"If it were, Bryce," he said, "we wouldn't be here talking."

I swallowed. He had a point. "Where do Colin and Ted Morse fit into this?"

"Colin is the unfortunate result of Ted's greed," Brad said.

"So he's right, then. Colin, I mean. My father . . ." I couldn't finish.

"Bought Colin, just like he bought your friend Justin Valente, who, as I'm sure you've already figured out, now goes by the name of Cade Booker."

Nausea crept up my throat. This was what pure disgust felt like.

"I thought . . ." I cleared my throat. "I thought they just stole kids and women. Why would my father . . . ?"

"Your father was a sick man. Sometimes he stumbled upon a certain person he had to have. Justin was one of those unfortunates. So was Colin Morse."

The nausea again. My throat swelled, and I inhaled deeply, trying to get air into my lungs.

Fuck. I was hyperventilating.

"Easy," Brad said. "You're a strong man. I helped raise you myself. I know what you're about. Breathe."

I put my hand over my mouth to force carbon dioxide back into my body. Soon I was breathing normally.

You're a strong man.

I didn't feel very strong at the moment.

"Once your father died," Brad said, "I knew Cade would come out of the woodwork and seek revenge any way he could. I needed to protect those who were the weakest, so I paid Dominic and Alessandra to take Daphne, Marjorie, and Colin."

"Marjorie would hate that you called her weak."

"Trust me. I know."

"Why not Jade and Melanie? They were carrying your grandchildren."

"They would have been next. I needed to make sure the safe houses were equipped to deal with pregnancy, and now they are. Plans were being made when... Well, you know how it all turned out."

"Why Colin?" I asked.

"Colin's in as much danger as anyone," he said. "Cade knows about Ted and Colin and their ties to your father. Ted's a mercenary, and he's been in touch with Cade."

Yes. It was all starting to make sense now. "I was wondering how Ted knew about Justin."

"He heard it from Justin himself, who is, of course, Cade."

"Why would Cade be interested in talking to Ted? Ted did the same thing to Colin that Cade's father did to him."

Rustling began in the nearby trees.

"You should go," Dominic said to Brad.

Brad nodded, covering his face once more with the black ski mask. "I'll be in touch." He disappeared quickly.

"I trust you'll be discreet?" Dominic said.

Being discreet meant lying to Marjorie about her father being alive. It was a promise I wasn't comfortable making, but I'd make it on one condition.

"You two keep Marjorie safe above all else, and I'll keep that promise."

CHAPTER FORTY

Marjorie

I was waiting in the guesthouse kitchen when Bryce returned.

"How's Dominic?" I asked, a little sardonically. Okay, a lot sardonically.

"He's fine."

"Of course he's fine. He should be in police custody like his bitch sister."

No response from Bryce.

"What did he need to talk to you about?"

Bryce cleared his throat. "Mostly stuff I already knew from what you and Jade uncovered."

"Mostly?"

"Yeah." Another throat clear. "But he didn't know... He didn't know my father had paid off Cade's father for him. That freaked him out."

"That would freak anyone out, even someone who kidnaps people for a living."

"I think Dominic is actually on the up-and-up," Bryce said. "He's not his brother's biggest fan."

"No one who kidnaps people is on the up-and-up, in my opinion." I sighed. "I have no idea what to think about Cade. He's a mess, and he's doing things he shouldn't be doing, but he's been through so much—"

"We don't yet know what he's been through. Remember, he got away. That almost never happened, except with Talon, and that was because he was never supposed to be taken in the first place."

"Still, you know what your father and the others were capable of."

"You don't need to keep reminding me." His lips straightened into a thin line.

"I know, but—"

"Cade isn't exactly innocent. He's been watching Joe and me for years."

"And how do you know that?"

"I just know. Trust me."

"I trust you implicitly, Bryce, but you can't just expect—"

His lips came down on mine in a crushing kiss.

Okay. He didn't want to talk. I could accept that, but we'd be resuming this conversation later.

I opened to his kiss, letting him take what he clearly needed. I'd always be here for him, always give him what he demanded.

Always.

Without breaking the kiss, he led me to the master bedroom and slid my tank off my shoulders to cup my breasts. He was still fully clothed, and my nipples abraded against his shirt. They were already hard, and the friction made them stiffen further.

My core throbbed. His mere touch, his mere kiss, turned me on, made me wet. I was wearing a loose pair of boxers that I used for pajamas, and he eased one hand down my arm to my ass and then slid it inside my boxers.

He groaned when he touched my wetness. His fingers

were smooth and warm against my folds, and when he slipped one inside me, I gasped, breaking our kiss.

"So wet," he murmured.

"Take off your clothes," I said. "Now."

He chuckled. "You think you're in charge here?"

"You think *you* are?" I retorted.

"We'll see who is." He picked me up and tossed me onto the bed.

I bounced slightly and then lay there, eyeing him. "Undress," I said again.

"You first." He tugged the boxers over my hips and discarded them. Then he spread my legs. "I need to taste you."

I closed my eyes, ready for what was to come. Bryce's tongue in my pussy. The best feeling...

He swiped his tongue over my slit. "God, you taste amazing. Always amazing." Then he thrust his tongue into my warmth.

My fingers trailed up my tummy to my breasts, and I began tugging on my nipples. So, so good.

Bryce was humming groans into my pussy as he ate me, nipping my clit about every other swipe. When he eased a finger inside me, touching that spongy spot of delicious nerves, I pinched my nipples and flowed into a shattering climax.

Energy radiated from my pussy outward, outward, outward... My arms and legs tingling, my fingers and toes sizzling.

"Yeah, baby," he said against my slick inner thigh. "That's it. Come. Come for me. Always."

"Bryce, I'll always come for you," I said, clenching my teeth as the shudders ripped through me. "Always."

He still hadn't undressed, but within seconds his belt was

unbuckled, his pants undone, and his hard cock inside me, thrusting.

"So hot," he said. "You're so fucking hot. God, the way you make me feel . . ."

I bit my lip as the climax continued to roll through me when his pelvic bone hit my clit with each thrust.

"You're amazing, baby. So damned amazing."

"Fuck me," I said. "Fuck me harder. Harder."

He obliged, increasing the speed of each plunge into me until he was panting above me, sweat dripping from his brow.

"That's it," I said. "Harder. Harder."

"God, baby. God damn!" He pushed into me, releasing.

I soared with him into his climax, our bodies one with each quaking contraction. Together we flew.

When I finally came down, Bryce rolled off me, his pants still around his thighs. I snuggled into his shoulder.

"Wow," I said.

"Double wow." His upper arm covered his eyes. "I needed that."

"I always need that," I said, "but that doesn't get you out of talking to me."

"I told you everything."

His eyes were covered, so I couldn't look into them. If I could, would I see a lie there? I wasn't sure. I did trust Bryce, but if he thought he was protecting me, he might not tell me everything.

"I'm going shooting tomorrow," I said.

That got him. He sat up abruptly. "Say what?"

"I want to learn how to handle a gun. Ruby's going to teach me."

"Ruby's a great shot, but if you want to learn, why didn't you ask me?"

"I didn't want you going all Alpha on me like my brothers would."

"What makes you think I'm anything like your brothers?"

"Bryce. Come on. You're blond and blue-eyed. There the differences end."

"Honey, I want you safe. Knowing how to protect yourself is a good thing. I'm the best. I'll teach you."

"Ruby's a trained police detective."

"And a great shot, but she doesn't love you like I do."

I laughed. "Well, I hope not, since she's married to my brother. Still, I'd like to go with her. I think I might respond better to a woman."

"Why?"

"Because I've been taught by men all my life. My father and my brothers taught me ranching. Most of my professors in college were men, for some reason. The guy I took my cooking classes from in the city was a man. I'd like to see how a woman teaches."

That was such a crock. I didn't for one minute think that all women or men were the same when it came to teaching. But I wanted to learn from Ruby. I wasn't exactly sure why.

Then it hit me.

I didn't want Bryce to see me shoot until I was good at it.

Stupid reason, but that was it. It was a matter of pride and vanity.

Bryce sighed. "Okay, if it means that much to you. But I'm coming along."

"Don't you have work?"

"Nice try. Tomorrow's Saturday. Though I've been gone so much this week, I'm sure I could find something to do at the office."

"Do that, then."

"Why don't you want me to be there? This is a proud moment for me. It would be for your brothers, as well."

I huffed. "Fine. I don't want you there because I don't want you to see me fail."

"What makes you think you'll fail?"

"I *don't* think I'll fail. But I won't be good at it at first."

He kissed my cheek. "You're adorable. All proud and indignant."

"I am who I am," I said.

"And that's who I love. All right. Go with Ruby. You're certainly safe with her."

"I'm safe at a shooting range," I said. "Everyone will be armed."

He removed his pants and rolled back on top of me. "I'm armed right now."

CHAPTER FORTY-ONE

Bryce

Watching Marjorie leave to go shooting with Ruby wasn't easy for me, but I did it. I had other things to attend to, like figuring out what to do about Brad Steel.

Why didn't he want his children to know he was alive?

Because they'd be mad as hell, and I was pretty damned angry myself.

I kept silent for one reason, and one reason only.

If Marjorie's safety was at stake, I'd keep silent about her father being alive. I'd do anything for her protection.

Absolutely anything.

In the meantime, I had to get back in touch with Dominic and get more information. Somehow, we had to find Cade Booker and find out what he was up to.

Marjorie felt sorry for Cade, and I understood her reasoning. Cade might have been taken against his will as a child, sold for cash by his own father, but he was not innocent in this. We had no proof that he'd killed his father and his mother, but if it was out there, I'd find it.

I also had to uncover the connection between him and Ted Morse. Knowing Ted, I figured it was probably money.

I swallowed the acidic taste in my mouth.

Keeping Brad's secret didn't feel right.

It didn't feel right at all.

★ ★ ★

Heading back to my father's cabin had happened on autopilot. I'd gotten in my car, determined to drive into Grand Junction and trade it in for another, something I'd been meaning to do since my father died.

Somehow, though, I'd ended up at the cabin.

Most of the furniture was still outside the cabin. Joe and I hadn't bothered moving it back in when we'd put it outside to lift up the floorboards. Oddly, the only stuff we found had been buried in the bedroom Joe and I had shared.

Typical of my father.

Hide in plain sight.

Where would we look if we thought he was hiding something? Certainly not in his son's room.

He was brilliantly psychopathic.

Yeah, the acidic taste was still on my tongue.

Brilliantly psychopathic.

Fuck.

I looked around the bare rooms, walking along the joists. It was daylight, so I could see clearly without turning on any lights.

Ghosts lived here. That eerie feeling I couldn't shake. Something was still hidden here.

I knew it.

I could feel it, like an ooze of evil crawling over my flesh.

Perhaps some memories are better left buried.

The thought speared into my head in my father's voice.

"Fuck you," I said aloud.

I forced him out of my head. It felt good. Damned good.

This cabin wasn't even in my father's name. It belonged to a company called Tamajor Corporation. Not a name I'd heard of, though I'd looked it up. Tamajor was a village development committee in a small district of Nepal. What was a village development committee? I still had no clear idea after reading up on it.

Not that it mattered. It wasn't incorporated in Colorado. It was a Delaware corporation, and its registered agent was a woman named Laura Clarke, who had recently passed away from colon cancer. Nothing else was available, so I'd given the information to Joe to give to Mills and Johnson.

Nothing so far.

Joe checked in with the PIs once every day, and so far, the best PIs in the business hadn't uncovered anything we didn't already know.

Which was strange.

Because they were the best PIs in the business.

"Damn it, Dad," I said aloud. "What are you hiding here? What the hell are you hiding?"

I didn't expect an answer.

So I jerked in surprise, nearly jumping out of my boots and falling through the joists, when I got one.

CHAPTER FORTY-TWO

Marjorie

"You did well," Ruby said, after swallowing a bite of her hamburger. "You're a natural, which doesn't surprise me, given your brothers are all excellent shots."

"Thanks. Bryce wanted to come today, but I asked him not to."

"Why?"

I laughed. "It's really silly. I didn't want him to see me screw it up."

She joined in my laughter. "I never would have guessed. You seem so put together all the time. So full of self-esteem."

Wow. What a crock. My scar itched. So put together? So full of self-esteem? Right.

"I'm just used to being judged by my father and brothers," I said. It wasn't a lie. It just wasn't the whole truth. "They're harsh critics, so I've learned to be good at anything I try before I make it known."

"I can understand that. Ryan's quite the perfectionist, especially where his wines are concerned. I've seen him chuck an entire barrel if it's not perfect. I'm learning, but I swear, the barrel he most recently tossed tasted delicious to me."

"All of his wines are great," I said. "He's the most creative of all of us."

"Don't sell yourself short. Cooking is another form of creativity."

Hmm. I'd never thought of myself as creative. I didn't draw, didn't write, didn't do any crafts. Cooking? I almost never followed a recipe as written. Yeah, it *was* creative.

I'd always assumed Ryan's creativity came from his mother, since Talon, Joe, and I hadn't inherited it. But maybe we had some creativity as well.

"How long until I qualify for a concealed carry?" I asked.

"You need to complete the required training. As an ex-cop, I'm a qualified instructor, so I'll sign off when you're ready. It won't be too long. Like I said, you're a natural."

I smiled. "Cool. It's very important to me that I'm able to take care of myself. I can't always depend on my brothers and Bryce to be there for me."

"Every one of them will always be there for you, but I get it. I like being able to take care of myself."

Ruby had the most fit body I'd ever seen on a woman in real life. Even Jade's mother, ex-supermodel Brooke Bailey, couldn't compare. Feminine, but lean and muscular and strong. She'd been on her own since she escaped her father's rape attempt at fifteen. There was a lot to admire about my pretty sister-in-law.

"I've been meaning to ask you," I said. "As a cop, have you come up with any insight into Cade Booker? He seems to be acting almost randomly."

"Like I've said before, there's usually a system to a psychopath that experienced cops can see, but you're right. Booker's an anomaly."

"You know who we should ask?"

"Melanie," Ruby said. "I agree. We're pretty close to the hospital."

"Joe won't want us to bother her."

"Baby Brad is doing well," Ruby said. "There's no reason for Melanie to be upset about anything. And what your big brother doesn't know..."

"...won't hurt him." I smiled. "Of course, it's Saturday, and he's probably at the hospital with Mel."

"Only one way to find out." Ruby stood.

★ ★ ★

Baby Brad had gained five ounces since his birth, and his skin was pink with a healthy glow. I kissed his little cheek before handing him back to the nurse to get his vitals.

"You just missed Joe," Melanie said. "He went out to get some supplies I need at the hotel."

Good. I loved my brother dearly, but Ruby and I wanted to speak to Melanie alone.

"How are you doing?" I asked. "Hanging in there?"

"I'm good. I miss being home, of course, but there's no place I'd rather be than with my child. He's everything I could have hoped for, and he's thriving. Life is good."

"He's beautiful," Ruby agreed.

"Are you and Ryan going to try soon?"

"We were just talking about that." Ruby rubbed her chin. "Ryan is so afraid of passing on the psychopathy from both our parents, but he's finally calming down about it. I never thought of myself as mother material, for that matter, but seeing little Brad changes things, to be honest. I've been on the pill for so long, though. I thought I'd see a doctor first."

"Always a good idea," Melanie said.

"Says the doctor." I laughed.

"What's going on with you two?" Melanie turned to me. "You doing okay?"

What she was truly asking was, *are you harming yourself?* I wasn't, thank God.

"Oddly, I don't feel overly traumatized by what happened. I guess I never really felt I was in any danger. Dominic was nice to me, and Alex was ... well ... Alex."

"All normal," Melanie said. "But don't be surprised if you don't get over it as quickly as you think. You *were* traumatized, Marj."

I nodded. Mel was right. Mel was always right. Just because I wasn't having nightmares didn't mean my scar wasn't tingling. "I'll get help when I need it," I said.

"I know." Melanie smiled. "Joe told me who Cade Booker is, and that Alex and Dominic are his half siblings."

"Cade Booker is a riddle," Ruby said. "As cops, we can usually see a certain logic in the psychopathic behavior of an individual, but Cade ..."

"I've been thinking about that," Melanie said. "Of course I can't make any kind of diagnosis without a thorough physical and mental examination, but my gut tells me he has a personality disorder, most likely borderline. He might also have some kind of mild dissociative identity disorder."

"You mean split personality?" I asked.

"Not in the sense you're thinking. Just an ability to go outside himself when he needs to. It's a self-protection mechanism."

I bit my lower lip.

I knew well about self-protection mechanisms. I used physical pain to disassociate from emotional pain.

Not a good idea, but I understood. I cleared my throat.

"What's borderline personality?"

"It's a disorder characterized by erratic and self-destructive behavior. The thing is, our personalities are formed by the time we're five years old, so personality disorders can't be blamed on any trauma that happened afterward, although such trauma can certainly exacerbate a disorder, as I'm sure it did for Cade."

"He was the son of a guy who ended up selling him for cash," I said. "Probably enough to help him form a personality disorder at a young age."

"True enough," Melanie agreed.

"How did Bryce and Joe end up in Cade's office anyway?" Ruby asked.

A question I wanted an answer to as well. I hadn't yet asked Bryce.

"I asked Jonah about that," Melanie said. "He said he'd done business with Cade in the past and thought he might know a hacker who could help."

"That's no reason for Cade to douse Joe and Bryce in pepper spray," I said.

"Erratic behavior," Melanie said. "It's textbook."

"There's still the question of Dale and the guy he saw stalking the playground," Ruby said. "I've been thinking about that, and it concerns me. First, Dale and Donny both said all of their abusers were masked, so how would he recognize this person on the playground?"

"Unless it was a person he recalled who wasn't masked," I offered. "Maybe whoever brought food didn't bother wearing a mask."

"Doubtful," Ruby said. "Even someone performing innocuous duties knew what was going on in that compound.

He wouldn't want to be recognized."

"Maybe it was his stance," Melanie said, "or his clothing. Something about that person spooked Dale. He hasn't been able to give me a clear answer as to why yet, but we'll get there."

"If it *was* Cade Booker," I said, "why would he do that?"

"Erratic behavior," Melanie said again. "It doesn't make sense to a rational person."

"Plus the stuff he left behind," Ruby said. "A cufflink that can be linked to Colin Morse, a baseball card that can be linked to Dominic Booker, and a rock that can be linked to Dale himself. It's a head-scratcher even for me."

"What if it wasn't Cade?" Melanie asked. "What if it was Ted Morse? He had access to Colin's cufflinks. Maybe the one we found at Bryce's cabin was the only one Tom had. Maybe Ted only gave him one."

"Why would Ted Morse want to stalk a ten-year-old kid?"

"Money," Ruby and Melanie said in unison.

"There had to be money involved," Ruby continued. "That seems to be Morse's motivation above all else, including his own son."

I swallowed. "This is all conjecture. We really don't know who the stalker is."

"True," Ruby agreed. "It also could simply be Dale's imagination."

"I don't think so," Melanie said. "I've talked to Dale at length about it. He's sure the guy was looking at him. Stalking him. What's in question is if he truly recognized the man. That part might be his imagination."

"Is Dale okay?" I asked.

"Dale will be okay," Melanie assured us. "He's not done healing yet. Something this traumatic can sometimes be a lifetime journey of healing. But he's making good progress, and he'll lead a normal life. He *wants* to lead a normal life, and that's a big thing."

I smiled. "I love him and Donny so much."

"We all do," Ruby said.

"I suppose we should get back to the ranch," I said. "Those little boys will be hungry, and Jade isn't much of a cook."

Ruby stood and gave Melanie a quick kiss on the cheek. "Call if you need anything."

"I will. Keep me posted on what's going on. Joe tries too hard to protect me from everything right now."

I nodded.

Boy, did I understand where she was coming from.

CHAPTER FORTY-THREE

Bryce

"I've looked myself."

I turned and jerked backward.

"Brad," I said as calmly as I could.

"Now that you know I'm not dead, I didn't think it would hurt to follow you out here."

"This isn't any of your business," I said. "It's my father's place."

"Actually"—he cleared his throat—"it isn't."

My brows nearly jumped off my forehead. "Say what?"

"It's owned by a corporation," he said.

"Oh, yeah. I know that. But he left it to me specifically in his will. I just assumed my fa—"

"Tamajor Corporation," Brad interrupted. Then, slowly, "Ta-ma-jo-r."

"Brad, I don't— Oh, for fuck's sake."

How could I not have seen it? Easy. I wasn't looking. Brad Steel was supposed to be a damned corpse.

"Talon, Marjorie, Jonah, Ryan." I shook my head. "When the hell did you buy my father's cabin?"

"The corporation bought it shortly before your father killed himself. He was low on cash, Bryce. He'd just paid a fortune for—"

"Colin Morse," I finished for him, my stomach turning over inside my abdomen. "Did my father know it was you?"

"Not that I'm aware of," Brad said.

"Why did he still leave it to me in his will?"

"He probably didn't get around to changing his will before he died."

"Why? Why would you want this stupid place?"

"Why do you think? Evidence, Bryce. This place is full of evidence."

"But my father and the others are dead," I said. "What good is any of the evidence now?"

"For putting your father and the others away? No good at all. But it has other uses. For example, you got your mother's inheritance back, right?"

The gems now resided inside the safe at the guesthouse.

"You know about that?"

"I know pretty much everything your father has done over the decades. I've kept close tabs on him."

I shook my head. "I'll never understand you. Why didn't you have him put away long ago? All of them?"

"It wasn't that simple," he said. "You know that. They had a lot of power, and Wendy had the most power of all. She'd threatened me with a fail-safe if anything happened to her and the other three—a fail-safe that turned out to be a hoax, but I didn't know that at the time. She was a loaded gun, and I had to protect my family—especially my wife, who couldn't protect herself."

Yeah, yeah, yeah. I'd heard it all before. I even understood it, for the most part.

"So you know about everything hidden here."

"Not everything. Just what you've dug up so far."

That rustling in the trees. I'd been sure we were being watched.

"I never thought it was you," I said.

"It wasn't actually me. I had Dominic and several others watching this place."

That eerie feeling that I was being watched. Turned out it wasn't just an eerie feeling. Never in a million years would I have thought it was my best friend's supposedly dead father.

"Are you the ones who bugged our phones, as well?"

He shook his head. "As far as I know—and I keep apprised on all of my children and you—your homes and phones are not bugged."

I sighed. "Ruby said she didn't see any evidence of surveillance. I should have believed her."

"Sometimes, the threat of being watched is worse than actually being surveilled. It's a mindfuck, Bryce, and your father was the best at that."

"My father's dead," I reminded him.

"He is, but in some ways, his legacy lives on."

"Legacy?" I scoffed. "They broke up the ring, Brad. What's left?"

"The mysterious phone calls you and Joe have been getting, for one thing."

"They're from Cade," I said. "They have to be. Though it's always a different number."

"An easy tactic."

I couldn't help an eye roll. "Why are you here, Brad? Why didn't you dig up this stuff yourself?"

"I had every intention of doing so. Just hadn't gotten around to it. Believe it or not, faking your own death is kind of a full-time job."

"Am I supposed to sympathize with you?" I shook my head. "Unbelievable."

"I don't want your sympathy. I want only your discretion. You and my sons went after Marjorie, Daphne, and Colin when I had them put away safely in a safe house. Now they're walking targets, and Cade Booker is a ticking time bomb."

"He disappeared," I said.

"He disappears from time to time, but he'll be back. He has a score to settle."

"With Joe and me? We were kids."

"That's not how he sees it."

"Then why not come after us? He pepper-sprayed us in his office. Why not just kill us then?"

"First of all, you took all his weapons."

"So? We were indisposed. He could have left us there and gone and gotten another weapon."

"He was in his place of business."

"Again . . . so?"

"I'm only guessing, but he has a certain image to maintain."

"He was the only one in the office with Joe and me. Everyone in his office knows that."

"But you and Joe didn't file charges. Why?"

Did Brad know about Joe's past dalliances at the leather club? He seemed to know a lot. If he knew, he'd have to be the one to bring it up. I sure as hell wouldn't.

"What good would that do? He already got away with offing his parents. He'd weasel out of a tiny assault charge. He's a lawyer, for God's sake."

"True. And a good one. Too bad he never actually went to law school."

My eyes widened into circles. "Talon was right. The

records were forged."

"You already had that figured out?"

"It was a hunch. Was he ever with the FBI?"

"No, he wasn't. That was another cover story. But he *is* trained in FBI tactics."

"Then who trained him?"

"Your father, Bryce. Your father trained him."

CHAPTER FORTY-FOUR

Marjorie

Joe cornered me as we were leaving the hospital. "Excuse me, Ruby. I need a word with my sister."

Ruby nodded and went back into the room where Melanie sat with the baby.

"Yeah?"

"What are you two doing here?"

"Visiting our nephew."

"Okay, I'll buy that. But not only that. Why else?"

"Do we really need a reason other than to see your son?" I smiled sweetly.

"No, you don't. But I know you, little sis. You and Ruby aren't that close. Why would you come together?"

"We're close enough, and Ruby is Mel's best friend."

"She's also an ex-cop. I don't want you bothering Melanie with—"

"Hold on." I raised my hand to stop his mouth from moving. "We're all in this, and Melanie wants to help. She's the one person who might be able to shed some light on Cade Booker and why he's doing what he's doing. Ruby and I were curious, and you know what? Your brilliant wife didn't let us down. She has a theory about Booker, a theory that makes an awful lot of sense."

"Still, I— Shit." His phone buzzed. "I have to take this."

"Good." I stood, tapping my foot on the floor. Joe infuriated me sometimes.

Ruby peeked out from the doorway. "All done?"

"As far as I'm concerned. Let's go."

★ ★ ★

"Cade must know that Dominic was working on the other side," Ruby said in the car as we were driving back to the ranch. "That's why he used the baseball card. And Colin as well. He used the cufflink to incriminate Colin, since Colin had been a victim of Tom Simpson. He was giving us two suspects."

"He was going to throw his own brother under the bus?" I said.

"Oh, yeah. Psychopaths will normally throw anyone under the bus."

"But then you have Tom himself, who went out of his way to keep his son away from this part of his life. Bryce is going crazy over it. He remembers Tom as a great dad, and it's killing him."

"Has he talked to anyone?"

"He'd planned to talk to Melanie, but then I got taken, and she had the baby early. There hasn't been time."

"I kind of get it," Ruby said, "in a weird way. My father was, in some ways, the worst of the three, but in the end, he saved my life. He also saved me from his goons when I was at the compound."

I opened my mouth, but she gestured me to stop.

"I know what you're going to say. He tried to rape me when I was fifteen. I haven't forgotten that, and I haven't forgotten all the heinous things he did to others. In the end, though, he saved my life. How can I not be grateful for that?"

"Have you talked to Mel?"

"Yeah. A little. More as friends than as doctor-patient. She's helped me see that it's okay to have a good memory of a bad person. It's not like they negate each other. My father was a monster, but I wouldn't be here without him. I wouldn't have this wonderful life I found with Ryan. So I'm grateful, in a strange way, and that's okay."

"Bryce needs to hear that," I said. "I've tried to tell him the same thing, but it will mean more coming from a professional."

"He will. Bryce is a decent guy. One of the good guys. He's struggling with the fact that he always thought his father was the same. In fact, every memory he has of his father would indicate that. So his situation is different from mine and harder. I always knew what my father was. The fact that he had a smidgeon of feeling for his only child at the end doesn't change who and what he was. What it does change is that I'm here, and I wouldn't be if he *hadn't* had that smidgeon of feeling."

"And Bryce has your feeling times a million," I said softly. "Poor baby."

Ruby smiled. "I don't know Bryce well yet, but I'm betting he'd hate being called a 'poor baby.'"

"I know he would, but I can't help it. I feel for him. I love him so much, the way you love Ryan. I feel everything he feels."

"I know." She pulled into the drive leading to the main ranch house. "He's lucky to have you."

"And vice versa," I said. "We had a rocky start, but I can't imagine my life without him."

Talon was outside on the front deck when we arrived. Odd. He didn't usually sit out front. He walked to the car as I got out, gesturing to Ruby. Ruby unrolled her window.

"Can you stay for a few minutes? Dale wants to talk to you."

"Sure." Ruby killed the engine. "Is he all right?"

"I think so. He just says he remembers a few things, and he wants to tell all of us together, including you because you're a detective."

"Was," Ruby said. "But of course. I'm happy to help."

My heart beat double time as we walked into the house. Dale was sitting in the family room with Jade.

"Where's Donny?" I asked.

"He actually had a playdate with a boy in his class," Jade said. "He was really excited."

Dale, at ten, was too old for playdates. Only three years separated the brothers, but at their current ages, it might as well have been a lifetime, especially considering what Dale had gone through to spare Donny. Dale wasn't smiling—he still rarely smiled—but he did look at ease. Not stiff and tense, the way he had for so long... before he'd found the polished rock where he'd seen the stalker standing.

"Hey, Dale," Ruby said.

"Hi."

"What do you want to talk about?" she asked. "Do you want us all here?"

"Yeah. That's fine."

"What's on your mind, then?"

He opened his mouth but then closed it.

"Whenever you're ready, son," Talon said.

"Sometimes things come back to me," he said. "I don't understand why I don't remember everything. Melanie says I was probably drugged a lot of the time."

Talon nodded. "You probably were. We're all glad it didn't do any permanent damage."

"Yeah. Me too," Dale said. "I mean, I kind of don't want to remember some of it, but Melanie says it's part of getting better."

"It is," Talon said.

"Anyway..." He sighed. "There was a guy where we were. He didn't do anything to us. He just..."

"Just what?" Talon asked.

"Um...he stood in the room and watched."

My throat felt raw and saliva pooled in my mouth. I held back a gag.

"Watched...what?" Talon asked slowly.

"Whatever. Whatever the other guys decided...to do to us...that day."

"He didn't do any of that?" Ruby said.

"No. He just watched. I only just remembered this today. This morning. I woke up, and I remembered."

"What did this guy look like?" Ruby asked.

"I don't know. He wore a mask like all the others. But he also wore a gray hoodie and jeans. Or dark pants. I don't know. The hood was always up."

"So you think..." Ruby began.

"I don't know. Something about the way he stood. That's what I saw on the playground. It was him. I know it was."

"So you *did* recognize him."

"I'm sure now. I know I wasn't quite sure at first."

"You were scared."

"Well...yeah." He gulped.

"It's okay to be scared, sweetie," Jade soothed. "You've been through a lot."

"No," he said. "I don't want to be scared. I don't want to be scared anymore."

"You don't have to be," Talon said. "The bad men who hurt you are gone, and I won't let anyone else hurt you. I promise."

That was a huge promise to make, but I had no doubt my brother meant every word he said to his son. If Cade Booker was indeed the person who had spooked Dale at the playground, he'd better not cross paths with Talon.

Or Joe, for that matter.

Or Ryan or Bryce.

Or me.

He'd put us all through enough.

"Is there anything else you want to tell us?" Ruby asked. "Remember, the more information we have, the more likely it is we can find this guy."

"I can't say how I recognized him," Dale said. "I just know it was him. The guy who watched. He was the same. And he was watching."

Ruby nodded. "Dale, there's one other thing."

"What?"

"You said you used to collect rocks."

"Yeah."

"Where is your rock collection? Your mom and dad said they couldn't find it at your old house."

"I don't know. I wasn't as interested after a while. It was kind of a little kid thing."

"But you recognized the snowflake obsidian we found outside the playground."

"Yeah. I had one like it. Most of my rocks were polished. I had a polisher of my own for a while, but when I stopped using it . . ." He paused a few seconds. "I think my mom sold it at a garage sale. She asked me if it was okay, and I said sure."

"So you had stopped collecting rocks?" Ruby asked.

"Yeah. It was a little kid thing, you know?"

I smiled. Was it really this simple? "Did you sell your collection at the garage sale?" I asked.

He smiled. Smiled! For the second time since he'd been here. "Who would want to buy a bunch of dumb rocks?"

"Didn't you say people carried rocks for good luck?"

"That's what my mom used to tell me. I don't really believe it. I don't believe in good luck anymore."

Silence for a few seconds. Not one of us knew how to respond to that.

However, one thing stood out. The rock collection had simply been misplaced because Dale was no longer interested in it. Kids were like that. They changed hobbies when the wind changed.

"Anything else, Dale?" Ruby asked.

"No."

"And you haven't seen that guy on the playground since the last time?"

Dale shook his head.

"Okay." Ruby smiled. "This is really good information, Dale. You're helping us a lot."

He smiled again.

And that was worth every dollar of the Steel fortune.

CHAPTER FORTY-FIVE

B r y c e

Your father trained him.

I opened my mouth, letting my jaw hang there. Words flew through my mind, none of them coming together as a coherent sentence to speak.

My father trained him.

"I don't understand," I finally said.

"I'm not sure I fully understand, either," Brad noted. "Now that your father's gone, we may never know unless Cade decides to come clean. But I have a theory. I think your father took him as a sort of . . . protégé."

I stood, my mouth still dropped open, most likely looking like an imbecile.

A protégé?

A strange wave of envy passed through me, and then I had to stop myself from doubling over.

Envy, Bryce? Really? That your father took a protégé other than you for his life of horror?

I was being stupid. Really fucking stupid.

"But he . . ." God, what a moron. I couldn't even form words.

"Like I said, it's only a theory. But we know your father bought Cade's father's silence."

Money buys silence for a time, son, but a bullet buys it forever.

"I just assumed he . . ." Again, the words stopped. Brad and I both knew what I meant.

"He probably did. I'm sure Joe told you what your father and the others went through in their training."

Again, the nausea. "Yeah. He told me. Who would do that?"

"Someone for whom money trumps all else," Brad said, shaking his head. "Your father wasn't always that way. Neither was Larry. They were corrupted."

"Sorry, I don't buy it. They had to have the propensity for it to even be corrupted like that."

"I won't disagree with you there," he said, "but they *were* corrupted."

"By whom?"

"Wendy. She was the mastermind behind it all, though I didn't see it quite as clearly when we were still in high school."

"You funded them," I said, more to myself than to Brad.

"I did. And I'll regret it for the rest of my life."

I couldn't help a sarcastic scoff. "The rest of your life was supposed to have ended eight years ago. Then again a few months ago. Spare me your regrets."

"I've never asked for your sympathy," he repeated. "Only your discretion."

"Joe's my best friend. And Marjorie . . ."

"You're in love with her. I couldn't wish for a better man for my little girl."

"So how can you ask me to keep this from her? From Joe? From the rest of them?"

"They've all found their happiness, Bryce, just as I knew

they would. I've done all I can, but my first loyalty is to my wife. You know that."

"Your wife is insane."

"Mentally ill," Brad said.

"Semantics. No offense, but she doesn't even know you exist."

"I'm the *only* one she knows, Bryce. She doesn't recognize any of her children, and she's caught in a time warp. She can't take care of herself."

"You can't take care of her either. Sure, you built a replica of your ranch house on that island—"

"I did that so I could take her home," Brad said. "I had to protect her from Wendy. She never got over her jealousy of Daphne. She would have had her killed. I did what I had to do. I've told you this before. My children were adults and could protect themselves. My wife could not."

"Why were you worried for Daphne, Marj, and Colin when Justin—or Cade, or whoever the fuck he is now—had a beef with Joe and me, not with any of—"

I stopped midsentence. My words were asinine, and I knew it.

"Daphne is the weakest link. Easy to target," Brad said. "And Marjorie . . . Well, she means everything to both you and Joe. It was a two-for-one deal."

"And Colin?"

"Colin is a little different. Cade seems to have an issue with him. I'm not sure why, but it's enough to make me concerned for Colin's safely. I was also protecting him from his own father. Ted has been working with Cade Booker since he uncovered his true identity."

"I always wondered how he found out," I said. "Joe and I

couldn't figure it out, especially since we had no actual memory of it ourselves."

"I can't help you there. My guess is that Cade contacted Ted, but that's just a guess."

"There had to be a trail somewhere. My dad took care of Joe's and my memory and he paid off Cade's father, but a whole town couldn't have forgotten a kid."

"Snow Creek is a small town," he said, "but if a kid was the invisible type—"

"But he *wasn't* invisible. He was a target for the bullies. That's why Joe and I befriended him in the first place."

"I wish I had an answer for you. We may never know how Tom pulled it off."

"It's all crazy," I said.

"Pretty much. I know you and Joe have been through this place, but I still feel like there's something else here."

"So do I. That's why I came here today. My father's darkest secrets are here, and I don't think we've uncovered them all."

"Then let's get to it," he said. "I have the time. Do you?"

I cleared my throat. "You do know you're a grandfather, right?"

He smiled. "I do. I've already sneaked in and gotten a good look at my grandchild. He's small but strong."

"Melanie went into premature labor. Probably because of all the stress of the situation. The stress that *you* caused, Brad. You had Marjorie and the others kidnapped."

He ignored my rant. "Thank God she and the baby are both fine. I had to be careful. Melanie never actually saw me, so I don't know if she would recognize me, but—"

"She'd recognize you. Joe looks exactly like you."

"I was careful. She didn't see me. I took a quick look at the baby while she was gone to the restroom."

"How did you— Oh, never mind."

"I'm pretty good at sneaking around these days."

Yeah, he was. Being "dead," he'd have to be.

"All right," I said. "Let's start looking. Do you have any idea what we're looking for?"

"No," he said, "but I bet we find it."

My phone buzzed in my pocket. Really? Dominic Booker again? "What is it?" I said into the phone.

"Hey, can you meet me again?" he asked.

"I'm pretty busy at the moment."

"Who is it?" Brad asked.

"Hold on," I said to Dominic. Then I muted the phone. "Dominic Booker. He wants to meet me."

"Great," he said. "Let's do it. Now."

★ ★ ★

Dominic met us at the cabin.

"How's your sister?" Brad asked.

"She'll make a full recovery," he said. "Luckily the paramedics got to her before she lost too much blood. She's home from the hospital and taking it easy."

"Maybe she should be taking it easy in a prison infirmary," I couldn't help saying.

"Alex was acting on my orders," Brad said. "I've taken care of the charges against her."

Of course he had. I opened my mouth but then shut it quickly. Nothing I said or did would change the situation.

Dominic continued, "Alex isn't one to take anything easy. She's been fretting over the whole thing, saying crazy stuff."

"Like what?" Brad asked.

Dominic shook his head. "She's convinced it all went wrong because she didn't have her lucky rock."

That got my attention. Marj had mentioned that Dale's mother had told him some people carried stones for luck— stones like the one Dale found where he'd seen the stranger lurking around the school playground.

"Lucky rock?"

"Yeah, this smooth rock she keeps with her. She lost it a couple weeks—"

"Smooth rock? Like black with white markings, maybe?"

"Yeah. How did you know that?"

I cleared my throat. "Lucky guess."

"She calls it snowflake obsidian."

"Damn. That's it."

"That's what?" Dominic and Brad both asked.

"That was the third thing Ruby found at the playground where Dale saw the strange man watching him. A baseball card, a cufflink with Colin Morse's initials on it, and a polished piece of snowflake obsidian."

"That bastard," Dominic said.

"He was trying to implicate the three of you." I inhaled. "But why the three of you? His beef is clearly with Joe and me."

"Who knows?" Dominic said. "The man is a mess. Maybe he didn't think anyone would believe you or Joe would stalk a little boy. Though why anyone would think Alex or I would—"

"Easy," Brad said. "He knew you and Alex were onto him, that you were working for me, and he was trying to get you out of the way."

"But Dominic makes a valid point," I said. "If his problem is with Joe and me—"

"His plans for you and Joe are much more sinister," Brad said. "Believe me. I've been dealing with psychopaths for the last forty years. One in particular had a beef with me, and she hurt me in the worst possible way."

Wendy Madigan. Wendy Madigan, who'd had Talon abducted, starved, and brutally tortured.

She'd gotten to him through his child.

His *child*.

I gulped. "Oh, God." I quickly texted my mother.

Mom, where's Henry?

He's right here with Vicky and me.
Getting ready to feed him.

How much could I tell her without freaking her out? He was most likely safe . . . as long as Cade Booker couldn't find him.

But none of us knew where Cade was at the moment.

"What?" Brad said.

"My son. He's with my mom in Florida. I'm just making sure—"

"I've got tails on them," Brad said. "I'll know if anything happens. The minute they're in even the slightest danger, I'll have them taken to safety."

Nausea welled within me. If that happened, my mother would be scared shitless. But at least she'd be safe. In the meantime, I wouldn't burden her with any of this. I didn't trust Brad to tell the truth about being alive, but I did trust that he had my family's best interests at heart.

For the first time since he'd shown up, I felt an

overwhelming gratitude to Brad Steel. "Thank you," I said softly. "But what about—"

"I've got a tail on Melanie and the baby as well. I told you that. I'll know within seconds if anything happens."

"Why didn't you have them taken to safety?" I asked. "Never mind. Stupid question. The baby needs medical care. Thank you."

"I'll do anything to protect my family," he said, "and to me, Bryce, you are family."

CHAPTER FORTY-SIX

Marjorie

Ruby and I sat with Jade on the deck after we'd shared a quick dinner of sandwiches. Talon was with the boys in the yard, playing with the dogs.

"He's like a little kid himself with them," Jade said. "Those boys have been so good for him."

"He's been good for them too," I said. "Having a father with that level of understanding . . ." I didn't need to finish. None of us wanted to say the words, but we all knew how special it was that Talon was now father to the two boys.

"It's so great to see Dale come out of his shell more," Ruby agreed.

Jade smiled and patted her belly, which now showed the tiniest baby bump. "I think they'll be good big brothers."

"Are you and Tal going to find out the sex?" I asked.

"I don't know. We haven't really talked about it. For a while, we were just hoping the pregnancy would continue. Now, with everything else that's going on, we haven't discussed it."

"Are you hoping for one or the other?" Ruby asked.

"I suppose it would be nice to add a girl to the mix," Jade replied, "but it doesn't really matter. I just want a healthy, happy baby."

My phone buzzed. I smiled. "It's Bryce. Hey," I said into the phone.

"Where are you?"

"Home. We just had a small dinner, and Jade, Ruby and I are chatting. Where are you?"

"On my way to you. Stay there. I have news."

★ ★ ★

"So the rock belongs to Alex Booker," Ruby said. "Cade Booker is trying to implicate everyone he has an issue with."

I grabbed Bryce's arm. "Have you checked in on Henry?"

He nodded. "He's safe. I've got someone keeping watch."

"Good." I was eternally glad Bryce had someone keeping tabs on his son. If anything happened... God, I couldn't go there.

"Why would he have an issue with Colin?" Jade asked.

"I've been thinking about that," Bryce said. "Believe it or not, I think it was jealousy."

"Jealousy?" Talon said. "That's nuts."

"To us, yeah. But to Cade? Cade was the first person my father liked enough to pay money for. As far as we know, he didn't pay money for anyone again until Colin."

Ruby nodded. "Booker is finally beginning to make psychopathic sense."

I said nothing. It made an eerie sort of sense to me as well, something I wasn't altogether comfortable with.

"But Colin escaped from Tom," Talon said.

"That doesn't mean Cade didn't know about him," Ruby said.

Bryce had already given us the theory that he thought

Tom had taken Cade as a sort of protégé.

"You think Cade thought he was being replaced?" I said.

"That's what it sounds like to me."

"Crazy shit," Talon said, more to himself than to any of us. He looked to the yard, where the boys were playing with the dogs. Dale didn't usually join in, but he did today. That made all of us happy, despite what else was going on.

"So the only question is," I said, "how did Ted Morse find out about Cade?"

"I've been thinking about that too," Bryce said. "Cade must have gone to Ted after he found out about my father paying for Colin."

"So Cade and your father were continually in contact," I said.

"That's my guess."

"Dale says the man at the playground was someone who watched at the compound. Not someone who hurt him, but watched him being hurt by others," Ruby said. "How does that fit in?"

"I have no clue," Bryce said. "I'm sure my father 'trained' Cade the way he himself had been trained. Maybe Cade couldn't do it to others. Or maybe he was in training himself, watching first. I have no idea."

"We need to find Cade," Ruby said. "That's the only way we'll get the real story, and that's only if he wants to tell us."

The rest of us nodded.

"You realize he's going to try to hit you or Joe," Ruby said.

"We've got Melanie and the baby protected," Bryce said.

"You do?" Bryce didn't normally keep stuff like this from me. "Why didn't you tell us?"

"Joe and I just got it done," he said. But he didn't look me in the eye.

There was something he wasn't telling me, but I wouldn't push it. Not yet. Not in front of my family.

But later.

Later, Bryce, you're going to level with me.

You're going to tell me everything.

★ ★ ★

Bryce went home, and after I'd helped Jade get the boys to bed, I headed to the guesthouse.

Bryce and I were going to have words.

I'd barely gotten through the door, though, when he grabbed me and crushed our mouths together.

No, talk first. We have to talk fir—

I opened for him in spite of myself. We were both so needy, so raw with emotion over everything.

I couldn't fight it.

I didn't want to fight it.

We kissed, hard and passionate, with a mixture of fervor and fury. Fury not at each other but at the situation. Fury because it was better than sadness and ache.

He ground his hard cock into my belly and deepened the kiss, our mouths fused together and our tongues dueling. I gave in to it, reveled in it.

We could talk later.

Now was the time to give to each other and take what we each needed in turn.

We kissed harder, harder, harder . . . until he finally pulled away and inhaled a gasping breath.

"Bedroom," he grunted, and he pulled me along until we were ensconced in the master suite.

I expected his usual command to undress. Instead, he frantically pulled off his own clothes until he stood naked, his cock hard and ready, his gaze raking over me as I quickly disrobed as well.

"Need you," he said gruffly.

"I'm here."

"Get on your hands and knees," he said. "I'm going to take you from behind. Like a damned animal."

His words set me on fire, and I obeyed him without question. I was already soaking wet. I could feel it. Feel every quiver between my legs as I imagined him sinking his cock into me.

Soon, he was behind me, the bed shifting with his weight, his cock slapping the cheeks of my ass.

"I'm going to fuck you hard, baby. So hard. I need it. And I need you."

I squealed sharply as he thrust into me.

I was ready. Wet and ready. But something was different this time. Was he more erect than normal? No, I'd looked at him. He was the same large size he always was.

No, it wasn't his size. It was his attitude. Something was different.

He slapped the cheek of my ass when he pulled out and then thrust back in.

He'd slapped me once before, but not like this. This felt different.

"Yes," he said. "Take it. Take all of it, baby. Take all of me."

I pushed my hips backward, giving him the best access I could. Whatever he needed, I would give it. I'd always give it.

He took me harder, harder, harder, thrusting, thrusting, thrusting... until my body was so ready, but the position didn't give me the friction I needed against my clit. I tried letting my legs relax so I could rub against the bed, but he pulled me upward, continuing to plunge deeper and deeper inside me.

"Need. To. Come," I said into the pillow. "Please."

With one swift movement, Bryce swiped his fingers over my clit.

That was all I needed.

I erupted, he still thrusting into me, my whole body singing a discordant melody.

Yes, discordant.

This was different. So different.

Yet no less passionate and amazing.

"Keep coming, baby," he said through puffs of his breath. "Keep coming for me."

The pulses of my climax increased, as though hearing and obeying his words. Vibrant colors kaleidoscoped behind my closed eyes.

Different. So different.

Yet still the same. Still Bryce. Still Bryce and me. Still perfect.

He pushed into me harder and harder still, and when my climax finally began to subside, he groaned and spilled inside me, the walls of my pussy clasping him with each contraction of his cock.

He stayed there for a moment, his cock sunk into me, his hands gripping my hips. I stayed still beneath him, letting him take what he needed from my body. From me.

When he finally let go, he rolled over onto his back and pulled me into his arms.

"Thank you," he said softly.

"For what?"

"For everything."

I stroked his chest, tangling my fingers through the hair coated with perspiration. *Give him a few minutes before you pounce on him with questions.*

I was determined. I closed my eyes and relaxed against his hard body.

Then—

"I needed to remember," Bryce said softly, his breath tickling my forehead.

"Remember what?" I asked.

"Who I am."

I lifted my brow. "Oh?"

"This won't make any sense to you," he said.

I moved away from him slightly and lifted my head to meet his gaze. "Try me."

He closed his eyes. "I experienced some strange emotions today, after talking to"—he paused—"Dominic."

"Dominic? Why?"

"I found out some stuff about Cade and my father. Stuff that shouldn't have bothered me but did a little."

"Bryce, you can be bothered about this whole situation. I certainly am."

"No. You don't understand." Another pause. "Dominic told me that Cade was . . . was my father's protégé."

"Why would that— Oh." I swallowed.

"Stupid as shit, right?" Bryce shook his head. "I was his son. I should have been— God, I can't even say it."

"He kept you out of that part of his life *because* you were his son. He loved you."

"I know. It's not enough that I feel tremendous guilt for that, but then he chose someone else to . . . I'm so fucked up."

"You're not fucked up, Bryce." I swept his hair off his forehead. "You're just a son who found out his father was a lot different than the great guy you remembered. I've been there. I get it."

He opened his mouth, but I placed two fingers on his lips.

"Don't. I know your father was worse than mine ever was."

"That isn't what I was going to say," he said.

"Oh. Then what?"

"It's the sliver of envy," he said. "How fucked up am I?"

"Bryce, do you truly wish your father had brought you into his other life?"

"No! Of course not."

"Then why are you torturing yourself over a stupid little slice of emotion that means nothing?"

"Because it sickens me. Seriously sickens me that I could even have the thought."

"That tells you something right there," I said. "You know the thought is wrong. Do you think you're the only one who's had a thought they didn't want? That stupid little imp in your mind plays tricks on you. Mel told me all about it. Give yourself a break. You're way too hard on yourself where your father is concerned, Bryce. First, you won't let go of the guilt that he didn't harm you and was a good father, and now you actually think that one morsel of envy actually means you wish he'd chosen you instead of Cade? That's not what it means at all."

"Yeah? What does it mean, then?"

"It's means you're a damned human being. You're normal. You're dealing with a lot. It's more guilt."

"More guilt? How is it more guilt?"

"Because Cade went through something you feel you should have gone through. That's all it is."

CHAPTER FORTY-SEVEN

Bryce

"Say that again," I said. "Please."

"What? You're a human being. Just like me. Just like everyone."

"No. Not that. The part about the guilt."

"Well, I can't take credit. I learned it all from Mel. But it seems like it's all part of the guilt you feel about having good memories of your father and more guilt about others having to go through hell while you had a good father. It's not envy. It's guilt that it was him instead of you."

God. So simple. And so clear once she said the words. "How can you see something that's right in front of my face? Yet I was blind to it?"

"Mel taught me a lot. I've done a lot of the same things."

The sliver of envy over my father choosing someone other than me as a protégé to his life of horror suddenly seemed like the nothing that it was. It stemmed from the guilt.

And it was damned time to let the guilt go. "I'm sorry. It's self-indulgent. This isn't about me. It never has been."

"It *is* about you, Bryce, but it's not your fault. There's no reason for the guilt, just like there was no reason for mine. Does it go away overnight? Of course not. But I no longer have to indulge it. I was only hurting myself. In my case, both emotionally and physically."

I cupped her cheek. "How did you get to be so smart?"

"I always was, babe." She smiled.

I kissed her lips. "I know. You're amazing."

"I still think you should talk to Mel," Marj was saying. "I'm certainly not qualified to—"

I silenced her with a kiss.

I had every intention of talking to Melanie once she and the baby were home. I knew these things weren't solved in a day. But a huge brick had been lifted off my chest by this wonderful woman in my bed.

I was okay. I wasn't jealous of Cade Booker. I felt guilty that it was him instead of me.

We had to find him. While he was out there, I could never be sure of Henry's safety or baby Brad's, or even Marj's for that matter. He blamed me—and Joe—for what he'd been through.

But part of me hoped Cade could find a life of peace eventually.

Being my father's protégé couldn't have been an easy life. Not at all.

Still, the man had been watching us for how long, now? I was pretty sure his so-called "friendship" with Joe at the leather club was all a part of him keeping tabs on us, and once my father died . . .

He came in for the kill.

I needed to talk to Joe.

Alone.

But right now I had my beautiful woman in my bed, and I'd take advantage of that. She'd helped me immensely. She'd let me fuck her hard and fast when I needed it to cleanse my soul of the blackness that sliver of envy had colored it.

In the end, though, her words, rather than her body, had helped most of all.

★ ★ ★

I woke to the sound of the shower.

I moved my arm to the other side of the bed. Still warm. Marj hadn't been up for long.

I sat up and stretched, yawning. I could join her in the shower. Yeah, that sounded good.

When I got to the bathroom, though, she was stepping out and reaching for a towel.

I smiled. "Guess I'm too late."

"For what?"

"To make love to you in the shower."

She laughed. "Just this time. Jade and I are driving into the city this morning to see Mel and the baby."

"What about Joe?" I asked.

"We didn't invite him." She laughed again. "He might be there. He spends about every other night with Melanie at the hotel."

"Do you have time for breakfast?"

She nodded. "Just let me get dressed. I'll make something. I want to talk to you anyway."

"About what?"

"It can wait for coffee. I started a pot. It'll be ready now. Go pour yourself a cup, and I'll be out in a minute."

Hmm. She wanted to talk. And she didn't want to talk in the bathroom while she was wet and naked.

That didn't sound too good.

I pulled on a pair of jeans and headed to the kitchen, texting Joe on the way. Marj might need to talk to me, but I needed to talk to Joe. I'd promised Brad discretion, but Joe and I were in this together. He had to know what his father had done, and together, we had to find Cade Booker and discover the truth, once and for all. I quickly texted Joe and got an almost instant response.

I'm heading to the north quadrant.
You can meet me there. I only have an
hour or so before I leave for the city.

That didn't give me a lot of time. I poured coffee into a travel mug and scribbled a quick note to Marj, apologizing and saying I'd see her later.

★ ★ ★

"He's trying to incriminate Dominic, Alex, and Colin," I said, after explaining how we'd inferred that the polished rock Dale had found probably belonged to Alex.

"Did she ID it?" Joe asked.

"No. Ruby has it. She's going to take care of that. Alex was just released from the hospital."

Joe nodded. "Why them? Why not us?"

"Evidently Cade hates his siblings nearly as much as he hates us. They work against him, after all."

"Makes sense. But why Colin?"

"That one's a little harder." I explained my theory of Cade's jealousy of Colin.

"Wow. Cade really had a number pulled on him."

"Yeah. Well, my father pulled a number on a lot of people." Myself included, to a much lesser extent—and not until his true self was revealed after his suicide.

"No one's blaming you," Joe said.

I exhaled slowly. "I know that. I'm beginning to see things a little differently."

"Oh? Did you decide to see a therapist?"

"Not yet. I'm still going to talk to Melanie, once she and the baby are home. It was actually Marj who gave me the epiphany."

"Ugh. Spare me the details of sex with my sister."

I chuckled. "It wasn't during sex, you idiot. Your sister is one smart woman."

"I always knew that."

"She wants me to talk to someone qualified, of course, and I will. But she basically told me to get over myself. That I was indulging myself, a lot like—" I stopped. Marjorie had trusted me with her secret, and I couldn't let her down.

"I know what you don't want to say," Joe said.

"You do?"

"Yeah. I know. I did the same thing. Feeling guilty because I didn't protect Talon. Feeling guilty because nothing happened to me. It was stupid."

Good save, Bryce. Actually, Joe had done the saving. He'd thought Marj had been talking about him.

"It's time we both got over it," I said.

"Can't argue." Joe tipped his Stetson. "That what you wanted to talk about?"

I swallowed. No. That wasn't what I'd wanted to talk about. How to bring it up?

By the way, your father's still not dead. Dominic and Alex actually do work for him. Oh, and he bought my dad's cabin.

Before I could get the words out, though, Joe's phone buzzed.

"Yeah?" he said into it. "Tell me some good news."

Pause.

"You're kidding. Excellent!"

Pause.

"We're on our way." He ended the call and stuffed his phone back into his pocket.

"Mills and Johnson," he said. "They found Cade Booker. He says he's willing to talk."

CHAPTER FORTY-EIGHT

Marjorie

I rolled my eyes, crumpled up Bryce's note, and tossed it in the kitchen trash. He could have texted me. Of course, had he texted, I'd have gotten it right away and run out to stop him.

Cute move, Bryce. But you and I are still going to talk.

I made my way to the main house. Jade was ready and waiting to go see Melanie.

"I can't believe I haven't seen that baby yet," she said. "I'm the last one."

"You've got two boys at home to take care of," I said. "She understands."

"Talon's got them today," Jade said. "He's taking them on an overnight in Denver. They're going to the zoo."

"You mean he actually left you alone?"

"I had to demand it," she said. "By the way, I promised him you'd be here with me at night. Sorry to cramp your style. You don't have to stay. I'll be fine. Or Bryce can stay here with you. Talon will never be the wiser."

"Works for me," I said. "I'm happy to look after you."

We drove out of the long driveway and onto the road that would lead us off Steel property.

A truck drove toward us and then whizzed by.

And recognition stabbed into me.

"That was Joe's truck," I said. "And Bryce was in the passenger seat."

"Hmm. I wonder where they're going?" Jade said.

"I have no idea. Bryce said he was going to talk to Joe this morning. I'm almost sure Mel said Joe was going to the hospital this morning, but they're headed the wrong direction."

"Something must have come up."

"Yeah. Something Bryce hasn't bothered to tell me about." I tossed Jade my phone. "Send a text for me, will you?"

"I can't get on. I need your thumbprint."

I took one hand off the wheel to access my phone for her.

"What do you want me to say?"

"How about 'where the hell are you going?'"

"Marj..."

I huffed. "Fine. Start with, 'Jade and I are heading into the city to...' Shit, I already told him what I was doing this morning."

"He knows we know they're going somewhere. Surely he recognized your car, with you driving."

"Was he looking at me?"

"If he wasn't, Joe was. Joe was driving, right?"

"Joe wouldn't forgo seeing his wife and son for just anything," I said. "I want to know what's going on."

"Okay. How about, 'What's going on?'"

"Good enough. Send it and tell me what he says."

She tapped into the phone and then the phone beeped when she hit Send.

A few seconds passed.

"He says, 'Stop texting and driving.'" She let out a laugh.

"Tell him to kiss my ass."

"Marj..."

"I'm serious." Then I thought better. "No, don't do that."

"I wasn't going to."

"Tell him I'm going to keep texting and driving until I get an answer."

"Seriously?"

"Yeah. Send that one."

Tapping and sending again.

"What'd he say?"

"Nothing yet. Okay, he's typing. Hold on."

She chuckled. "He says, 'Hi Jade.'"

"Oh, for God's sake." I was tempted to stop the car abruptly but not with my pregnant best friend in the passenger seat. I slowed to a crawl and pulled over to the side of the road.

I took my phone from Jade and called Bryce.

It rang.

And rang.

Just when I thought he was going to ignore me, he finally responded. "Hi, honey."

"Don't honey me. Where are you two going? Joe was supposed to go to the hospital, but it doesn't take a genius to see you two are headed in the wrong direction."

"Tell Melanie Joe will be there as soon as he can."

"Sure. Be glad to. Now where the hell are you going?"

Silence for a few seconds that seemed like forever.

"Mills and Johnson found Cade Booker. We're going to talk to him."

I gulped. "He's dangerous, Bryce."

"After what he's put us through, he'd better think the two of *us* are dangerous," Bryce said. "We'll be okay, baby."

"I'm tempted to turn around and follow you, but . . ."

"But you've got Jade in the car."

"Yeah, and she hasn't seen the baby yet."

"Go. Enjoy yourselves. Visit your nephew and Melanie. Joe and I will take care of Cade Booker."

I nodded, knowing he couldn't see me. "I want to talk to my brother."

"He's driving."

"So? I am too."

"No, you pulled over."

How did he know?

"I know you," he said before I could ask. "You wouldn't put Jade in any potential danger. That's how I knew you weren't the one texting."

"I'm pretty sure my brother can walk and chew gum at the same time. Put him on, please."

Some rustling. Then, "Hey, sis."

"I just want to remind you that you have a newborn baby and a wife who adores you."

"You think I ever forget those two things?"

"Well . . . you're walking into a situation without thinking it through, as usual. How do you know this isn't Cade Booker screwing with you?"

"Mills and Johnson found Booker, and we're going to—"

"What if the phone call was a fake?"

"It was their number. And it was Trevor Mills's voice."

"And Booker could have been holding a gun on him. Just be careful."

"I always am."

"I know. But this time you have the love of my life with you." I closed my eyes, unwilling to let an emerging tear fall. "Please."

"We both know what's at stake here, Marj. I have a family,

and so does Bryce. We get it."

"Just don't be a hothead."

Stupid words. Words had no effect on whether my oldest brother went into "Red Joe" mode. But he did love his wife and son. I knew that as well as I knew anything. Bryce loved his son as well.

And he loved me.

"Just be safe," I said. "Both of you."

CHAPTER FORTY-NINE

Bryce

"I suppose she has a point," I said. "Booker could be deceiving us."

"It's possible. But is it enough to make you not go?"

I shook my head. "Hell, no. We need answers, and I aim to get them. Today."

"One way or the other. If it *is* a trick, we know he'll be armed in at least three places, which is why I'm armed in two. You?"

"Right there with you." I patted my shoulder holster and pointed to my ankle. "How much longer?"

"About ten miles. Mills says they've got him in an old ranch house just outside the Belldore property."

"I sure as hell don't want to be blinded again, even if it is temporary."

"Fuck. Me neither. That's why we're going in with guns drawn."

I nodded. Sounded damned good to me.

★ ★ ★

"What the hell do you mean he got away?" Joe grabbed Trevor Mills by the collar of his shirt.

I held my gun steadily on his partner, Johnny Johnson.

"Let go of me," Mills said. "Right fucking now."

"For what I'm paying you clowns, you'd better find the bastard." Joe let him go.

I forced back a sigh of relief. Joe was on edge, and Joe on edge could easily turn into Joe in a rage.

"We had him locked in a bedroom with bars on the windows," Johnson said.

"Is he goddamned Houdini?" Joe said sarcastically.

"No. He must have picked the lock."

"With what?"

"I have no idea. I frisked him good. There was nothing on him. We took his shoes, too, so wherever he is, he's in his stocking feet."

"Did you strip search him?" I asked.

"Uh . . . hell, no," Mills said.

I swallowed. "This guy is dangerous and unpredictable. Hiding a bobby pin or anything else up his ass would be nothing to him."

"You two should have foreseen that," Joe said. "Why didn't you tie him up?"

"Because we're PIs, not lunatics. It's bad enough we took him against his will."

"The mercenary PIs with a conscience." Joe rolled his eyes. "You two take the cake."

"He couldn't have gotten far," I said to Joe. "Let's go after him."

"I wish we had two trucks," Joe said. "We could cover more ground. What if we miss him?"

"He didn't have access to a vehicle, did he?" I said to Mills.

"No. Our vehicles are accounted for."

"Then he's on foot, and he hasn't been gone long," I said.

"We'll take the truck and drive all around here. Good thing you've got four-wheel drive."

Joe grunted.

I replaced my pistol in my holster. "We could use some help," I said to the PIs.

"Can't do it," Mills said. "We've got another job."

"That pays as well as I do?" Joe said.

"It's all green to us."

No. No one paid as well as the Steels. This didn't make any sense, unless—

"You motherfuckers," I said through clenched teeth.

Joe eyed me.

"They let him go, Joe. They fucking let him go."

"Hey, we didn't—"

I drove into Mills this time, slamming him against the wall. "Mercenaries. What did he offer you?"

"Nothing. He doesn't have—"

"Bullshit. He might not have Steel money, but he's rich. He was my father's protégé. His real father was loaded too. What the fuck did he offer you?"

"You've got—"

"You gave him a car, didn't you?" I tightened my hold. "*Didn't* you?"

Joe had drawn his gun on Johnson by this time. "You'd better start spilling, or I'm going to start shooting. And I never miss."

CHAPTER FIFTY

M a r j o r i e

"He said he and Bryce had something to attend to, and he'd be here as soon as he could."

Melanie rocked baby Brad, trying to nurse him. "He's starting to get it. He's latching on, but it sure hurts."

She smiled, though. Clearly she didn't care about the slight pain. Who would? The baby was so beautiful, and he'd gained another ounce.

I didn't want to worry Melanie, but something didn't feel right. Bryce and Joe were walking into something that wasn't going to end well. I felt it deep in my bones. I looked sideways at Jade. She and I had discussed what they might be up to during our drive to the hospital. I didn't want her talking.

She didn't.

As much as I loved seeing the baby and Mel, I was antsy to get moving. I wanted to get Jade safely home and then figure out how to get to Bryce and Joe before they did something stupid.

My brother was a big hothead, and so was Bryce when they were together. Both of them knew the dangers of what we were all dealing with, but leave it to the two of them to go running in without backup.

I tried not to check my phone too often. I didn't want to be too obvious. Not that I thought Bryce would actually call me, but I had the urge to look at my phone anyway, even though the ringer was on. Call it a compulsion. It was better than cutting myself open.

Though my scar still tingled sometimes when I was tense, I'd kept the desire to slice myself open at bay. Perhaps it was my promise to be less self-indulgent. Perhaps I was conquering the problem. Or perhaps by helping Bryce with his self-indulgent behavior I had also helped myself.

Whatever it was, I felt an odd sort of loss. Nothing horrible or unbearable. Just the end of something that had given me a modicum of relief. The end of something that had been mine and no one else's. Something that had served a purpose that no longer existed.

Strange, to mourn something that had only hurt me.

I could ask Melanie about it, but she was enjoying her son, and I didn't want to ask her to work at the moment.

The scar tingling reminded me constantly that Bryce and Joe were out there, and they could be in danger.

I smiled. "You about ready, Jade?"

"Whenever you are."

Great. That meant the decision to leave would be mine. I was hoping Jade might play the pregnancy exhaustion card. No such luck.

Minutes stretched into another hour. I took leave to get us all some drinks and tried calling Bryce.

No answer.

Not that I expected one.

I left a pleading voicemail, got the drinks, and headed back to NICU.

Come on. Ring. Ring. Ring!

My phone remained silent, but as if in response, Jade's phone buzzed.

"Oh, no," she said. "It's Colin's father."

"Ted Morse?" I said. "Why is he calling you? And how did he get your new number?"

"I have no idea. Should I take it?"

"I guess so," I said. "If you're up to it."

Yes, take it. Take it. Take it.

"Hello," Jade said into the phone. "Yeah, hi, Ted. What? Are you kidding me?" She turned to me. "Colin's missing again."

I grabbed the phone from Jade's hand. "Yeah? Who paid you this time?"

"Who is this?" Ted Morse said.

"Marjorie Steel. I'm a friend of your son's, and I know exactly how Tom Simpson got hold of him. You sold him."

"Sold him? What are you talking about?"

"You know very well what I'm talking about, Mr. Morse. You took a payment from Tom Simpson, and in return, gave him access to abduct your son."

"This is ridiculous. I'm calling the police."

"Do it. I have proof of what you did." A lie, but Colin had the proof.

"You have nothing."

"Are you willing to bet your life on that?" I asked. "I'd think long and hard first."

"This conversation is over. I want to speak to Jade."

"Sure." I handed the phone to Jade.

"What am I supposed to do now?" she said after pressing her mute button.

"Keep him on the line. I want to get the call traced. Find

his location." I quickly called the number I had for Mills and Johnson.

"He's probably in Denver at home."

"We don't know that for sure."

"What am I supposed to say to him?"

"I don't know. Just keep him talking. Tell him you have the proof, but you're willing to listen to his side of the story. Whatever it takes to keep him on the phone. Damn! The PIs aren't answering."

"Call Ruby," Melanie said. "She'll be able to do it."

"On it."

Within a minute, Ruby was working on the trace.

"I've known you for so many years," Jade was saying to Ted Morse. "Please tell me none of this is true."

Apparently he was telling her just that. A few minutes passed, and Ruby was back on the line. "Done. He's actually here. In Grand Junction."

"Okay. Last I heard, Colin was in Glenwood Springs. Give me Ted Morse, Jade."

She handed me her phone.

"Mr. Morse? When was the last time you saw Colin?"

"I haven't seen him in a week."

"He was in Denver a day ago."

"He won't see me."

"Gee," I said sarcastically. "I wonder why."

"This is all bullshit," he said. "I'd never harm my son."

"Nah, you'd just have others do it and pocket their money."

"This is—"

"Spare me your fake outrage, Ted," I said. "We'll find Colin ourselves, and we'll get to the bottom of this." I ended the call and handed the phone back to Jade. "Man, he's rotten.

I'm glad he's not your father-in-law."

"Me too," Jade agreed. "More than you can ever imagine."

"Ruby gave me an address. I'm going to get you home and then go see Morse."

"Bull. We're already here in Grand Junction. If you take me home, he might move."

"I can't have you involved in this," I said. "You're pregnant. Talon would never forgive me if—"

"Sorry. I'm going. I actually know this man. Maybe he'll talk to me."

I sighed. "I wish Ruby were here."

"Me too. But I'm all you've got."

"That's not what I meant."

"It's exactly what you meant. Sorry. Your pregnant best friend will have to do."

"No one I'd rather have at my back."

True words. Just maybe not today.

CHAPTER FIFTY-ONE

Bryce

Johnson gulped. "Put the gun down, man. You know I'm armed."

"I can have a bullet between your eyes before you even think about reaching for your piece," Joe said, "and Bryce has fifty pounds on your partner. Start talking. And don't leave out a single dirty detail."

"Fuck it," Mills rasped out, choking against my hold on his neck. "Just tell them."

"Fine. Put the damned gun down."

"Nice try," Joe said. "No deal."

"For Christ's sake. We've been working together for months now. Where's the trust?"

"It went out the window when you let Booker go," I said. "You heard your partner. Start talking."

"Fine. Yeah, we let him go."

"What'd he pay you?" Joe said.

"Not much. You were right about one thing. No one pays as well as the Steels. But he did have one valuable thing to offer."

I shook my head, scoffing. "Your life."

"Give the man a silver dollar," Johnson said. "You were right about him hiding something up his ass, only it wasn't a bobby pin. It was a fucking switchblade. Somehow he picked the lock and got out of the room."

"And somehow, one man with a knife outmaneuvered two men with guns?" Joe said. "I don't think so."

"He had moves I've never seen before," Johnson said. "Tell them, Mills."

"A little hard to talk," Mills choked out.

"Tough," I said. "Talk."

"Some kind of martial arts thing. Nothing we've seen," Mills rasped.

"He was able to hold one knife on both of you?"

"Not exactly," Johnson said. "He had me in some kind of headlock against the wall and the knife at Mills's throat. It wasn't pretty."

"Do you know where he was going?"

"Do you really think we interrogated him while he was threatening to kill us?" Johnson said.

I couldn't help a laugh. I finally let go of Mills's throat, and he crumpled to the ground, clutching his neck. I pulled one of my guns and held it on him.

"So there *is* something more important to the two of you than money," Joe said. "Who'd have thought?"

"I'm not sure they ever gave it a thought," I said. "Did you?"

"Not really. We've never been in the situation. We're usually one step ahead of whoever we're tailing. Hell, we went underground and turned the tables on Wendy Madigan when she tried to frame us. But this guy is something else."

"Yeah, well, *this guy* was trained by the best," I said. *Trained by the best. Just like I was.*
No. Don't go there. No more self-indulgence.

"I ought to blow your brains out on principle," Joe said.

"Not worth it," I said. "We're not killers. We're not my father."

I'm not my father.

I took my gun off Mills. "Any more information you can give us?"

"Sorry. I can only tell you one thing," Johnson said. "If he got the best of us, he can get the best of just about anyone."

"Not us," I said. "Let's go, Joe."

★ ★ ★

"Where do we start?" Joe asked once we were on the road.

"Colin was in Denver, last I heard," I said. "Booker's probably headed there."

I checked my phone. "Shit. I've got about a hundred text messages from Marj. She knows something's up."

"She's too smart for her own good sometimes," Joe said.

"I agree, but it didn't take a lot of smarts to figure out something big was up for you to miss a visit with Melanie and little Brad."

"True that."

My phone dinged with another text. Yup. Marjorie.

*Jade and I are headed to see Ted Morse
in Grand Junction. Apparently Colin
is missing again. He's not answering
his phone.*

"Fuck," I said.

"What is it?"

"Marj is going to see Ted Morse in Grand Junction, and she's got Jade with her."

"Oh, hell, no."

"Oh, hell, yes. Do you think we can stop them? We're over an hour away. She says Colin's missing again."

"Fuck. Fuck, fuck, fuck." Joe swerved, turning the car around in the middle of the country road.

"Damn, Joe!"

"Sorry. I guess we're going back to the city."

"I guess so. But we won't make it in time. If Ted has something planned, we won't have time to stop him."

I frantically texted Marj back.

We're on the way. What's the address?

Jade and I can handle this.

Address, please.

A few seconds later, the address came through.

We're on our way.

I turned to Joe. "If Booker just got loose a couple hours ago, he couldn't have gotten to Colin yet. Morse says he hasn't heard from Colin in a week, according to all these texts from Marj. But Marj says she's heard from Colin and he's in Glenwood Springs."

"Maybe Booker's been in touch with Colin," Joe said.

"Colin would have told—"

But would he have told us? He'd just found out his father

had taken money from my father as payment for him. If Booker had gotten to him and they'd exchanged information, they had something in common. Something to bond over.

Of course, Booker had also tried to frame Colin, along with Dominic and Alex, by leaving his cufflink at the playground where he was watching Dale.

What was the connection?

Maybe Booker never actually harmed any of the children. Maybe, as Dale had said, he just watched.

"I have no idea where to look," Joe said.

"Then we get to Grand Junction and take care of Marj and Jade."

"I can't believe Talon let her go into the city without him."

"She was with Marjorie," I said. "Talon may think he controls his wife, but he doesn't."

"Talon doesn't think that. He just worries about her. She's pregnant, or have you forgotten?"

"Of course not. Jesus, Joe."

"Sorry. I'm a fucked-up mess."

"That makes two of us." I sighed. "We need to get to Marj. I can't lose her, Joe. I just can't."

CHAPTER FIFTY-TWO

Marjorie

Ted Morse looked a lot like an older version of Colin.

Except, unlike Colin, his eyes were not kind. His eyes were . . . What were they, exactly? Just on the edge of menacing, but not quite. They were eyes that had something to hide, eyes that were well regulated to not give anything away.

They were not the eyes of a nice man.

"It's nice to see you, Jade," he said. "Come in. Take a seat."

We walked in and he closed the door.

Morse wore a navy-blue suit. An expensive navy-blue suit with a black paisley silk tie. His shoes were Louboutins, I was certain, and he was impeccably groomed.

"You don't look like a man who's concerned about his son," I said.

"What is that supposed to mean?"

"It means you look like a silver-haired mannequin at Saks," I said. "Right down to your manicured fingernails. Did you have a two-hour massage this morning, too?"

"Marj . . ." Jade said.

"Come on. Look at him. Does he look like a worried father to you?"

"I'm sure you didn't come here to insult me, Jade. I'm sure you're concerned for Colin."

"As much as she could be concerned for a man who left her at the altar. Or the man who convinced him to do so."

Jade hedged a little. "She has a point."

"You think I convinced him to cancel your wedding?"

"You're not that good an actor, Mr. Morse," I said. "And he didn't *cancel* the wedding. He didn't show up to the wedding because *you* told him Jade wasn't good enough for him."

"That's preposterous."

"Either you're lying or Colin's lying," I said. "Hmm, I wonder which one would lie?"

"Look, Ted," Jade said. "We're concerned about Colin. We want to find him. If you haven't seen him in a week, how do you even know he's missing?"

"Because of this." He thrust his phone at us, revealing a text.

I have your son.

"When did this text come in?" I asked.

"Right before I called Jade."

"And I suppose you've considered that it's a hoax?"

"Of course I've considered that it's a hoax, but it was an Iowa area code. Not a lot of hoaxes come out of Iowa."

An Iowa code. All the texts Joe and Bryce received had come from an Iowa area code.

"Okay, let's assume it's real," I said. "Has he asked for anything?"

"Money."

I laughed. "Poor guy. He has no idea you'd give up your son sooner than you'd give up money. In fact, you *did* give up your son once. For money."

"You have no proof of that."

"I have all the proof I need. You. Standing there looking like a fashion plate when your son is missing. If anyone ever accused my father of selling out one of his kids, he would not take it lying down. The most you can come up with is some false outrage. You're a phony, Mr. Morse."

Jade was ominously silent, both hands on her belly.

"Jade?" I said.

"It's nothing. Just a little cramping. Probably gas. I'm okay."

Shit. I really shouldn't have let her come along. "We're going back to the hospital."

"No, really, I'm—"

"No arguments. It's what Talon would want. I'll be calling him too, by the way."

"No! Please let him have his little overnight with the boys. They all need it. Please, Marj."

"My brother would never forgive—"

We all jerked at the fierce pounding on the door.

"Open up, Morse!"

Bryce! I nearly flew to the door of the condo where Ted Morse was staying.

Bryce and Joe stood outside.

Bryce pulled me into a hug. "Honey, are you okay?"

"I'm fine, but I need to take Jade to the hospital. She's having some pain."

"Oh, shit."

"I'm okay," Jade said. "It's just a little cramping."

"Still," Joe said. "You two get to the hospital. Bryce and I can handle this clown."

"For once I agree with you," I said. "Let's go, Jade."

CHAPTER FIFTY-THREE

Bryce

"Start talking," I said to Ted Morse.

"My son is missing. I showed the girls this text."

I eyed his phone. "Iowa. Check your old texts and calls, Joe." I frantically looked through mine. None matched the number.

"Bingo," Joe said.

"You got a match?"

"Yeah. The first call I got. Looks like he got lazy and reused one of his old phones."

"He probably didn't think we'd be talking to Colin's father."

"Do you mind including me in this conversation?" Ted said. "It *is* my son who's missing."

"Spare us your fatherly concern." I drew my gun on him.

He visibly shuddered. "I don't want any trouble."

"Just tell us what we need to know, and there won't be any," Joe said, pulling his weapon out as well.

"Look, my son—"

"How did you find out about Justin Valente?" I demanded.

"Look, I—"

"No excuses," Joe said. "We're here for the truth. If you're truly concerned about your son, then you know we're your best chance of finding him. Start talking."

Ted sighed. "Can I at least sit down?"

"Sure. In fact, we'll be happy to tie you to a chair."

"That's not necessary. You've got two guns on me. I'd be stupid to try to run."

"Yeah?" Joe said. "You once tried to extort money from me, to frame me for what Tom Simpson did to Colin. I didn't realize at the time that you'd do just about anything for money, including pimping out your own son. I'd bet you'd try to run if you think there's a buck in it for you."

"You've got the wrong idea about me."

"I don't think so," I said, pushing him into a chair. "You got any rope around here?"

"Like I'd tell you," he said.

I pushed the barrel of my gun to his temple. "I'll ask that again. You got any rope around here?"

"D-Duct tape. Kitchen cabinet over the dishwasher."

I nodded to Joe. He returned in a few seconds with the tape. I continued to hold the gun on Morse as Joe taped his ankles to the chair.

"False imprisonment is a crime, you know."

"Is it?" I said. "Gee. Didn't know that. By the way, so is selling a human being to my psycho father. And maybe it's just me, but I think that's a whole lot worse than tying the perpetrator up while I'm questioning him."

"I agree," Joe said. "Now. How the hell did you find out about Justin Valente?"

"What makes you think I know anything?"

"You knew we weren't alone during that one camping trip with my father," I said. "Even Joe and I have trouble remembering that trip. But you knew about it."

HELEN HARDT

"As I understand it, you two were around nine years old at the time," Morse said. "How exactly do you expect me to believe you didn't remember?"

"You've dealt with my father. It shouldn't be any surprise to you that he would drug his own child."

"You seriously didn't remember? You didn't remember taking the kid camping and then he didn't come home?"

"No," Joe said. "We didn't fucking remember. We were nine fucking years old, Morse. We didn't commit a crime by inviting a friend to go camping."

Ted Morse met my gaze. "Do you really expect me to believe that not once in over thirty years did you ever have a clue what your father was capable of?"

"I'm not sure your son ever knew what you were capable of either. You sold him to a psycho."

"I find it hard to believe—"

Joe cocked his gun. "*I* find it hard to believe you're still talking without answering a question. Now where the hell did you learn about Justin Valente?"

Ted's lips trembled. "To be honest, he came to me."

"Bull," Joe said.

"Wait a minute, Joe. He might actually be telling the truth."

"Of course I'm telling the truth."

"You can stop talking now. I have a million more questions for you, but right now, I'm talking to Joe. This actually makes sense. Marjorie and I were talking about it. I think, in some warped way, Booker was jealous of Colin."

Joe raised his eyebrows. "Say what?"

"Yeah. Think about it."

Then I stopped speaking abruptly. I had learned that my

father had taken Justin as a protégé from Brad Steel. I still hadn't told Joe that his father was alive. Now wasn't really the right time to have that conversation, but I didn't have a choice. I put my gun down and grabbed the roll of duct tape. Quickly, I taped Ted Morse's chest around the back of the chair and then also stuck a strip of tape over his mouth.

"We need to talk," I said to Joe. "Alone."

CHAPTER FIFTY-FOUR

Marjorie

"I told you everything was fine," Jade said, once we got home.

"How was I supposed to know that pain was normal?"

"Because I told you it was."

"My brother would've never forgiven me if you'd had any issue while you were with me," I said. "He was really glad I called."

"It took me a long time to talk him into not cutting his trip with the boys short," Jade said. "And he only agreed if I went straight home and went to bed. I don't like lying to Talon, so I guess that's what I should do."

"Absolutely. Get to bed. I won't be leaving your side until Tal gets home tomorrow."

"What about Bryce and Joe?"

"They'll have to get along without me this time." I smiled.

Jade returned my smile. "The two of them can certainly handle Ted Morse. Do you think Colin is really missing?"

"I wish I knew. I don't trust Ted Morse as far as I can throw him, but after all Colin has been through, it wouldn't be unusual for him to take off."

"Or for Cade Booker... Honestly, Marj, I've given up trying to understand anyone in this whole situation anymore.

Oh!" She clasped her hand to her mouth. "I didn't mean . . ."

"It's okay. Why would anyone understand why a person would cut herself open to relieve emotional pain? It made sense to me. It worked for me. But it was self-indulgent. Counterproductive. The physical doesn't take away the emotional. You have to work through all of it."

Jade smiled. "Melanie is a wise woman."

"Do you need anything? Water? Herb tea? A grilled cheese and tomato sandwich?" I smiled.

"Actually, a grilled cheese and tomato sandwich sounds great."

"I'm on it."

CHAPTER FIFTY-FIVE

Bryce

Joe stared through me as though I were invisible.

Not the reaction I expected from my hotheaded best friend.

Of course, it wasn't every day you learned your father had faked his own death.

Again.

I'd been ready to take a punch for not telling Joe as soon as I found out about his father.

"You okay?" I said.

He shook his head slowly. "Not even fucking slightly."

"I know."

"You don't. I appreciate it, man. I do. But you don't know."

I nodded. No use restating the obvious. He didn't know what it was like to find out your father was a psycho pedophilic rapist, and I didn't know what it was like to find out your father had faked his own death. Twice.

"When I saw him on the island, found out he was alive the first time, I nearly fucked him up good I was so mad. Then I found out he'd been keeping our mother from us. At that point, fucking him up was too good for him."

"Honestly, I think he was doing all of it to protect your mother."

"From her own kids?"

"From Wendy and the others, the first time."

"What's his excuse now?"

"Cade Booker. He's known about him all along. Dominic and Alex have been working for him for years."

"Why didn't he just tell us?" Joe demanded. "We're strong. We're financially independent. We could have dealt with Cade Booker."

"He knew we didn't remember," I said. "He didn't want to traumatize us."

"Unbelievable." Joe rubbed his forehead. "Un-fucking-believable. As if finding out our father faked his own death again isn't traumatic."

"The way he put it to me was that you and your siblings could take care of yourselves, but your mother couldn't. His first loyalty was to protect her above all else."

"Fucker," Joe said again. "*We* could have protected her."

Except that Brad took her from the facility without Joe's or his siblings' knowledge. But now probably wasn't a good time to remind Joe of that.

"Where is he? How do I get in touch with him?" Joe demanded.

"I don't know where he is. He wouldn't give me that information."

"Fucker!"

"Look, Joe, we've got more important shit to deal with. We have to find Booker."

"I'll bet the great Bradford Steel already knows where he is."

Good point. Brad seemed to know everything. I didn't agree with his methods, but he did stay on top of things.

"He probably knows where *we* are right now," Joe continued. "Come on out, Dad! I know you're here. Get your ass out here, and you're going to answer to me!"

No response, of course. Brad Steel wasn't here, not in Ted Morse's condo.

"Come on. Let's go deal with Ted," I said. "We can't keep him tied up forever."

"I don't know about that," Joe said. "I hate the shithead."

Yeah, Joe had a particular ax to grind with Ted. I got it.

"Come on." I nodded to him.

We both walked back into the living area where Ted was still taped to the chair. I ripped the tape off his mouth without warning.

"Ow!"

"Get over it. Time for you to talk, Morse."

"Not feeling real talkative."

I pulled my gun out and pressed it to his forehead. "Feeling a little chattier now?"

Joe looked down, and I followed his gaze. Morse's crotch was wet. He'd pissed himself.

Sure, he could play the tough guy, but his body didn't lie.

"You'd better start talking now," I said, "before the other end releases."

"I told you. Cade Booker came to me."

"Why? Why would he come to you?" I asked.

"He wanted..."

"What?" I pushed the end of the gun into his forehead, leaving a mark on his skin.

"He wanted to know about Colin."

"Why?"

"About Colin and...your father."

"And what did you tell him? That you'd sold Colin to my father just like his father had done to him?"

"I didn't—"

"Spare me," Joe said. "Colin has proof."

"Whatever Colin thinks he has isn't true."

"Sell that somewhere else," I said. "Right now, we need to know about Booker."

"He was weird," Ted said. "Sort of . . . obsessed. He wanted to know about Colin, how Tom got hold of him."

"Because you pimped him out," Joe said. "Go on."

"That's not true!"

"Don't say that again," I said through clenched teeth. "Now keep talking."

"I told him Colin had been held prisoner by your father, but he already knew that. He also knew that you"—he nodded toward Joe—"rescued him."

"Does he know you tried to extort money from me by telling him to name me as the perp?" Joe said.

Easy, Joe. While I understood Joe's anger—especially now that he'd found out about his father—we didn't have time to rehash old news. I had to keep both Joe and Morse on track.

"Keep going," I said. "What else did he tell you?"

"He told me his story, that his real name is Justin Valente, that he'd been abducted by your father on a camping trip that you two invited him to go on. That your father let him move around on his own for the last ten years but kept him on a pretty short leash."

"And . . . ?" I said.

"You sure you want me to go further?" He eyed Joe.

"Go," Joe said.

"Really? You want your friend here to know—"

"He already knows. Now you tell us what *you* know."

"He's been watching both of you for years, but while your father was alive, he kept it under wraps. He befriended you at the club."

"And...?" I said again.

"He blames you two for what happened."

"We were nine," I said. "Neither of us knew who my father was."

"He thinks you lured him into a trap. I told him that wasn't true."

"So you're on our side now?" Joe asked sardonically.

"Of course he's on our side," I said. "I'm holding a gun to his head. We just learned from Mills and Johnson that the one thing that trumps money to a mercenary is life."

"You say Colin is missing," Joe said. "You sure you didn't lead Booker right to him? For the right price?"

"Why would I—"

"Shut the fuck up," Joe said. "We all know why."

Morse closed his eyes. "Maybe you should just pull the trigger. I deserve it."

"I won't argue," I said, "but you're not done talking yet."

"I didn't sell Colin. I didn't."

"Then what did you do?"

"I took some money from your father, and I gave him information."

"What information?"

Morse sighed. "Apparently your father witnessed an encounter between Colin and you and your brothers," he said to Joe. "Simpson came to me, said he was interested in talking business with Colin, maybe had a position for him with the city, and he offered me a large 'finder's fee' if I let him know how to get in touch with Colin."

"How large?" I asked.

"Really large. Seven figures."

"Sounds like a finder's fee for his next plaything." Joe said.

"I honestly didn't know—"

"What a crock," Joe said. "Didn't you wonder how the mayor of Snow Creek had access to that amount of cash?"

"I didn't think about it! You really think I'd sell my own son out?"

"For the right price?" I scoffed. "Hell, yeah."

"It wasn't like that. It wasn't—"

"What did you tell Booker?" I demanded. "About Colin?"

"Nothing. Not a thing. After what happened the first time, do you really think I'd accept money for information on my son?"

I looked to Joe. "Do you believe him?"

"Fuck no. No one pays a seven-figure finder's fee for a job with a small town."

My initial instinct was to agree with Joe. After all, it gave me a certain constancy to think there might be another father on the planet who was horrid like mine. But Ted Morse wasn't Tom Simpson. He was more like Mills and Johnson than my father, if he was telling the truth. He liked money and would do just about anything for it. Perhaps he truly thought he was getting a finder's fee for my father offering his son a job. My father was the mayor of Snow Creek and a respected attorney, after all. Ted could have convinced himself my father was on the up-and-up, so he had an excuse to take the money. "For God's sake, Bryce. You're not buying this horseshit, are you?"

"I'm not buying into anything," I said, still poking my gun into Morse's forehead. "But we need to find Booker. Does

Colin ever go off by himself?" I asked Morse.

"I don't know. He's an adult."

"If he went somewhere alone, where would it be?"

"We have a place in Glenwood Springs," Morse said. "This condo here in Grand Junction, although he's not here, obviously."

"Anything else?"

"We have some rentals here and in Montana and Florida, but they're all currently leased."

"Glenwood Springs, then. What's the address? And is there a landline there?"

"Yeah, yeah. You'll have to untie me so I can write down the information for you."

"Nice try," Joe said, pulling out his phone. "Give it to me."

Morse sighed as he recited an address and telephone number and Joe typed the information into his phone.

"Anything else?" I said. "How well do you know Booker? Where would he go?"

"I don't know." A tear slid from Morse's eye. "I truly don't know."

"Damned cry baby," Joe said. "I don't believe you."

"He only wanted to know about Colin," Morse said. "And he told me the story about your father and the two of you."

Joe sighed. "Fine. Now, how much is it going to cost me for you to forget we ever had this conversation?"

"Nothing," he said.

"Right," I scoffed.

"No. Nothing. Truly. I've learned my lesson after what happened to Colin. I didn't take any money from Booker, and I tried to warn you. I did. Why do you think I got in touch with the two of you in the first place?"

"Money," Joe and I said in unison.

Morse sighed. "I can understand why you'd think that. But I tried to warn you. I said all I could without putting my son's and my life in jeopardy." He shook his head. "My son is wrong about me. I did a lot of things wrong as a father. I know that. I was way too hard on him, and I thought he'd have the strength to stand up to me about marrying Jade. Everything I did was to try to make him stronger. But I never intentionally gave him to your father. I didn't know who your father was at the time."

"Whatever," I said. "What's done is done, and there's nothing you can do to change it. Now answer Joe's question. How much is it going to take?"

"Nothing," he said again.

"And we should trust you because . . ." Joe said.

"You shouldn't," he said. "But you can."

I put my gun away and started to unwrap the duct tape around Morse's chest.

"What the hell are you doing?"

"What else can we do? We have to go after Colin and Booker. We can't just leave him here stewing in his own piss."

"Sure we can."

"Leave me if you want," he said. "It's no less than I deserve."

"For once we agree," Joe said.

I quickly unwrapped the tape from Morse's ankles. "There. If you care about your son as you say, you'll let us do what we have to do."

He nodded, trembling.

"And take a damned shower," Joe added.

CHAPTER FIFTY-SIX

Marjorie

Going to Glenwood Springs
to look for Colin.

I read the text from Bryce again for the umpteenth time since it had dinged four hours ago. I'd texted back a quick "*Be safe, I love you,*" and that was that.

My feet itched to move, to run to my car and chase Bryce and my oldest brother all the way to Glenwood Springs.

But I'd promised Talon I'd stay with Jade.

Jade was fine. She said so herself. The cramping was normal, and her ultrasound had shown that the baby was healthy. She wasn't bleeding, her blood pressure was normal. Everything was A-okay.

No.

No. No. No.

I couldn't leave. She'd promised Talon she'd stay in bed, and I'd promised I wouldn't leave her alone.

I sighed, placing Jade's sandwich plate in the dishwasher. I'd just checked on her, and she was sleeping. We'd been home several hours, and all was fine.

The house was so big and quiet without Talon and the

boys here, so I jerked in surprise when the doorbell rang. I shut the dishwasher and walked to the door before it could ring again and disturb Jade. Chills erupted on the back of my neck. It was dark, and Jade and I were alone.

I drew in a deep breath, gathering my courage. I looked through the peephole—

I opened the door. "Colin! What are you doing here?"

"I need to see Jade," he said. "Quickly. I don't have a lot of time."

"What's going on?"

"I've got someone in the car. He's skittish, and I don't want—"

We both looked toward the sound of a car door. A man with dark hair and olive skin walked toward us.

"Who's that?"

"You were supposed to stay in the car," Colin said.

"Sorry. I'm not sure I trust you quite yet."

"Trust him? Who the hell are you?"

"Marjorie," Colin said, "this is Cade Booker."

I gasped, my jaw dropping.

"Also known as Justin Valente."

I gulped. "Colin, this man is dangerous. What the hell are you doing?" I quickly scanned Booker. "He's armed. Probably in three places."

"Only in one place," Colin said. "Show her."

He pulled at his jeans to reveal an ankle holster.

"He's the one who—"

"I know," Colin said. "He's not here to hurt anyone. I promise."

"Sorry. Don't trust him." I reached for my phone in my pocket.

"Don't call the police, Marj," Colin said. "Please."

"Why shouldn't I? He pepper-sprayed Bryce and Joe. That's assault."

"They barged into my office," Booker said.

"Yeah? Well, you kidnapped me and—"

"That was his brother and sister," Colin said. "You know that."

"Are you trying to tell me that Dominic and Alex are the bad guys?"

"No," Colin said. "They were acting on your father's orders."

"My dead father's orders?"

"You think Brad Steel can't control people from the grave? Come on. He put systems in place. They were telling the truth."

"Just who is the bad guy here, then?"

"There isn't one. Not now, at least."

"Sorry. Not buying."

"Let us come in," Colin said. "I came to talk to Jade, but it might be good for you to hear everything from Cade."

"I'm willing to work with you, Colin," Booker said, "but I'm not setting foot in the Steel house."

Just as well. Jade was in her bedroom resting.

"Then we'll talk out here," I said. "Pull up a chair."

The front deck wrapped around both sides of the house. I gestured to the Adirondack chairs to the side.

"Can you get Jade?" Colin asked.

"Sorry. She had a scare at the hospital today, and she's resting."

"All right," Colin said. "Go ahead, Cade. Tell her what we're going to do."

He opened his mouth when Joe's truck came rumbling up the drive.

"Shit," Booker said.

"Hold on," I said. "If you're willing to tell me, you should tell Joe and Bryce."

"They let that bastard take me."

"They were nine!" I said.

"I've been talking to him about that," Colin said.

Joe and Bryce exited the truck, and both came running toward the front deck, their guns in their hands.

"Cade Booker," Joe said. "We've been looking all over for you. I ought to shoot your brains out."

"He's armed, Joe," I said.

"I'll have his brains splattered on the deck before he can draw his weapon."

"Don't be so sure," Booker said. "Same man who taught you taught me."

Tom Simpson. Bryce's father.

Bryce was holding a gun as well. He nodded to me. "You okay, honey?"

"Yeah. I don't think they're here to hurt anyone."

"We're not," Colin said. "We're here to say goodbye."

"Right," Joe scoffed.

"Hear us out," Colin urged.

"I fucking trusted you, you son of a bitch. I vouched for you with my closest friend. I asked you for help finding a place for my mentally ill mother. You're not even a real lawyer!"

"I'm as competent as any lawyer." He looked at Bryce. "Your father saw to that."

"Shut up," Joe continued. "I don't trust easily, and I rarely make a mistake. You slipped right by me, and that pisses me off." His cheeks were red with rage, his free hand curled into a fist. "You attacked us."

"You barged into my office and disarmed me," Booker retorted.

"You've been watching us for years." Bryce this time.

"I won't deny it." Booker stared straight at Joe, who still held a gun on him.

He wasn't frightened. Not at all. Could he really draw before Joe shot him? No. No way. He wasn't frightened because he'd already been through hell. Death couldn't be any worse.

"You're going to have to answer for what you've done," Bryce said.

"For pepper spraying you? I don't think I'll get prison time for that."

"Not that," Bryce said. "For killing your parents."

"I didn't kill my parents," he said. "Though they both deserved it."

"Pretty convenient, their deaths," Joe said. "A drive-by shooting in a nice neighborhood and a holdup at a convenience store. What are the chances they both would die by getting shot? Right around the same time you showed up at your mother's?"

"Chances were good," Booker said, turning to Bryce. "Your father was behind it."

Bryce gulped and turned white.

I went to him and hugged him. "Not your fault," I whispered.

"We're supposed to believe that?" Joe said.

"Why the hell not? You know what that psycho was capable of. Killing two people with a gunshot, instant death, was probably one of the nicer things he did."

Bryce tensed beside me, and his countenance became rigid. He dropped his gun and held it at his side.

"I'm willing to hear you out, Justin," Bryce said. "Let's end this. Once and for all."

CHAPTER FIFTY-SEVEN

Bryce

My father was involved in killing Justin's parents?

Yeah, I had no problem believing it. It almost seemed *too* normal for him.

"Why would Bryce's dad have your parents killed?" Joe asked.

"Easy. My father demanded more money. Tom killed him."

Money buys silence for a time, son, but a bullet buys it forever.

I had no difficulty believing my father lived by his own words.

"And your mother?" Joe said.

"When I left, I went to her. Tom was afraid she'd soften me, so he offed her. He went after Dominic and Alex as well, but *your* father"—he nodded to Marj—"put them under his protection."

I swallowed down the nausea that had become such a big part of my life. None of this was hard to believe. It could easily be true.

"You're saying you've never killed anyone?" Joe asked.

"No. I've never killed anyone. I've never abused anyone. Never. Not *ever*."

"You pepper-sprayed us," Joe reminded him.

"Self-defense," Booker said. "You took my weapons."

"What were you planning, then?" I asked. "Coming after Joe and me? If you're not a killer, then what?"

"Truthfully? I have no idea. I always thought I'd make you pay somehow. Torture you. Maybe kill you, but I didn't have anything mapped out. I've had vengeance on my mind for so long, I didn't know what I'd do once I actually had you."

Cade's face seemed to morph before my eyes. He was Justin again, nine years old, running from Taylor Johns and the other bullies.

And suddenly everything was clear.

Even his sexual preferences at the club. He couldn't decide. My father made him the ultimate victim, and that was ingrained in his personality. When he finally got a small taste of freedom, he desperately wanted to break free of the victim role. He toyed with the other side, hoping it would cure him of his victimhood, but inside, he was still a frightened little boy. He'd even created a separate identity—the Spider. The role of switch fit him perfectly.

"You do know, don't you, that we had no idea what would happen to you on that camping trip?" Joe said.

"Maybe. You were kids. So was I."

"We were friends," Joe said. "At least I thought we were."

I waited for Joe to say more, but he didn't. How could he? It would mean talking about his leather club affiliation with his little sister present.

"We were never friends. We hardly knew each other."

"We protected you from Taylor Johns and the others," Joe continued.

"We don't have to defend ourselves," I said to Joe. "We were nine."

Cade looked to me then, and I couldn't read his eyes.

"I was watching you. Waiting," he said. "When your father died, I figured it was time for me to act. He no longer controlled me, so I could finally take revenge. Only I never thought it through. Never thought about *how* I'd actually take revenge."

"He's not a killer," Colin said. "Despite what he's been through, he's not a criminal. Just like I'm not."

I opened my mouth, but Colin gestured to me.

"I'm not saying what he's been through and what I've been through are equal. He's had it much worse. I get that."

I turned to Booker. "Tell us, then. What you've been through. How my father continued to control you after he let you go."

"You can't," Colin said. "You can't ask that of him. It wouldn't make sense to you anyway."

"And it makes sense to you?" Joe asked.

"Parts of it. I don't claim to understand everything, but I understand some."

Talon.

The name popped into my mind.

Talon might understand.

But Talon wasn't here. He was in Denver with his sons, and he was living a good and happy life.

I wasn't about to suggest he be brought into this mess.

"Why are you here, then?" I asked. "If you're not going to give us the information we want, why?"

"I came to speak to Jade," Colin said. "To say goodbye, probably forever. Cade and I are going away."

"Together?"

"Not 'together' together. Just as two men who have something in common and need to heal. Far away from here."

"Why?" Marj asked.

"My therapist suggested I get away, take some time to relax and truly work through what happened to me," Colin said. "Cade showed up in Glenwood Springs where I was staying, and we talked."

"You mean he didn't try to harm you?"

"I thought about it," Booker admitted. "But Colin was frightened, and when I looked at him . . ."

He saw himself. He didn't have to utter the words. It was written in the sunken depths of his eyes. He saw another victim of Tom Simpson.

He saw someone who understood.

Colin continued, "I convinced him to come with me. We can work through this together. My therapist has arranged for us to work with his colleague in Bora Bora. We both have the money to do it. We have a lot in common."

True. What they had in common was my father.

"And we're supposed to just let you walk out of here," Joe said.

"Yeah, you are," Booker said. "The worst I've done is pepper spray the two of you and send some emails."

"You stalked a little boy on the playground," Marj reminded him.

"I didn't stalk anyone," Booker said.

"So that wasn't you? You didn't leave evidence to incriminate your brother, your sister, and Colin?"

"I did," he said. "I was angry. I was hurt. Yeah, I took the cufflink I'd stolen from Tom the last time I saw him. I took one of my brother's baseball cards and my sister's stupid pet rock. I left them there to be found. But I swear I wasn't there to hurt the kid. I recognized the boy. I wanted to make sure he was okay."

"Right," Joe scoffed.

"You have no idea. I saw what they did to him. What he went through. They made me . . ."

"Stop it," Colin said. "He's had enough."

"No way," I said. "They made you . . . what?"

"Watch!" Booker raked his fingers through his hair. "They made me watch as they tortured that kid! Is that what you want to hear? You want all the gory details? Because they're all in my head, like a fucking cinematic masterpiece. Things I'll never be able to unsee."

"Easy," Colin said.

I regarded Booker.

And again, I saw the scared little boy he'd been. Justin Valente, who'd been relentlessly bullied by a prepubescent thug and his band of lemmings thirty years ago.

I'd felt sorry for him then. I'd wanted to help him. So I did what I thought would help. I invited him to go camping with me and my dad. My amazing, great dad.

And I'd made things worse.

So much worse.

I cleared my throat softly. "Joe, we need to let them go."

"Are you kidding me?"

"Please."

I could have said so much more. That he'd be with Colin, and Colin seemed to trust him. That these two men were my father's last victims, and I owed them something. That they hadn't asked for what happened to them, and they were trying to heal. Booker might have been set on revenge, but in his heart, he wasn't a criminal. I could see it now. I could see it in his eyes. Those sad, sunken eyes.

Joe would balk at that last thing. What did eyes say?

Never once had I seen a criminal in my father's eyes.

Not once.

But my heart, my soul, was telling me to believe Colin and Booker. To give them the benefit of the doubt. They'd both been victims of the man who'd fathered me, and though I wasn't guilty of anything, I felt some responsibility. I wanted to see them heal. They might see my father when they looked at me, but I wasn't my father. I knew that now, and I could prove it to his last victims.

Booker would never again be the innocent little boy he once was, but maybe he could live a good life. Maybe he and Colin both could.

Marj took my hand, entwining our fingers together. "I agree with Bryce."

Joe seethed, his jaw tight and tense.

"Please," I said. "I can't erase what my father did to them, but I can let them go in peace."

Joe raked his fingers through his dark hair. He didn't speak, but finally, he gave a slight nod.

"I just want to see Jade," Colin said once more. "Only for a minute. To say goodbye."

Marj sent a quick text. "She says to go on in. She's in the bedroom."

True to his words, Colin didn't stay inside for long. Within ten minutes, he'd returned.

Marj hugged Colin.

Booker didn't hold out his hand. Neither did Joe or I.

Some things were just too hard.

As they walked to their car and then drove away, I kissed the top of Marjorie's head and whispered, "*Vaya con Dios.*"

Then my phone buzzed.

CHAPTER FIFTY-EIGHT

M a r j o r i e

Bryce pulled his phone out of his pocket. He showed his phone to Joe.

"Damn." Joe shoved his hands into his pocket.

"What is it?" I asked.

"We need to get the whole family together. Except for Melanie and the baby. I'll talk to her myself."

I gulped. "You guys are scaring me. What is it?"

Bryce pulled me into his embrace. "It's okay, honey. It's not bad news."

★ ★ ★

I blinked.

Then I blinked again.

No. No. Couldn't be.

"Motherfucker," Ryan said slowly.

The boys were outside with the new housekeeper and nanny Talon and Jade had hired. Only the adults sat in the formal living room of the main house.

The adults.

And a ghost.

The ghost of my father.

Sounds buzzed around me. Talon yelling. Ryan yelling.

Joe yelling. Bryce trying to calm everyone down.

Then only two words emerged from the cacophony of chaos.

"Baby girl."

The voice. The voice that had comforted me as a little girl. That had scolded me, told me to work harder. That had apologized for leaving me only months ago. That had uttered its last words in this very house . . .

Not one word escaped my throat.

Because this wasn't happening. It just wasn't.

I couldn't deal with this. My scar itched and sizzled. Itched and sizzled. Itched and—

Then blackness descended around me.

★ ★ ★

"I think she's coming around."

Gentle hands wiped a cool cloth over my forehead.

"Marj? Honey?"

Bryce. I reached for him.

My rock.

My heart.

My everything.

Bryce would help me. Bryce would tell me I was seeing a ghost and nothing more.

"It's okay," he said in a soothing deep voice. "Everything is okay, sweetheart. Can you sit up?"

I nodded and attempted to pull myself up. Where was I? I quickly recognized my bedroom. I'd been in the dining room, hadn't I? No, the living room. How had I gotten here?

"What happened?"

"You fainted, baby."

Fainted? I'd never fainted in my life. Fainting was for girls.

"Where is everyone? Tal? Joe? Ryan? Jade?"

"They're all fine. They're still here. I told them I'd take care of you." He smiled. "In fact, I want to take care of you for the rest of your life."

A proposal? My mind was muddled. Was Bryce proposing to me in my bedroom when I couldn't yet think straight?

"I..."

"You don't have to say anything."

"I thought..."

My father.

My father's body. My father's face. My father's voice.

But that was impossible. He was dead.

I'd watched him die in this very house months ago.

"Easy, baby. You okay?"

My head spun a little as I gazed into Bryce's sparkling blue eyes. Such love was reflected there. Love for me.

I was the luckiest woman in the world.

"My fa... I saw him. I heard his voice."

"Yes, honey. You did."

No. Couldn't be. Couldn't be.

"I didn't. I didn't. He's dead."

Bryce cupped my cheek. "He's alive. And he has a story to tell. But he's not staying long."

I melted into Bryce's arms, tears welling in my eyes.

Should I be angry? Happy? Surprised?

I didn't know. Myriad emotions bubbled through me, weakening me.

I didn't like to feel weak.

Weakness was for girls.

Not for a Steel.

"Do you want to see him?"

"Bryce, why? Why would he...?"

"He had his reasons. Again. But the reasons no longer exist. He'll tell you everything."

"I don't want to see him. I don't want to..."

Didn't want to what?

I had no idea what I wanted, other than to stay in Bryce's arms for eternity.

"Sweetheart, I know this is a lot to take. Your brothers all gave him holy hell for this latest escapade, and he admitted to deserving all of it and more. He won't be here for long."

"Won't be here for long?"

"No," Bryce said. "He turned himself in. He self-surrenders tomorrow."

I gulped down a sob. "What?"

"He's ready to pay for his crimes, honey. He worked a deal so Dominic, Alex, and the others won't be charged. He's paying for everything he did to cover up the trafficking ring."

"But he had reasons... He was just..." I stopped, shaking my head. Yeah, he'd tried to protect my mother, but there was no justification for the lengths he'd gone to. No justification for faking his death not once but twice.

Bryce kissed the top of my head. "He's going to prison for the rest of his life."

"But he's sick... isn't he?"

"No, Marj. He's not."

So he'd lied about his cancer. About his death. About so much.

But he was my father. The father I'd loved. What was I supposed to feel?

The door creaked open.

"You okay, baby girl?"

His voice. His soothing voice. The voice that taught me right from wrong. The voice that helped me when I needed it, the voice that told me when I didn't need help and could figure it out on my own.

The voice that had made me strong.

The voice that would be so ashamed if he knew what I'd resorted to . . .

No. I wasn't ready.

"Not yet," I said into Bryce's shoulder.

"Give her some time," he said.

The door creaked gently shut.

Crying was for girls.

I didn't cry.

Give her some time, Bryce had said.

If he was going to prison tomorrow, he didn't have time. I'd have to suck it up. Talk to him. Yell at him. Tell him he'd fucked up. He'd violated our trust. He'd aided criminals in his attempt to keep our mother safe. Then I'd have to hug him. Tell him what he meant to me. Tell him that I loved him.

"Marjorie," Bryce said, "listen to me."

I wiped my nose on his shoulder, looked up, and met his gaze.

"You're going to have the chance at something you thought was lost to you."

Yeah. My father was alive. I still didn't quite know how to feel.

But Bryce continued, pulling a small box out of his pocket. It was black velvet tied with a golden ribbon. "Your father's attorney already got the warden to agree to a furlough when we decide on a date. If you want, he'll be able to walk you down the aisle."

EPILOGUE

B r y c e

Golden.

Everything about this day was golden.

I stood at the makeshift altar in the backyard of the main ranch house. A little over a year ago, I'd been at this same spot as a guest at Ryan and Ruby's wedding.

Joe stood next to me in a black tux that matched mine. I'd insisted on a tux. A man didn't marry the classiest woman on the planet in anything but a tux.

Melanie sat with baby Brad, now eight months old, perched on her lap. He was a gorgeous child. His hair was dark like Joe's, his eyes sparkling green like his mother's—his mother, who'd been a guide to me, helping me deal with the guilt. Finally, I was ready. Ready to marry the woman of my dreams. Ready to move on with my life—my amazing life.

Talon sat next to Melanie with Diana Jade in his arms. The baby's big brothers doted on her. We all hoped she'd sleep through the ceremony.

Ryan and Ruby sat on the other side of the aisle, next to my mother's empty chair. At Marj's bridal shower a week ago, Ruby had announced she was expecting. Her pretty face glowed.

Colin had kept in touch with Marj. He and Cade were

slowly healing. Ted Morse had tried to reconcile with his son but hadn't had a lot of luck. None of us were going to put a good word in for him. His wife had left him high and dry in a highly publicized divorce when everything went public after Brad's incarceration. Losing his money and lifestyle was the ultimate punishment for Ted Morse.

I looked down the aisle at my beautiful little son, his hand tightly in my mother's. His blondness was so like my own at that age, my mother said constantly. So like mine, and so like...my father's. We could both say it now without wincing. We didn't have to banish all the good memories...though I had finally gotten rid of his cherried-out Mustang in favor of a more conservative set of wheels that would keep my family safe.

I'd also worked out a deal with Henry's mother. Marjorie and I had full custody, but she had visitation rights four times a year. My father had indeed forced her to sign away her rights, and I felt I needed to help make up for that.

My mother had to help Henry get down the aisle. He was nearly two now but still needed Grandma's assistance so he didn't drop the rings.

The notes of Mozart's "Wedding March" from *The Marriage of Figaro* drifted across the gorgeous evening like the soft melodies of a quartet of songbirds.

I smiled.

My little son, blond and blue-eyed, held on to the gold pillow with both hands as my mother guided him toward me. He smiled when he reached me, and my mother took her seat.

Next came Jade, Marjorie's matron of honor, in a golden gown.

And then...my love.

With her father. She hadn't forgiven him yet. None of us had. That would take more time. But she'd allowed him the ultimate honor on this day.

Devastating in ivory, Marj carried a bouquet of her favorite yellow Asiatic lilies. The canary diamond engagement ring—the stone a gift from my mother—sparkled on her left ring finger.

Pure beauty. I'd never quench my desire for her. Day after day after day we'd be together, and my love and passion for her would always be insatiable.

I took the pillow holding the rings from Henry, handed it to Joe, and then hoisted my son in my arms.

Yeah.

Everything about today was golden.

"Ready to get married, buddy?"

Henry smiled and nodded, the sun gleaming on his golden hair.

We were both more than ready.

CONTINUE THE STEEL BROTHERS SAGA
WITH BOOK THIRTEEN

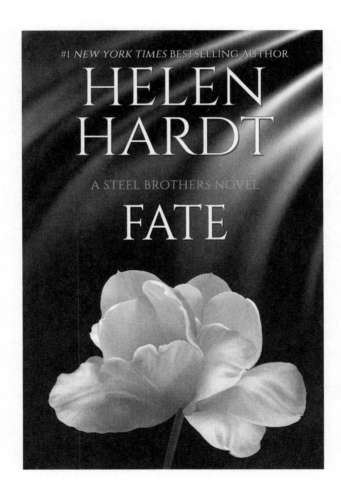

MESSAGE FROM HELEN HARDT

Dear Reader,

Thank you for reading *Insatiable*. If you want to find out about my current backlist and future releases, please like my Facebook page and join my mailing list. I often do giveaways. If you're a fan and would like to join my street team to help spread the word about my books. I regularly do awesome giveaways for my street team members.

If you enjoyed the story, please take the time to leave a review on a site like Amazon or Goodreads. I welcome all feedback. I wish you all the best!

Helen

Facebook
Facebook.com/HelenHardt

Newsletter
HelenHardt.com/SignUp

Street Team
Facebook.com/Groups/HardtAndSoul

ALSO BY HELEN HARDT

The Steel Brothers Saga:
Craving
Obsession
Possession
Melt
Burn
Surrender
Shattered
Twisted
Unraveled
Breathless
Ravenous
Insatiable
Fate
Legacy
Descent

Blood Bond Saga:
Unchained
Unhinged
Undaunted
Unmasked
Undefeated

Misadventures Series:
Misadventures with a Rock Star
Misadventures of a Good Wife (with Meredith Wild)

The Temptation Saga:
Tempting Dusty
Teasing Annie
Taking Catie
Taming Angelina
Treasuring Amber
Trusting Sydney
Tantalizing Maria

The Sex and the Season Series:
Lily and the Duke
Rose in Bloom
Lady Alexandra's Lover
Sophie's Voice

Daughters of the Prairie:
The Outlaw's Angel
Lessons of the Heart
Song of the Raven

Cougar Chronicles:
The Cowboy and the Cougar
Calendar Boy

ACKNOWLEDGMENTS

Huge thanks to the following individuals whose effort and belief made this book shine: Jennifer Becker, Audrey Bobak, Haley Byrd, Yvonne Ellis, Jesse Kench, John Lane, Robyn Lee, Jon Mac, Amber Maxwell, Dave McInerney, Michele Hamner Moore, Keli Jo Nida, Lauren Rowe, Chrissie Saunders, Scott Saunders, Celina Summers, Kurt Vachon, and Meredith Wild.

Thanks also to the women and men of Hardt and Soul. Your endless and unwavering support keeps me going.

To my family and friends, thank you for your encouragement.

Most importantly, thank *you* for reading *Insatiable*.

ABOUT THE AUTHOR

#1 *New York Times*, #1 *USA Today*, and #1 *Wall Street Journal* bestselling author Helen Hardt's passion for the written word began with the books her mother read to her at bedtime. She wrote her first story at age six and hasn't stopped since. In addition to being an award-winning author of romantic fiction, she's a mother, an attorney, a black belt in Taekwondo, a grammar geek, an appreciator of fine red wine, and a lover of Ben and Jerry's ice cream. She writes from her home in Colorado, where she lives with her family. Helen loves to hear from readers.

Visit her at HelenHardt.com